COODER CUTLAS

COODER CUTLAS

ELIZABETH BALES FRANK

1 8 1 7

HARPER & ROW, PUBLISHERS

Cambridge, Philadelphia, San Francisco, Washington, London, Mexico City, São Paolo, Singapore, Sydney

NEW YORK

"Give Me Jesus" by Fanny J. Crosby and John R. Sweeney, used by permission of Hope Publishing Co., Carol Stream, IL 60188.

Designed by Joyce Hopkins
1 2 3 4 5 6 7 8 9 10
First Edition

Library of Congress Cataloging-in-Publication Data
Frank, Elizabeth Bales.
  Cooder Cutlas.
  Summary: Lonely and grieving over his girlfriend's death, Cooder hooks up with a New Jersey rock band and falls in love again.
  [1. Rock groups—Fiction. 2. New Jersey—Fiction] I. Title.
PZ7.F84915Co 1987   [Fic]   85-45822
ISBN 0-06-021859-2
ISBN 0-06-021860-6 (lib. bdg.)

To Linda East and to Lonnie Carter

COODER CUTLAS

Soon enough I was gone, driving north, lead footed and light-headed, on Route 1. I had meant to make the trip as a favor, but I had decided that morning to make my escape. So I'd packed, after Eddie woke me up by calling to tell me he was ready and waiting. As soon as I came back into the bedroom and saw the exhausted roses trying to peel themselves from the wallpaper, and the mascara-stained pillow, I began packing in a frenzy, as though I had the law after me or someone on my tail, as though Sally would wake up and fling herself at my feet and beg me to stay. I stuffed my duffel bag with my clothes, the few books I still carried, my tool kit, my maps, my worn-in cowboy boots, and the shaving kit that I hadn't used in three days and would have used then if I hadn't thrown myself into such a rush. I reached for my Bible, where

I kept all my photographs. I grabbed it by the spine and all the photos fell out, and then Sally did wake up, but she didn't fling herself anywhere. She scowled at me and muttered, "What?"

I left the photos on the floor long enough to shrug on the jacket that everyone loved, a perfectly faded jacket with suede collar and lining. Then I picked up the photos and replaced them carefully. Sally squinted at the clock.

"What're you doing up this early?"

"I'm driving Eddie to Jersey. Remember?"

"Oh, yeah."

I shoved the Bible into the duffel bag and zipped the bag closed, straightened up, and pulled my old Strat out of the closet, where it had been gathering dust since I had placed it there the day I moved into Sally's room. I turned to her and found her watching me.

" 'Bye. I won't be coming back."

She shrugged, pulled the covers up to her chin, and turned away from me to face the faded roses on the wall. I walked down the stairs, through the evil-smelling bar, and out into the parking lot, where the air had the happy carbonated scent of midmorning by the sea. I pulled away quietly.

Eddie was pacing, practically dancing, on the sidewalk in front of his former apartment building when I got there. His drum set and luggage were heaped on the curb between a No Parking sign and a streetlight, and as soon as I parked by the No Parking sign and opened the trunk, he began throwing his luggage into the trunk and his snares into the backseat, talking the entire time, filling me in on all the local gossip, mostly

4

the gossip about his former band, a group of worthless idiots who had split up to go their separate hallucinogenic and criminal ways. Eddie was the only ex-idiot not in a local jail or hospital, and that was because he had somehow seen during the winter that the band would be lucky to make it through the spring, and he had spent the spring running up and down the coast trying to find a new set of guys to play with. He had found a band in Jersey that had just fired its drummer, and he had had to run back to Virginia to get rid of his apartment, furniture, and cat and make it back to Paradise Beach in time for the band's first summertime show at the local boardwalk dive. I had agreed to drive him up because I figured a change of beach town would be nice for a while, if not for good, and because I liked him. He was a big, dumb, friendly drummer who wasn't afraid of me because he was so big and dumb that he wasn't afraid of anyone; he was just a pretty good drummer and all he wanted was a good band made up of some decent guys like him who wanted to play music and chase girls.

"So you and Sally are quits, huh?" he said, glancing at my luggage.

"Yeah."

"How'd she take it?"

"She went back to sleep."

"I think she really liked you, in her way," Eddie said. "You know? I think maybe you expected too much from her."

"Expected too much?"

"You . . . expect a lot."

"What do you think I expect?"

Eddie stuffed his hands in his pockets and shrugged.

5

"Oh, well . . . I don't know. You know, you're pretty strict. I mean, you're a real cool guy and everything, real cool . . . but you're pretty strict. I mean, that's okay, though."

I should have taken the time to shower, shave, and eat, or at least have grabbed a chocolate milk shake. I realized that part of the anger in my head was a hangover, and when I had a hangover I craved a quiet bed and something made of chocolate. I shivered, shrugged my jacket closer, and reached for the tape deck. Eddie pulled a tape out of his pocket and waved it at me.

"You wanna hear Jack's tape?"

"Jack?"

"My new band," Eddie cried proudly. "Jack Armstrong and the All-American Band."

"Hope these guys are better than your old bunch."

"They don't even compare. I mean, these guys . . . they've got a *record* out and everything. They're local *heroes.*"

"Every town has a local hero."

Eddie placed the tape on the dashboard, looking slightly hurt. He examined my collection of tapes.

"What *do* you want, then?"

"Soul. For now."

He slipped in a tape, and instantly Gladys Knight began telling me how wonderful it would be for me if she were my woman and I were her man. I sighed and settled back and adjusted my shades, and tried not to think about chocolate.

"*What*'re they called?"

"The All-American Band."

"Stupid name."

"Yeah, I know. They know, too. But it's what they're called. It's after the old radio show. You know that old radio show? *Jack Armstrong, the All-American Boy*?"

"No."

"Well, I don't either, but Jack's mother does."

"Jack's *mother* named the band?"

"Well, I guess so. She named Jack, and then she . . . named Jack's band. I'm really excited about these guys, Cooder. I'm real glad to be gettin' out of Virginia, too. That place was gettin' to be a real drag. I guess you think so, too. Anyway, I think you'll like Jack. Jack reminds me of you, a lot. He's real strict, too."

"Yeah?"

"I told 'em about you."

"What for?"

"Well, they were askin' me all these questions. They were real *serious*. What kind of music did I like? Not just that, but how did I think it all fit *in* to everything? You know, I couldn't say, 'Hey, great way to meet girls, beats working,' or any of that. So I thought about you. What you would've said. I said, 'I can't really put it into words myself, but I got this friend down in Virginia and he told me once how he felt about it.' And I told 'em how it's, like, kind of religion because it gives people hope they don't get from anything else anymore. How you had to be rich to get rich people's culture, and if you weren't rich you got poor people's culture, and poor people's culture was music and movies and stuff like that. How music didn't have to, like, lull you to sleep or nothing, but it didn't have to preach at you, either. How the best kind of song didn't have to be about much at all, like a girl or a

7

car or a lonely night, but as long as it made you cry or made you . . . glad to be alive, it was something. It was something, for three minutes, that made you cry or made you glad to be alive."

Eddie let out a long sigh of relief when he was finished making his slow way through the words.

"You remember telling me that, Cooder?"

"No!" I said sharply, then added, when I saw his face fall, "I mean, I've said that, Eddie. But I don't remember saying it to you."

"Well," Eddie mumbled. "You were pretty drunk."

Drunk, I thought, I must have been insane. That was her talk; that was Maude's talk. The culture was her part and the music was my part, and she had combined the two of them one night when she was trying to figure out how she could possibly be in love with me when we had nothing in common except for a future bright with all the things that we deserved and never had until we met each other. I had nothing left of Maude but her talk, and I remembered every word she'd said, and held all her words deep inside, because they were more precious to me than the words of the Bible, words that had been drilled into me when I was a kid. They were her words, our words, and I had never tried to tell them to anyone; I didn't trust anyone to understand, and I didn't trust anyone to touch me the way she had. But I had obviously spilled it to Eddie one night when I must have been stupid drunk, insane drunk, drunk and missing her so hard I wanted to cry, but knew even drunk that I couldn't cry in front of Eddie, and so I must have talked instead.

I shifted my eyes ahead, staring at the green signs

sweeping over the windshield, with their white lettering advertising destinations I would never see unless I pulled off right then and took a look. I used to think of all those place names as half-spoken promises, as "This might be home," but now I knew that those towns already were home, and not home to me, because I would not stay there long enough to outgrow being the stranger. To outgrow being the stranger you had to stay there a long time, and it says somewhere in Proverbs: "He that keepeth his way preserveth his soul." That wasn't all there was to it, that wasn't the whole verse Aunt Jane Ellen read to me, as she read to me from the Bible every single night, except when her eyes grew bad later on and I read to her, because we had to remember each word of the Bible. The whole verse was: "The highway of the upright is to depart from evil: he that keepeth his way preserveth his soul."

"So you gave them that whole speech," I said. "And they told you you were in the band—just like that, huh?"

"Well, no. I mean, I auditioned with them, and we played some stuff together, and then the other guys left, and we just sat around talking—Jack, and this guy Delrone who writes the music, and me. Then I told them about what you said, and Delrone got this look on his face, I couldn't tell what he was thinking, and he looked at Jack, and then they looked at each other and they didn't say, 'Okay, you're in,' or nothing like that. They just started telling me about their manager and their deal with the record company and how they got Lee, their piano player, and how their bass player, Billy, puts grease in his hair, and then they told me they had a show Saturday and if I didn't have

9

a place to stay I could stay with them. And if you wanna stay with me for a few days, Cooder, that'd be great with me, you know, while you figure out what you're gonna do next. I think you'll like these guys, Cooder, I really do. I mean—lemme play the tape, okay?"

Jack Armstrong was standing on the pier at Paradise Beach. He was gazing out over the ocean so intently that he didn't notice us walking toward him until we stopped right in front of him and Eddie said, "I'm here, Jack." He looked at us and nodded in an amiable, vague way before his eyes grew confused and uneasy and then cleared. "Oh. *Right*. Eddie, man. How ya doin'?"

"This is my friend, Cooder Cutlas."

Jack nodded and held out his hand. His eyes were dark, naturally kind, and friendly-shy, but at the same time they were very alert, taking in everything. He had tousled hair flopping everywhere and terrible clothes: a decrepit gray sweatshirt with the sleeves torn off, a pair of ragged sneakers, and jeans held together by tattered threads and sheer affection for their owner, in memory of his better days. I was taller, sharper, and even unshaved and unshowered, cleaner, and I reckoned I could take him in a fight, but it seemed somehow that he had the advantage, or maybe I was just imagining it. When I took his hand, I saw nothing in his face but the cheerful charm that probably kept all the Paradise Beach girls calling his name at night.

"He's the one I was telling you about," Eddie added.

"Oh. *Right!*" Jack looked at me more carefully,

grinned suddenly and let the grin die slowly. His grin was fantastic, flashing over his face like a flood of white spotlights, center stage.

"*That's* where . . ." Jack began, then let it drop and looked out at the ocean again for a few seconds. He muttered, "A girl, a car, a lonely night . . . right. Hey, listen," he went on, in a brighter voice, turning back to me, "Eddie told us you fix things."

"Well, I'm a mechanic."

"My guitar? You think you can fix my guitar? I was playing 'Twist and Shout' last night, right, at the Outer Limits, right, and I'm into it, and suddenly *boing! boing! boing!*, three strings down, then *neeeeeng!*, not transmitting to the amp anymore. I mean, Cookie's looking at it, but I don't think it's going real well, 'cause she sent Stevie and Billy to the hardware store to get all kinds of stuff and usually she just puts a hairpin in it. And they don't any of them seem real happy."

I barely had time to nod before he was dragging us down the pier to the boardwalk, down the boardwalk until it ended, down the beach until we hit a stretch that had fallen into disuse, grown into weeds and was spotted with dead wood, then finally off the beach and across Seaside Boulevard, past Angie's Clams, and half a block down the street to a surf-beaten cottage with peeling paint and a sagging roof, trying to hide behind thatches of wild grass. Jack strolled up to the screen door and held it open for us to go inside.

We walked into a blast of decayed wood, warm salt air, mold, and beer. The front room was a grown-up playpen, the floor covered with mattresses, crumpled heaps of blankets, jeans, sneakers, guitars, dishes and

11

beer cans, triple cheeseburger paper wrappings and empty doughnut boxes, scraps of notebook paper and magazines. The walls were also covered—with an ambitious mural that had been abandoned, with a furious volley of graffiti, with a poster from the Elvis Presley movie *Girls! Girls! Girls!* There were handbills advertising local groups who had played the Shore in summers past, a framed photograph of a high school track team, a map of the United States with small red x's dotting the Northeast coast, a photograph of someone's parents sitting on a front porch and waving at the camera, and lots of photographs of Jack and the All-American Band—in a concert hall, in a club, on the beach. Then there were other photographs of Jack with his arm draped around a pretty girl in long blond braids. The girl smiled as though she were friends with the photographer, friends, really, with everyone in the world, her eyes bright and cheerful, while Jack alternated between smiles of sheepish pride and cool-guy expressions of quickly donned bravado. I stepped closer to examine the girl more carefully, but then the screen door slammed and I turned to see a tough-looking droopy-eyed guy saunter in, carrying a paper bag in an impatient fist. He was followed by a very tall man in tight black jeans with slicked-back blond hair, wearing hipster-style wraparound shades.

"Hey—" Jack began.

The first guy cut him off, shaking the bag at him.

"She can't fix it, it goes, Jack. Got that? She can't fix it, you're getting a new guitar."

"This is Cooder, Stevie," Jack said sunnily, waving

12

at me. "Eddie's friend. That's Stevie Delrone, Cooder. And that's Billy," he added, pointing to the hipster. "Listen, guys, he's gonna take a shot at it."

Delrone glanced skeptically at me, his dark eyes sagging with doubt and wariness. He had wide shoulders straining the neck of his black T-shirt, hard muscular arms, large hands and a grim expression, and he looked more like a blade-flicking street punk than the man who helped Jack with the pretty melodies of the songs Eddie and I had listened to on the way up. Billy turned down the hall with a noncommittal salute, and Delrone, after answering Jack with a dubious grunt, turned to follow. Jack trotted after them, and Eddie and I followed along, glancing quickly at and just as quickly away from the saucepan and cereal-bowl junkyard that served as their kitchen. Right across from the kitchen was a small bedroom, severely tidy in comparison to the rest of the house. The girl was sitting on the bed, her hair not braided as it had been in the photographs, but pulled back into a ponytail. Her head was bent over the guitar, which she held like a baby in her lap.

Delrone threw the bag on the bed next to her.

"It's no use," the girl said very quietly, and Billy, hanging over her shoulder like a vulture, patted her shoulder.

"Faint heart ne'er crossed home plate," he told her.

"Cooder's gonna try to fix it," Eddie said.

The girl looked up and smiled.

"Oh, hello, Eddie. Did you just get in?"

"Right on time," Jack answered for him. "And he brought the man who will fix my guitar. Cooder, this

13

is Mary Catherine O'Donnell, but you may call her Cookie."

She wrinkled her nose at him, then smiled at me and said hello—at least, I saw her lips move. I didn't answer her because I was too busy staring at her, at everything I hadn't seen in the photographs: the teasing blue eyes, the calculated delicacy of her nose, her mouth, her cheekbones. I suddenly remembered my hometown in Florida, and the mocking but tempting teenage girls who would come down on spring break and buy my Coca-Colas and flirt—"You live here, honey? All year *long*?"—until their boyfriends, big confident monsters like Delrone and Billy, snatched them away from local trash like me. I didn't last more than one summer hawking Coca-Colas to those girls before I walked off the beach and into town, and went to one of the mechanics and asked him to teach me the trade. His name was Cal. He was a devout and lonely lame man who became a brother in exile. My uncle, the Reverend Aaron Cutler, called him a "God-fearing man who knows his place in the world," and that was the highest praise I ever heard him give anyone. He sure as hell never gave me any. Knowing your place, to my uncle, was all you had to know, but I never caught on to what my place was, and Cal never tried to teach me. But he did teach me about cars and machines and wiring and a few other things that helped me survive, like how to keep your mouth shut and how to walk with dignity in a town that didn't have much use for you and how to never look straight into the eyes of the teasing blond tourist girls who thought you were just part of the vacation package.

14

Cookie's smile became puzzled as I continued staring, and Jack took the guitar from her, handed it to
me, and pulled her to her feet. He cupped her face
with both his hands and kissed her.

"For a noble effort," he said.

"Take your shot, then," Delrone said.

"I can't watch," Billy cried dramatically, throwing
his hand over his already-shaded eyes. "C'mon, Eddie,
let's get your stuff."

I tossed Eddie the keys. Then I sat down on the bed
and studied the guitar. It was a toy. It was painted
white, had a frail dark-brown plastic pickguard, and
looked as though it would crumble at a touch, much
less an attempt to deliver "Twist and Shout." I dumped
Delrone's paper bag onto the bed to see what he had
brought: a spool of wire, three new strings, four new
tuning pegs, a small wrench, nuts and bolts. I turned
the guitar all around, searching for the name of the
manufacturer, but I wasn't surprised to find that no
one had dared to claim responsibility for creating it.

"His mama gave it to him," Cookie explained. "To
keep him out of trouble. Pulled it right off the rack
on his fifteenth birthday."

"I love this guitar," Jack said, and sat down on the
floor to watch.

"You're the only one who can play it," Delrone said.

"Remember what that fortune-teller lady said!" Jack
answered. "This fortune-teller lady," he went on, ad-
dressing me, although I hadn't raised my head, "was
on her way to Atlantic City and she had a flat tire and
I changed it for her—"

"*I* changed it for her," Cookie corrected.

15

"And in return she read all of our fortunes, and she said I was gonna become a big rock-and-roll-star. Said it was in the cards. Said it was in my stars, read 'em and weep!"

"That's because she saw my guitar in the backseat of the car," Delrone told him. "A good guitar. Not yours."

"Said it was in my stars," Jack repeated, his voice pleasant and distant.

"Yeah," Delrone sighed. "She said I would do much traveling and never have a home and that Cookie would have many children. So what?"

"What's your name again?" Cookie asked me abruptly.

"Cooder Cutlas."

"That's a nice name. I love that jacket. Don't you love that jacket, Jack? What do you do, Cooder?"

My face was starting to get hot. I kept my eyes on the tuning pegs and pulled off the broken strings. If I glanced to one side, I could see her ankles peeking out from under her rolled-up jeans, and I sighed very slowly through my teeth and tried to concentrate. Soon I was lost in the work, and the next thing I knew, Eddie was peering over my shoulder.

"Bring in my guitar, huh?"

He nodded and retreated to the front room, then returned with my Strat. I started to remove a string from it, but Delrone pulled it out of my hands.

"There's a nice guitar. Jack, look at that. You could use this for tonight. Eddie, you don't mind if Jack uses your guitar, do you?"

"It's not mine, it's Cooder's."

16

Delrone looked at me and I looked at Jack. Jack was watching me with the hope of a patient child, and with a strange look of recognition, as though we had been through something like high school together and he couldn't place the memory.

"How's she coming?"

"I want to pull off a string from mine and put it on yours. Then we'll see."

Jack nodded and I took the Strat from Delrone.

"You play that?" Delrone asked carelessly.

"Not anymore," I told him, and loosened one of the pegs.

"He used to have this band in Atlanta, this great blues band, and there was this crazy guy who played sax and flute and clarinet," Eddie blurted. "And harmonica, too, right, Cooder? And he looked like a gangster or something—"

"Who told you all that?" I snapped, knowing that it must have been me, knowing that I must have spilled it the same night I spilled my Maude talk. I must have been better than a movie that night. Delrone gave me a thin smile I tried to ignore. I took a deep breath to keep my fingers steady. I was getting edgy to get out of that room.

"So where are they now?" Delrone drawled.

"It was a long time ago."

"So what happened to them?"

"Stevie," Cookie said.

"Just a hobby?" Delrone asked. "Or were you really good?"

I stood up and handed the guitar back to Jack.

"Not good enough for Paradise Beach, I guess."

17

"My God, it's fixed!" Jack shouted, strumming his guitar. "He *fixed* it! The show goes on! Cooder! I owe you my life! Let me buy you a cheeseburger!"

"Later," I said, and strode out of the house, letting the screen door slam behind me.

I walked down toward the beach and back toward downtown, passing a girl flopped on a towel and reading a beauty magazine while her transistor radio finished up a car commercial and charged into "Burning Love." I walked by two teenage boys who were muttering to each other about their romantic ambitions for the summer. The boardwalk had the same casual air, gearing up for the summer, some of the souvenir stands opened up and airing out last year's pennants and T-shirts, other stands still boarded shut.

Paradise Beach was a failed dream. They must have started on it just before the First World War, I reckoned, when the people from New York City would come all the way down here to fix up summer homes for their wives and children, and the town must have thrived during the twenties, but then there had been the Depression and then the war and then, with Europe only a jet trip away and other holiday towns close enough to the city to make day trips, the people from the city must have found better places to go when the weather got hot, and now in the middle of the seventies the dream of Paradise Beach was left unfinished, drifting off into a deep sleep. The town was gearing up for the summer out of habit, and the ocean breeze floated toward the fast-food stands with an amiable sigh. Like a rejected lover, the place was still quietly pretty, but it lacked the old charm and sparkle. It had hoped to be a nonstop dance party.

18

Instead it was as stale and sweet as a week-old birthday cake.

The place was half the hometown of my dreams and half the hometown I had really lived in, the town where by day I had sucked in grease and blasted rock and roll out of Cal's radio and watched the forbidden girls go by, and by night I had listened to Aunt Jane Ellen's prayer readings. It was half Disneyland and half never-quite-fashionable Belleau Beach just north of Tampa–St. Petersburg, the town where I had created myself, where I had fooled nobody with the arrogance of changing two letters in my last name; they all knew I was the illegitimate son of the Reverend Aaron Cutler's errant sister, Martha Jean, but I fooled myself with dreams of the day when I would be famous, when they would all know my name, when I would have them all beat. How could I ever think I had them all beat? They had all forgotten me once I was out of sight, but somehow I had taken them with me when I left town, like a pair of shoes a size too big that I kept tripping over.

There was a loud mechanical groan and whine, followed by the hesitant, breathy voice of a calliope, piping out its first cautious notes of the summer, piping out, I realized after a few bars, "And the Band Played On." The music was coming from the carousel just off Seaside Boulevard and hidden from the boardwalk by the pinball arcade. As I walked closer to it, I saw that it was beautiful—the horses, sculpted out of wood, their saddles and bridles trimmed with gilt, wore fierce, proud expressions, the only ones left who remembered what Paradise Beach was supposed to have been.

I felt a hand on my shoulder, and a voice said, "Hey, hey."

I turned and saw Cookie. Her ponytail was pinned into a bun, and she was wearing a pink dress that looked like a uniform, with a short skirt and low lacy neckline, and white Keds with ankle socks.

"So you found the carousel. Jack stares at that thing night and day."

I glanced back at the carousel and looked at her again.

"Jack's very happy about his guitar."

I shrugged and cleared my throat, stared down at her feet, then at mine.

"He really ought to get another one, though," Cookie continued. "I mean, he's got the money from the advance and everything. It's really silly for him to play that thing, but he's attached to it."

I nodded.

"I'm going to work if you want to walk with me," she said easily, and I fell into step beside her, shoving my hands into my pockets. Her eyes fluttered over me for a second, and then she continued her low, casual chatter.

"I usually manage the morning shift, so I can watch the boys all night and sleep all afternoon, but one of the girls just called the house and said she's sick, so I'm taking her shift. The malt shop. Have you seen it? It's a pretty place, nice tile floor. . . . Have you been exploring? Eddie says you're from a beach town in Florida."

"Small town," I mumbled, when I realized that she was waiting for an answer. "North of Tampa."

20

"Well . . . Eddie says you've left Virginia for good. Where are you headed?"

"I'm not sure."

"Maybe you ought to hang around for a while. At least stay tonight and see the show."

"So they're really hot, huh?"

"They're wonderful," she said, and her face was glowing.

"But you'd say that anyway."

She looked at me sharply. "No, I wouldn't."

She had a deep husky voice, relaxed and kind but with a rasp that hinted at sweet mornings after warm, warm nights.

"Give me some credit."

"I didn't mean not to. I just meant—well, you have your loyalties."

"I also have taste."

"So if they did a record and they're so good, what are they doing in this place all summer?"

"Jack's doing his second album, starting July. He grew up here. He tries out his new stuff at the Outer Limits. It's family down here for him."

"How long have you known these guys?" I asked.

"Well, Stevie and Billy since high school."

"High school," I echoed, fighting down a disappointment that had no business being there.

"In Maryland," she went on serenely. "They were a few years older. Stevie played defense on the football team. I barely knew him. Billy was a track star, and I was on the school paper. He won All-Maryland for the hundred-yard dash and I interviewed him for the paper and I guess he kind of got a crush on me. But

21

then they graduated and I still had two more years. They moved up here and I forgot about them. Then . . . but you don't want to hear all this."

We were standing in front of the malt shop now, and she was studying me. Billy kind of got a crush on her, she guessed. She guessed guys were getting crushes on her all the time. My hangover rushed back at me in one big splash. My hair was sticking to my forehead and my eyes ached. I thought for one moment that she would brush my hair back for me, and I begged God to make her do it. I could tell that she was playing with the idea, and then I could tell that she wouldn't do it.

"Go ahead."

"So I came up to New York to go to school, anyway," she went on. "And I came down here the summer after my first year to work at the Shore, because I thought it would be fun, and Jack and Billy and Stevie came into the malt shop . . ."

"Ah. Right."

"No," she chided. "Listen, I have to go in. Come on, I'll make you a chocolate milk shake."

They had them prefrozen in the dairy case, but she pushed the other malt-shop girl aside and made me one from scratch: chocolate ice cream, chocolate syrup and milk.

"I didn't want to get involved with any rock and rollers," Cookie explained, which brought a snort from the other malt-shop girl. "They all asked me out. I don't mean to sound conceited, but they did. So we went out as a group a lot. I was like a den mother. Near the end of the summer, Jack told me that the band took up his whole life, he didn't have time for a girlfriend. I said, 'Fine, I don't have time to be a groupie, either.' So I went back to school kind of mad. And then he came up, oh, I guess it was near Christmas. He was just there in the dorm. In his black leather jacket. And that was three years ago."

The other girl looked up with a smile.

"Three years in the ice-cream business," Cookie said with a sigh. "But I'm *manager* now. I run the jukebox."

I read the jukebox when the other customers started coming in. There wasn't a record on it that wasn't at least ten years old, and they were all by girl-groups: the Crystals, the Ronettes, the Shirelles, the Marvelettes, the Chiffons, the Dixie Cups. Then there was a masterpiece called "Don't Say Nothin' Bad About My Baby," by a group I had never heard of, the Cookies.

The local kids did love him. They screamed when he came on as though it were a rare appearance, as though he hadn't promised them every Saturday night in June. Jack stood at the microphone and waited for the screams to subside. Then he started in, very slow, very soft, like lighting one match in a dark room. It was a long quiet ballad from his new album and it grew lighter and brighter, while the lights came up on the rest of the band, until the whole song burst into a shower of sparks and died with a shout. Lee, the keyboards man, seemed to be a quiet sort, leaning over his piano and whispering instructions to Eddie, who was blind behind his drums, but right at home onstage. Billy and Delrone had a routine down, checking one another out, switching places behind Jack, both restless and prowling, watching Jack's every move.

After he let his ballad drown out in applause, Jack

23

paused for one heartbeat and then slid into "I Only Want to Be With You," a slowed-down, bluesy version of what I remembered as a happy-go-lucky, slightly sappy pop song. Cookie rose and leaned against a pillar, her arms folded across her chest, small smile dancing around her mouth. Jack closed his eyes and held his hair with both hands while he moaned for four bars, and then he looked right at her and flashed her a smile that would have broken your mother's heart.

> *'Cause you started something, oh can't you see*
> *That ever since we met you've had a hold on me*
> *No matter what you do*
> *I only want to be with you.*

It was a sleazy, sticky-tabled, fishnetted, dollar-at-the-door joint, but it was home to him. Everybody in the place belonged to Jack. I was astonished by their innocence, their good nature. They were like no crowd I had ever played to in the days when I had played. My crowds had been concerned with social issues and the blues, but all this bunch wanted was Jack. He danced across the stage with their collective grace, wearing their collective crummy summer clothes, telling them about themselves, the summer that had been and gone, the girls he had known and left behind, the cars he had met cruising down the road, the guys he had tried to beat, the mornings that had greeted him when the night finally went to bed. There was always something to celebrate.

I moved to the bar to watch them, although Cookie had given me a seat at what she called "the Table for the Select Few," the up-front table reserved for herself

24

and the other malt-shop girls, Trudy and Sara and
Cindy and Robin, and a mysterious group they called
"People from New York." The audience knew all
the words to Jack's songs, and they sang along at his
signal, a call-and-echo performed with a spirit, on
both sides, that I hadn't seen since my last revival
meeting. He paused after a long run of songs, all the
rhythm-and-blues and rock-and-roll snacks of glory
that had made sense to me back when nothing else
did, the seventy-two-greatest-hits-of-all-time, here-for-
the-first-time-ever-on-this-five-record-set, not-available-
in-stores, call-this-number-before-midnight-tomorrow
rap that had blasted out at me on late-night television
in so many motel rooms, and he formed a huddle with
the guys onstage. The bartenders hurriedly began re-
moving all glasses and bottles from the bar. Then Jack
burst into "Twist and Shout" with an explosive glee
that set my ears back an inch. It was a cue for a dance
marathon and a temporary shutdown of the bar for
reasons of public safety.

The only kids who weren't dancing were watching
Jack with looks of "How's he do that?" gliding over
their faces. I turned from them to watch Jack, sliding
and skipping and stepping and turning with a style too
perfect to have ever been learned, a style heaven-sent.
Then Cookie was tugging on my arm and laughing.

"The girls want to dance with you," she shouted,
waving back at the Table for the Select Few.

"I'll dance with you first!" I yelled, and then Jack,
bless him, began a sweet old last-song-at-the-sock-hop
number, and I slid my arm around Cookie's waist.

"All right," she said, nervous and pleased.

She rested her chin on my chest. She came just to

25

my breastbone. She had let her hair down and combed it away from her face, and I could see that the roots of her hair were darker than the blond tips. I kissed those roots and she looked up, but I gazed off across the room and pretended I hadn't done a thing.

I was too old for it, a summer on the beach watching girls. I was twenty-three years old, and if everything had worked out according to my plan, I would have already had a wife and at least one baby and a classic hit record. If everything had worked out, I would have had it all, but instead it had all fallen through. And I had nothing except pride, telling me I was too old to pretend I had all the time in the world.

Except that Jack was my age, and he wasn't worried. He did have all the time in the world, because he had the music, he had his band, he had a summer stretching ahead and a beach that hadn't yet disappeared into the ocean, he had his girlfriend, he had his turf. He had so much that he could afford to be generous. And he was generous to me in a way he didn't even know, in giving me what I could not give myself when everything had fallen through, in giving me a second chance.

"Where did 'Cookie' come from?" I asked.

"Jack."

"I like Mary Catherine."

She smiled, but pulled her hands out of mine, shook her head at me slightly, then jerked her head back toward the Table for the Select Few.

"You have to dance with Trudy now. She's almost dying, waiting for you to ask."

"Okay," I said. "Which one's Trudy?"

*   *   *

26

The next afternoon I was sweeping out the inside of the car and fixing the radio. Some kids had vandalized it during the night, before we got back from the Outer Limits; they had not been clever enough to remove the radio and had only mangled it, so in frustration they had made off with the blades to the windshield wipers. Jack had stood over it and clucked, "You know, there's so many *thieves* around here, and the cops bother us with *noise* complaints," before he strolled away to see if he could "find Carl." As soon as I got the radio fixed and playing "Brown-Eyed Girl," Jack returned with a short, thin, rodent-featured man who walked around the car, nodding as though he intended to buy it.

"Cougar XR7-GTE," he said.

"That's right."

"This is Carl," Jack said, and Carl handed me two windshield wiper blades.

"You should keep it parked near my place," he told me. "Kids don't come near my place. They know better. So, you're a mechanic?"

"That's right."

"Good?"

"I can make anything run."

Carl raised his eyebrows. "Worked on Corvettes?"

"Corvettes? Yeah. Good little cars. Not really my taste."

"Your taste doesn't really matter," Carl said curtly. "Your skill does."

"Well, I know my way around a Corvette."

"That's fine. Okay. Well," he added, clapping his hands once and rubbing them together, "you can come by tomorrow, if you want."

27

I watched him walk away, then squinted at Jack.

"Carl the Corvette Specialist," Jack explained. "He has a garage. He needs an assistant."

"Does he?"

"He mentioned that. I mentioned that you might be interested."

"Did you?"

"Well, hell, Cooder, he's a good guy, and we've got plenty of room, and it's a fun town come summer, and the malt-shop girls all like you, and you've got . . . what did Chuck Berry say . . . ?"

He knew damn well what Chuck Berry said, and he knew I knew he knew it.

"No particular place to go," I finished.

"I mean I don't know if you're in trouble or what, but if you need a place to sort things out, this is it. I know. I've spent my *life* here sorting things out, right?" Jack grinned, that grin that made me wonder how Cookie could have spent an entire summer refusing him. "And my guitar, you know, it's temperamental. It might break again."

"That's true," I said.

"Great," Jack said, and leaned into the backseat to grab my tool kit and duffel bag. I took the tool kit and he leaned in again for my Bible.

"Careful—" I started to say, but he had already picked it up by the spine and the photographs had already fallen out.

"Oh, sorry, man," he said, and bent to pick them up. Then he set down the duffel bag, tucked the Bible under his arm, and studied the pictures. I winced but I let him look. The silence seemed to grow as loud as "Twist and Shout."

28

"This is your band," he said at last.

"Yeah."

"Who's this guy?"

"Dark Mark Clark."

Jack whistled. "He looks mean as hell."

"He played mean. We were a mean bunch."

Jack continued staring, then transferred the stare to me in a long hard look, as though by searching my face he could hear what we had sounded like. Then he turned his attention to the next few photos.

"This girl doesn't look mean. She looks nice. She's pretty. She sort of"—he stopped short when he heard me suck in air, then he raised his eyes and finished quickly —"looks Irish."

"Yeah."

He placed the photographs back in the Bible and picked up the duffel bag. I picked up the tool kit, and as we walked to the house he clapped me on the shoulder and said, his voice all smiles again, "Irish girls. Best in the world."

So I stayed with them and fell into the pattern of their days. I took the job with Carl the Corvette Specialist, and I bought a mattress and threw it down on the floor in the living room beside Eddie and Billy and Delrone. In the mornings we slept as the sun crawled up the outside walls and finally broke through the window, until Cookie returned from her morning shift at the malt shop and threw us our breakfast, a box of day-old doughnuts. Then she went into the bedroom she shared with Jack and shut the door on us firmly.

The band rehearsed at the Outer Limits in the early

afternoon, then the boys left Jack to tend to business while they cruised the beaches. Johnny Streeter, the band's very young manager, had not booked them studio time in Manhattan until July, so they relished June, knowing that in a short month they would be making long three-day trips into New York to record. Johnny Streeter was a thin, excitable guy who moved constantly when he spoke, and he always spoke in violent staccato bursts, as if he had been holding his comment in for hours and couldn't restrain himself any longer, although the All-Americans were always willing to give him the floor. They treated him with respect since he was their manager, and he had thrown himself into the job from the moment that Lee, his friend from music school, had suggested it to him. Johnny Streeter brought a tape of Jack and the All-Americans to his father, John Streeter, Sr., a record company executive who signed up the band. Johnny Streeter and Lee dropped out of school. Jack and the All-Americans played up and down the east coast in clubs like the Outer Limits and made one album, which sounded flat, compared to their stage work, and hardly sold at all.

So while Delrone, Billy, Eddie, and I walked up and down the boardwalk and lay out on the beach, Jack and Lee sat with Johnny Streeter at the piano on the darkened stage of the Outer Limits trying to learn how to translate all the fun and energy on stage into a record that would bring the boys the glory they deserved. The boys warned me that Jack was a stickler in the studio. He could spend hours perfecting a chord change and time was money and spending all that time in the studio left them with no money to spend.

Delrone and Billy said they didn't mind the money, they were used to being poor. It was the wear and tear on their nerves, they said, and being in the dark all through July.

The band kept their fears to themselves, though. Jack seemed too absorbed in writing and rehearsing to bother with concerns like fame and capital gain. He ran the guys through new material, left lyrics on fast-food wrappings scattered around the front room of the house, spent long nights talking with Lee about arrangements, and played around with my guitar as Delrone nagged him to go shopping for a new one.

Carl the Corvette Specialist let me come in late because I stayed late, and I didn't mind staying late because nights out with the All-Americans didn't begin until around ten o'clock. If the guys were rehearsing in Paradise Beach, I sat and watched them and drank beer and flirted with the malt-shop girls, Trudy and Sara and Cindy and Robin, one of them always in uniform and arriving late after she closed up shop, the other three always dizzy and brown from a day in the sun, Trudy plump and sweet and friendly, Cindy lean and sleepy-eyed, Sara pretty in a preening way, Robin aloof and preoccupied. If the guys were going out, they went all out, piling into cars and barhopping their way north until the bars in Jersey closed, and then, what the hell, it was only a hop over to Manhattan, where the bars were open all the time. We returned home from the late salty nights and crashed on the floor until the late salty mornings; there was always the salt of the popcorn, the salt of the pretzels, the salt from the sweat of dancing, the salt of the sea that sprayed all over us when we walked down the beach, clinging to us so that we could taste it without opening our mouths.

I awoke before the rest of them, to the beer-drenched damp smell of the house, with a dry thirst, pulling on my jeans and shuffling off to work to the beat of the music that was always in the air. It was the music of Jack's guitar tuning up as I headed for the door. It was the music of the calliope as I hurried down Seaside Boulevard on my way to Carl's. It was the music of the pop tunes that snapped and crackled out of the transistor radios of the suntanned girls who passed me on the boardwalk on my way to Carl's, pounding those jingles and rhymes and rhythms into my head all day long, interrupted only by the news of the Watergate drama, down the shore and far away, and of more sunny weather to come.

Girls were everywhere. They clustered around Jack after seeing his show, and he was kind and shy but made it clear that he was taken, and Eddie and Billy found that it was easiest to stand around Jack and pick up his discards. Billy, a rockabilly junkie who would have given his soul to be born again in Mississippi, turned on a sweet-talking Southern accent so thick it made me wince to hear it, until he caught me wincing and demanded that I give him lessons. Eddie abandoned any attempt at sharp suave banter in favor of the classic line: "Hey! I'm the drummer in Jack Armstrong's band, you know!" to all the girls, their memories Ringo fresh, who still thought all drummers were adorable. Delrone was more or less hooked up with Cindy from the malt shop. And Lee lived in Manhattan and came down only when he was needed.

"So what's the story with Lee?" I asked Jack one

afternoon when we were both free from work, walking along his favorite highway and leaping out of the traffic.

"Eddie told you about Lee, right?"

"Just that he was at music school with your manager, Johnny Streeter, and he was some kind of piano genius, and now everybody hates him because he's a rock and roller."

"Naw, they don't hate him. They don't *understand* him. He's been studying for, like, sixteen years. His mother is some opera singer and his father's some kind of conductor. Lee was studying with this guy Zamenak, some really important famous guy. I met him once, Zamenak; Lee wanted us to meet each other, God knows why. So I played a little for him and he starts muttering in German and waving his hands at me. So Lee says, 'He thinks you should study,' and I said na na na. I did study once, you know; my dad said, 'Well, if you have to be a *musician*, at least know what you're doing,' and Mama thought I should study composition. So I tried to be a good son, right? I knew they were wrong, but I went. And I had this old drunk for a teacher, really sad guy, and he wanted us all to write chorales, man, you know? Like in church, dirges for four voices. So I gave it a good shot, you know, I tried to make it like doo-wop, but the guy didn't want to have anything to do with that, so I quit after two months."

"But how did Lee get in the band?"

"Oh, well . . . like, he was up at Juilliard, practicing ten, twelve, fourteen hours a day. So he decides he needs a few days off and he comes down to the Shore and he walks in and sees us."

"And saw the light?" I teased.

33

"Right," Jack said solemnly, then caught my eye and shrugged, smiling. "Well, we *had* a piano player at the time, this guy Mike, used to play the piano with the heel of his shoe. Like Jerry Lee Lewis. You know? Made Lee sick. Lee goes up after the show and tries to tell him he shouldn't treat his instrument that way, and Mike snaps off, 'Right, you think you can do any better?' and Lee does, he gets up there and plays this boogie-woogie walking bass bit, you woulda died to hear it. Then he was just gonna go. But I dragged him over, I bought him a beer. I tried to talk him into playing with us. He came down a few more times that summer and played. He was great. You could tell he'd never had so much fun in his life. At the end of the summer, he wouldn't say yes, he wouldn't say no. Like Cookie, you know? He went back to school. She went back to school. I fired Mike anyway. That kind of showing off, that's not what we're about."

"What do you mean," I asked carefully, "like Cookie?"

"Oh, well, I met them the same summer. Billy and Stevie, they were all excited when they saw her in town. They knew her from high school. They kept asking her out, but she said she didn't want no rock and roller. Of course, she didn't. She was pretty and real smart, top student at this fancy school. They kept asking her, though, like, why not? It's just a summer romance. But she was tough tough tough. Finally, they said, 'Hey, Jack, I think she wants to go out with *you*.' And I thought, no way. But I started going to the malt shop more, hanging out, playing the girl-group songs on the jukebox for her. She knows all those songs. She sang along with them. She knew them by heart. And that's when I started, started . . ."

He sighed and ruffled his hair, and I had to smile.

"C'mon, man, let's get off the highway. It's too dusty."

We headed for the boardwalk and stopped along the way to buy a couple of soft ice creams.

"Anyway, so Mike was acting up and the drummer, hell, was on drugs half the time. So they were out. And who was in? Lee, why would he want to leave that silver-spoon life of his, and Cookie, she was probably used to guys in ties. So then winter came. And I went home. The band was on, like . . . *hiatus*, I guess you'd have to say. And Dad started in. 'Jack, get a job.' I already felt like Scruff King of the Universe. 'Get a job. Go to college.' And I was beginning to have my doubts."

"A crisis of faith."

"Exactly, man. So then Mama was making Thanksgiving dinner. And this song came over the radio, the Chiffons singing, 'One fine day you're gonna want me for your girl.' And I don't know what happened, but suddenly Mama was saying, 'Jack, what's wrong?' and I was spilling my guts. And she was *so happy*. I'd never had a steady girl, you know, and I guess Mama was gettin' kind of *worried*," Jack laughed, a raspy gurgle that sounded like a wheezy puppy trying to bark. "And Mama said, 'Jack, go and get her.' And I said, 'Ma, I got the band, I don't have time for a serious girlfriend.' And she said, 'So, when are you gonna have the time? When you're fifty years old?' "

He paused for so long that I prompted, "So you went and got her."

35

"That part wasn't easy, either. I was on her turf, and she let me know it. And I didn't like it. We used to fight like dogs. I was going from her school to Lee's school, begging, 'At least *one* of you say yes.' And one time, after a big fight with Cookie, I went up to Lee's school, and he comes out of his practice room, it's the dead of winter, he has circles under his eyes, no color. And I grabbed him—"

Jack grabbed me by the shirt collar with surprisingly strong hands and shook me.

"—'What's so great about this life, huh? And what's so rotten about mine? I'm talking to *kids*, man. I'm talking to people who *need a voice*. Who are you talking to, except a bunch of snotty old rich people who think they own the world? The kids *listen* to me. Who listens to you, shut up in your little room all day, studying studying *studying*?' "

He shoved me away on the last word and I stumbled back. He didn't even notice, his hand in his hair and his eyes on the ocean, lost on memory lane.

"I guess I took him by surprise," he said.

"I *guess*," I answered, straightening my shirt.

"Of course, it was her I was really mad at."

"But you got her," I snapped, suddenly irritated. "And she was worth the wait. And all in all, you're pretty goddamned lucky."

His eyes were puzzled and almost hurt at my tone, as though he hadn't one minute earlier tried to shake my teeth out. He continued walking, but he pulled his gaze away from the ocean, away from me, and his voice fell down to earth. "She reminds you of that girl, doesn't she? That girl in the pictures?"

I stopped short and looked at him. He scowled at

36

the horizon. There was a similarity in their features that even Jack could see, but it was more than that. It was her voice, I realized, her voice and her husky giggle, a giggle that was three fourths whisper, a sleepy, happy, just-us-two-awake-in-the-whole-city giggle.

"The voice," I said slowly. "Low like that. And the eyes. The same eyes. Different color, but the same eyes."

"What happened to her?"

"She's dead."

"How long?"

"Three years. Three years in September."

"Nobody since?"

"I don't know if you get another one. Not like that."

He was watching me with that same look of recognition he had had on the day we met, and I remembered how he'd looked straight at me when we were introduced, straight into my eyes, and kept his gaze there until I turned away. His vision, in that and everything else, was not so earthshatteringly keen, just very steady and constant and gentle. I thought I was a tough guy with the hard blank face of a master poker player. But there must have been times, maybe when Cookie laughed, maybe when a certain song came over the radio, when he could read my face like a road map if he was looking. And he *had* been looking. His sympathy penetrated as far into the depths as I would allow anyone to go, and then we both came up for air, glanced at our feet, glanced at the beach.

"Maybe you don't," Jack said quietly, "if you don't let it go."

"Maybe you don't know a damn thing about it until you've lived through it," I said, the words coming like

37

a knee-jerk curse before I could stop them. I wished he'd never brought her up, but I knew it wasn't his fault. I felt like a whining fool.

Jack cuffed my shoulder and spoke very casually.

"Probably not. Maybe you could fill me in some-time."

"Yeah," I said. "Sometime."

One Sunday afternoon we were in the malt shop, Delrone and Cookie huddled at a corner table while Cookie fretted over the work-week schedule, thrown into an emergency because one malt-shop girl, Robin, had just quit. I was sitting at a table with Lee and Johnny Streeter and Carl the Corvette Specialist, dis-cussing a new paint job and complete overhaul for Lee's teacher's 1956 white Mercedes.

"Wait 'til you see this car, Cooder, your mouth'll water. He bought it with the money he got from win-ning his first international piano competition. Had it shipped over to the States and everything. My parents want to fix it up for him. The engine knocks, rat-tles . . . I don't know. Needs a whole new paint job. And we want to put in a four-way speaker cassette tape deck so he can listen to his students, on tape, on his way to school." Lee sat back and smiled thinly. "They want to do it for his birthday, and also to thank him for spending ten years with me, teaching me to play classical piano so I could turn around and run off with a rock-and-roll band."

"When's his birthday?"

"August."

"I'd like to help you out," Carl said, "but I don't have time for it. I've got two Corvettes to customize

38

and a Camaro that a guy wants to have painted with flames on the hood. You want it done fast, you'll have to take it somewhere else."

"Couldn't Cooder do it?" Lee asked.

Carl looked at me inquiringly. "You wanna do it, you'll have to do it on your own time."

"Can I use your paint compressor?"

"Long as you clean up before I come in mornings. I don't want your stuff in my way. These Corvette guys are my regulars. I promised 'em. Deadlines, and stuff."

"I'll keep it clean."

"Okay by me," Carl said, standing up. "You find your own paint, don't let it get in my way, it's okay by me. See ya round, Lee."

"Thanks a lot, Carl," Lee said. "Listen, Cooder," he added, as Carl waved good-bye to Trudy and strolled out the door, "I wanted you to do it all along. Carl, he's a great guy, and Corvettes, they're great cars, but a Corvette isn't a Mercedes."

"I haven't done that much foreign work myself, Lee."

"It doesn't matter. You have an eye for it. I can tell. You have a respect for it. Also, you can charge my parents anything you want."

"Whatever's fair," I said.

"Just put a sign in the window," Delrone was telling Cookie. "All the kids around here need a summer job."

"We can't take just anybody, Stevie," Cookie said. "We need a *malt-shop girl*."

"So she'll learn to be a malt-shop girl."

"Whatever's fair!" Johnny Streeter repeated sarcastically. "What do you mean 'fair,' Cooder? We're talking about your labor here. You probably have the same idea of 'fair' as Jack. You probably need a manager."

"I thought we had an exclusive deal."

"Oh, *there* you are," Johnny said to Jack, who had just come in with Billy. A young girl was in their wake.

"You trying to steal my manager?" Jack teased.

"Isn't Carl here?" Billy asked. "I thought you guys had Carl in here."

"He took off," Johnny Streeter said.

"He took off," Billy told the girl.

She twisted her fingers and looked ready to cry.

"But *Cooder's* here," Jack said cheerfully.

She looked at me with a kind of shy fear. She had wide startled eyes, dark soft hair pulled into a loose ponytail, a long thin nose and pale baby skin. She was wearing a dark-blue school sweater with a broken-heart emblem inscribed with Latin words on the right breast pocket, a blue pleated skirt, white cotton blouse, bobby socks, and blue sneakers. She seemed ready to recite a lesson. She looked so out of place in there that Trudy, Cookie, and Delrone stopped what they were doing to look at her.

"He works in the garage," Jack said, pulling up a chair for her, then explaining to me, "She's had some car trouble."

She sat down primly, arranging her skirt. Lee studied her carefully, and ran a finger across her broken-heart emblem, then translated for us the Latin words underneath.

"Courage, charity, and grace."

"Oh—that's the school motto."

"CCGA," Lee read.

"Creve Coeur Girls' Academy."

"Creve Coeur Girls' Academy?" Lee asked Johnny, who had been thrown out of almost every prep school on the East Coast.

"Never met any Creve Coeur girls."

"It means 'broken heart,'" Lee told them. "Nice name for a girls' school."

"We found her creeping around outside Carl's."

"I want to know how much it would cost to have my tires replaced," the girl said.

"How many did you lose?" I asked.

"Four."

"Four!" Johnny exclaimed. "That's pretty careless."

"They were stolen. I left my car in front of the Sandpiper Motel, and when I got back, they were gone."

"Did you tell the police?"

"Oh, no, I can't. Well, it's . . . it's not my car," she admitted. Her voice trembled slightly, and she stared down at her fingers in her lap.

"Whose is it?" I asked.

"Jimmy's. He's—he was my boyfriend."

"And where is he?" Johnny asked.

"I don't know. I don't care, either."

"Does he know you have his car?"

"I guess he's figured it out by now."

"What do you mean?"

"Well, when he comes back and finds me gone . . ."

She raised her eyes suddenly, looking weary and defeated, and looked right at me. I stirred my Coke with my finger and nodded at her to go on.

"We ran away together," she said breathlessly. "From St. Louis. Three days ago. And now I'm running away from him."

"In *his* car," Johnny Streeter pointed out.

41

"Well, I'm gonna give it to his father when I get back!" she burst out indignantly. "And I don't care how he gets back—he took all my money and he left me alone in the motel room, and he said he was going to find someone who wasn't such a baby. He said he was gonna find someone *else*. He *hit* me and said he was gonna find someone else."

Cookie scowled, laid down her pen and scooted over near Jack. Delrone stood up and joined the group around the table.

"Where was this?" I asked.

"New York. Not New York. Somewhere outside New York. He left his jacket. His keys were in his pocket." She lowered her eyes again and spoke rapidly. "He said he was going into the city, but he didn't want to take his car there, so he left me, he left his car, and I just wanted to get away from him. He knew that, that's why he took my money. He's been so mean to me, ever since we left. I just wanted to spend the summer on the beach, but he . . ."

She started crying, and Jack and Cookie, who had been waiting for the tears, handed her napkins. Jack stroked her hair soothingly.

"See, back in St. Louis, I did a little modeling. Nothing major, just girls' juniorwear and stuff. The department store owner was a good friend of Daddy's, so I did it. And Jimmy thought I should—well, I wanted to, too, I guess—come to the city and try it. Try to be a model. A real model. But when I went in there, I went into one of the agencies, and there were so many girls, *so* many. I thought, Oh, they'll never want me. I just turned right around. And that made him mad. That and . . . other things. Oh, I don't know. It was

42

going to be so simple, just us, just the beach. And I just wanted to drive home, I was just going to wire Daddy and have him send me some money and say I'm sorry and I don't want to . . . go back, but I don't know what else . . .''

She leaned forward to cry into her hand, and Cookie kindly but firmly removed Jack's hand from the girl's hair. Cookie patted the girl's shoulder and waited until the girl's tears had subsided into violent sniffing before she said mildly, "But you're kind of off the beaten track. How did you end up here?"

"I wanted to see it, before I went back. I didn't want the trip to be a total waste."

"Wanted to see *what*?"

"Paradise *Beach*," the girl said, wiping her eyes and setting the napkin down. She looked at me with embarrassed but resolute eyes. "Paradise Beach, like the Paradise Beach album. You know that album? By Jack Armstrong and the All-American Band?"

I bit my lip and nodded as sincerely as I could, fighting to keep my eyes on her and not look at the rest of them.

"You like that album?" Johnny Streeter asked, his voice thick with restrained glee.

She nodded, and looked up at their grinning faces. Her face puckered again to see them laughing at her, and she turned back to me quickly.

"Jimmy and I listened to it all the time. Nobody else seemed to know it— What's wrong? It's a good album!"

"It's a fine album," I assured her gravely, and that was too much for Delrone, who made a wild sound that was half a cough and half a dog's bark, and clutched

43

helplessly at Billy, who could not restrain himself in the face of Delrone's yelping laughter.

"Stop it, Stevie," Cookie ordered.

The girl, too confused and exhausted to fight them, started crying again in the circle of grins, and Jack, who had not laughed at all, pulled up a chair and wiped her tears away for her. He put his arm around her shoulders and shushed her.

"You came all the way from St. Louis to see this place because of the album, huh?"

"Don't make *fun* of me!"

"No, no, I'm not. I think that's nice. I think that's real nice."

"And it wasn't just the album, it was Jimmy," the girl said, too tired to quit and ready to spill the whole story. "It's always been school and dancing lessons and piano lessons and painting lessons and then the modeling, and my aunts didn't *approve* of the modeling, and Jimmy was the first boy they ever let me go out with and now I'll have to go back there and I'll be in all kinds of trouble."

"Well, listen—Shut *up*, Stevie—listen, no garage in town is gonna fix your car today, because they're all closed. You'll just have to relax."

"But I can't—"

"Look, have you eaten? Are you hungry? Trudy, fix the girl a cheeseburger! What's your name, anyway, honey?"

"Madeline Deene Simmons," she answered, and then amended, after Jack frowned, "But you can call me Macky."

Macky was sworn in as the new malt-shop girl and member of the All-American household without much fuss, aside from a small tiff in the kitchen on the night of her arrival, after we had brought her home and Cookie had lent her a towel and shown her to the shower.

"Nobody'll come looking for her," Jack said. "She's seventeen. That's old enough to leave home."

"Seventeen?" Billy repeated. "She looks twelve."

"Naw, thirteen," Eddie corrected, with a leering gleam in his eye. "Thirteen, at least."

"Look, Jack," Cookie said. "I know you're a sucker for a good runaway saga, and I know she came to Paradise Beach because of you, but if she makes any trouble and they ask about her, we don't know—"

"Her? Make trouble?" Delrone scoffed.

"She just wants a summer," I said. "She just wants a summer away from them all. Hell, she told me on the way home she'd never even seen the ocean before."

"Wow," Jack said softly. "See, Cookie, she's never even seen a *beach* before. She came out to see a beach because she heard *me*."

"Look, I'm sure lots of girls would like to do that—"

"It's not against the law, is it?" Jack asked. "Seventeen is old enough, right?"

"Old enough for one thing, anyway," Eddie said, grinning.

I leaned back, curled my foot around the rung of the chair, and jerked the chair out from under him. He swiped at the table on the way down, upsetting Jack's Coke, then frowned at me from the floor.

"Guess that means hands off, huh?"

"Guess that means mouth shut," I answered.

"If anyone *asks*," Cookie continued, "we don't know a damn thing about her and she's just staying here 'cause she's Cooder's girlfriend. If anyone asks."

"How come she can't be staying here 'cause she's *my* girlfriend? If anyone asks?" Eddie whined, struggling to his feet.

"Because you're filth," I told him.

"Right, and I guess *you* just wanna play hopscotch with her," he sneered.

She had eyes like molasses, dark and slow and sweet, and a soft, clear, childish voice. And when she talked to me, I stared at her evenly until a blush crawled slowly up her neck to her face and she looked down, then raised her eyes again, and I had to look away.

She fought her way through her crash course in being a malt-shop girl and being a member of the All-American crowd with every bit of the courage, charity, and grace inscribed on her sweater. The girls teased her at the malt shop and the boys teased her at home and I never teased her at all, and she turned from their teasing, her cheeks pink and her eyes sparking and her braids flying, to me. Her eyes were still innocent, and appealing for protection, but it was an appeal wiser than it would have been even a few days before she arrived in Paradise Beach; it was not an appeal for protection from danger and disrepute, since she, with her seventeen-year-old heart, thought she had experienced both already, but an appeal for a partner in crime.

"You're new, too, aren't you?" she asked me that first night in the living room while she waited in vain for Cookie to throw Jack out of the bedroom and welcome Macky in as a sister. Eventually, she realized that the girls were not going to be with the girls, that Jack and the bedroom were taken, and that she was stranded in the living room with the guys in the band. She chose my mattress to share, maybe because it was the cleanest. She turned pink when Eddie winked at me, and she hurried into the bathroom. She came out with her hair down and a teddy-bear-patterned nightgown on, and hurried under the blanket, breathing bravely until the lights were out and Billy whispered loudly, "Good *night*, Macky," and I could feel her blushing on the other side of the bed. I let her have her distance and watched her sleep, with her mouth half open, her hands tucked under her chin. Her face while she slept was serene, relaxed now that

47

she did not have to blush or wrinkle her nose or stand on guard. Her hair, as fine and clinging as a spider's web, spilled everywhere, and I allowed myself to play with one lock of it while I stared at the soft pouty curve of her mouth, her skin, the opened buttons at the collar of her stupid teddy-bear nightgown.

And all those nights when I did not dare touch Macky, I thought about Frannie Kirby, my dream girl back in Florida. Frannie used to sit in my uncle's church with all her Kirby brothers, scratching her legs and sneaking looks at me during the hymns, twisting one curl around her forefinger while my uncle sneered at lust from the pulpit and the congregation muttered fervent A-*men*s and I burned hot. She played softball with her brothers in the churchyard on Saturday afternoons and I joined them, after sweeping out the church and cleaning the yard, just so I could watch her slide home. I had pined for her, with an intensity that made me wonder whether the congregation was right about me, that I had bad blood, my mother's wild and my father's unknown, that no baptism could bleed out.

Frannie and I started dating when we both reached fifteen, although her father objected, as every father in the congregation would object to having his daughter in my company, except that the Kirbys weren't that all-fire religious, and Mr. Kirby was bothered by the thought that a tomboy like Frannie would never get a date. He didn't have to worry: I discovered, on the night she became my first lover, that she had had at least one before me. But I was glad about it, because I didn't want to repeat the crime of a father I had never seen. I didn't want to cause a girl to be driven out of town the way my mother had been. All the girls in the rock-and-roll songs I turned to knew exactly what they had and what to do with it, and all the girls I had ever turned to had known that, too. So I did not dare touch Macky, on all those nights when it would have been so easy, until she came to me first.

Soon enough she fell into step beside me when we all went out as a group, and soon enough I persuaded her to come out with me alone. I took her on long drives and taught her to dance like a pro, and kissed her in the alley behind the Outer Limits during Jack's last June show before he spent his weekends recording in Manhattan. She slipped her hand over my knee while I drove, and fought hard not to look at her feet when I taught her the dances, and kissed me back with a mouth that was small and fragile but very quick to learn. And then one night we were left alone in the house.

It was the night after the Fourth of July, and the afternoon air smelled of departing smoke and oncoming rain—a slow day of hazy, crowded air, still and poised and waiting to explode into water and wind. The boys were recording in New York that night, and when they were through they would stay at Lee's parents' townhouse, and Cookie would be with them. I chewed my nails down to skin and clicked off the storm-staticky radio. I heard thunder coming off the sea. I pinched my finger in a wrench and stubbed my toe on the paint compressor and banged my head on a car door handle. On my lunch break, I walked halfway to the malt shop, then stopped in front of the carousel with my hands in my pockets. I remembered how she'd looked at me when I'd dropped her off at work that morning, the dark bright flash in her eyes. I would be seeing her that night, seeing her all night, maybe all of her all night. I went back to Carl's and leaned in the doorway. There was a teasing seethe in the air and a chill in my stomach. I wished to hell it would rain.

When evening finally came, it started sprinkling as I closed up the garage. It started raining harder as I walked back to the house, and when I got to the end of the block, thunder cracked the sky and the downpour soaked me in one quick rumble and I ran like a Derby horse for the house. The front yard was one wide puddle by the time I slid in through the front door.

I let the screen door slam and called her name, but there was no answer. I ran into the bathroom, peeled off my clothes, threw them into the tub and grabbed the nice terry-cloth bathrobe that Cookie had given Jack on their first anniversary. I wrapped it around myself and toweled off my hair. I had just fallen into the easy chair in the living room when the screen door slammed and Macky stood in the doorway, panting and dripping wet, holding a soggy bag. She looked at me for a moment, breathing quickly, while the rain ran down her face.

"Ice cream" she said finally, nodding at the bag, and I said nothing. She lowered her eyes after a few seconds and hurried into the kitchen and dropped the bag on the counter. She came back and stood right in front of me, one foot on the mattress, shivering. She shuffled her hand through her wet hair, and sent droplets flying. Then she sprang swiftly, leaping almost like a dancer, and killed all the lights in the room, so that I could only see her by the light in the kitchen. She half turned away from me, then kicked off her shoes, peeled off her socks, reached up to unzip her wet uniform and down to grasp the hem of her skirt. And then she pulled the uniform off slowly over her head. She threw Delrone's blanket around herself and turned her back to me, wriggling as she pulled everything else off, and then turned back to me and jumped into my lap.

She dried her face on the lapels of the robe, slowly, the left lapel for the left side of her face, the right lapel for the right side of her face, and then she bent her head dangerously low to gather more fabric to use to dab at her hair. I grabbed her chin and lifted her mouth up; she leaned up to me like a stretching cat, her kisses eager and soft, still breathless from the run across the yard, still exhilarated from the rain.

I slid my hands under the blanket and pulled her in. I could feel her muscles tense; she moved her mouth away suddenly and pressed her forehead against my neck. I pushed the blanket down and found myself staring at fading brown bruises, shaped like fingertips, right below her shoulders. I slid my hands around her arms and held them in a careful grasp, in a very gentle imitation of what I reckoned her old boyfriend, Jimmy, must have done, and felt a quick surge of anger when I saw that my grasp almost met the marks. I looked up and saw that she was watching me, wincing. I let her go and circled the bruises lightly with my fingertips. Her eyes were shy, frightened, and her mouth flickered in an attempt to smile. I kissed her softly; her mouth went briefly electric and then collapsed into trembling again.

51

"I do it all wrong," she murmured, half apologetic, half desperate.

I swallowed a burst of sympathy and shame, and ran my fingers down her face.

"No, you don't."

"He told me . . ."

"Never mind him. He's gone."

"I got scared at the last minute, and he got mad at me," she said, and then she seemed angry with herself, and shook her head rapidly, and added in a whisper, "I'm sorry. I don't want to say anything wrong. I want to do everything right."

"So do I."

I gave her time; we had all night. She had small mouthfuls of breasts, acorn shaped—small and tense, every part of her was small and tense, ready to spring. When I kissed her throat I could feel her heartbeat, rapid and unsteady as her breathing, so I waited until she was lulled, lulled by my hands, lulled by the loud drumming of the rain, lulled by the whispers and the pauses and her renewed courage, until her trembling was forgotten and her hair was almost dry, until her eyes were hot and languid and her hands were brave. Then she was saying my name deep in her throat and she was murmuring to me, and I never thought about whether she was doing everything right, I only thought that we had the house, that we had all night, while the rain kept coming down and the ice cream in the kitchen melted over the floor.

I fell asleep with her arms wrapped around my neck, and woke in a faceful of soft hair, her arms still around me, her breathing deep and sweet. The horses of the carousel down the street were already working,

52

prancing up and down to the music that floated over the sleeping town, chiming with the soft bittersweet insistence of chapel bells on Sunday mornings when you no longer go to church.

I worked on restoring Zamenak's white Mercedes for the next month, to the beat of the news of the downshore drama of the noose slowly tightening around the neck of President Nixon, the man in the White House running scared, his face sagging with all the lies that had caught up with him. The All-Americans surrendered their weekends to work and stomped in on Monday night keyed up and rowdy, or depressed and exhausted. Macky and I pitied them but enjoyed the time alone together. Now, on the weekends, when Cookie returned from work and shut her bedroom door, it was for the sake of our privacy, not hers.

"Poor Jack," Macky whispered to me one night when they crashed in late and woke us up, and we could hear Jack in his bedroom yelling at Cookie about some recording engineer. "I thought being a rock star was a little more glamorous."

The next afternoon I finished all but the final stages of the Mercedes. The engine was purring and the tape-deck system was thundering. Macky, who had come by on her break with a chocolate milk shake and the latest malt-shop gossip, sat in the front seat with me and listened to the only cassette tape I could find, one of Lee's last recital at Juilliard. I switched the sound from the front to the back speakers.

"It sounds wonderful," she said. "Lee was really good, wasn't he?"

"He's still good."

"Trudy says he's having a nervous breakdown. She says last night they had a really bad session. He burst into her apartment around two and said he wished he'd never left Juilliard. He's going out with her now," Macky added. "Did you know that?"

"No," I said, switching the music to the front speakers again.

"And *Cindy* says Delrone is in a *terrible* mood. She went up to hug him, you know, make him feel better, and he *pushed* her out of the way."

Macky watched me as I played with the balance.

"Don't you think that's really rude?"

"Well, they're working really hard."

"So? *You're* working hard, too, Cooder, and you don't act like that. I mean," she went on, and I leaned back and swallowed a smile, "you would never push *me* out of the way. Would you?"

"Well, I don't know. You never come up and hug me, so I couldn't say for sure."

She slid her hands around my neck and brushed her lips over mine. Then she slid her leg over mine and hugged me so hard I would have had to peel her off if I had wanted to push her away.

"I'm glad *you're* not a rock star," she whispered, and then I felt her pull away quickly and saw her face flush pink. I turned and saw Jack, all dressed up, for him, in a clean white T-shirt and a borrowed suit jacket of Delrone's, and dollar-ninety-nine reflective mirrored sunglasses. Macky released me and, blushing harder, said "Hi, Jack."

"Heya, Mack," Jack rasped. "How ya doin'?"

"I gotta get back to work," she said, and raced away before I could give her a good-bye kiss.

Jack walked around the car, eyeing it critically, then slid in on the passenger side where Macky had been.

"Does this thing run?"

"Seventh heaven on wheels," I assured him, with the confidence of a used-car dealer.

"It doesn't look so hot."

"Neither do you," I said. "Needs a paint job, that's all. What do *you* need?"

Jack leaned forward, scowling, and ejected the tape of Lee's last piano performance at Juilliard. He held up a cassette he'd pulled from his coat pocket.

"Mind if we hear this—

"Actually," he added before I could answer, "I *do* need something. Mr. Streeter wants to talk to me about what went down last night, and I'm late for a meeting with him."

"You want a ride to the city?"

"You can just take me to Hoboken. I'll take the train in from there."

"Right," I said, and backed the car out. Jack leaned back and sighed. He held on to his tape for so long that I turned on the radio. He sighed several times before we reached the highway, sighed and stretched and rolled his head around. I knew he was exhausted. After a while, I sensed that the radio was bothering him, perhaps because he wasn't on it, so I turned off the radio and listened to the pleasant, hushed hum of the engine. Jack groaned then, and I laughed, thinking of Macky, glad that I wasn't a rock star.

"Something funny?" he rasped.

"Something Macky said last night."

"Did I keep you guys up last night?"

"You mean, when you were yelling at Cookie?"

"Oh, Christ," he sighed. "That's another thing I wanted to ask you. I wanted to ask you about that girl."

"Macky?"

"Naw. The other one. You know. You never told me her name."

"Oh. Maude."

"Yeah. Okay, like, when you were going out with her, and you had your band . . . I mean, could you handle both things? I mean, they were both really important to you, right? Did you ever feel like you were, I don't know, robbing Peter to pay Paul?"

"No. But it was probably different with me. Maude *was* my music."

"You mean she was your inspiration, like?"

"Well. More than that. For one thing, she had a lot of money. She *owned* a lot of our instruments. For another, she helped me write a lot of our songs. I don't mean that we sat down together. But she was my best critic. She was the only one I could depend on."

"That's my problem," Jack said. "I don't know *who* to depend on. It seems like everyone's depending on *me.* Like, last night. It wasn't right. It just wasn't *right.* And everyone else thought it was. The guys, the engineer, Johnny Streeter. And I couldn't explain what it was. Or what it wasn't. It's this song I wrote for Cookie. I wrote it one night for her when she was asleep. And that's all right. I mean, I don't mind that it's so personal. I mean, it's *gotta* be personal, it's gotta *mean* something, or else it's nothing. You know? Did you feel that way? When you were writing songs?"

"Yeah."

56

"Yeah, I figured you would. Anyway, it sounds like a music box. Everyone kept saying last night, 'It sounds real pretty, Jack.' But that's not what we *are*. Pretty. There's gotta be more *bite* to it, like there is to us. And I got crazy. I guess I wasn't like"—he let out a hiss between his teeth—"*professional*. But I kept thinkin', if I could get this, this synthesis between her and the music, maybe I could have both. You know? Like, maybe I could really have both. Like, you thought you could have both."

He took off his shades and looked at me, his eyes so tired and urgent that I knew I had to drop my guard.

"Listen, Jack. It was different with me. When I pictured myself making it, making it big, I didn't picture what you picture. I pictured my voice coming out of a car radio while some cool dude raced down the road. I pictured my album covers. The concert scene . . . I wasn't comfortable with that. You—I know you picture the kids. You live on the stage, Jack. You belong there. You're one of them, except that you've been . . . blessed. You're one of them, and I wasn't. I just wanted my *voice* out there. When I pictured making it, I pictured us, me and Maude, and our farm in Georgia. We had it all picked out. And kids, our kids, running around. Home."

Jack slammed his sunglasses back over his face and looked away. Then he said, his voice level and low, "You think I don't want that?"

"It's not for me to say."

He shoved the cassette into place. The song began with Lee's piano tinkling, as Jack had said, like a music box, before the guitar started strumming along.

"Sounds like it was recorded from down the hall," I said.

"Let's not talk about the quality of the mix," Jack said through his teeth. "Sore spot."

I listened, then, to how each instrument entered, to the melody, to Jack's singing. The mix was so poor that I couldn't make out the words very well, but I didn't have to. I knew what he was saying. It was nighttime, his time, and the band was snoring in the other room and Cookie was breathing soft and he could hear the waves rolling in and it was one night he wanted to keep forever, one moment almost complete except that the waves were reminding him that he wanted more. He wanted to crawl back into bed with her, but he had to stay up and write the song, because maybe this would be the song that would bring it home for him, that would let him watch her, some future night, sleeping in a bigger bed with finer sheets in a house all their own with no band in the next room. Yet without the band he would never get that house, without the band he could never explain how much he wanted and how much he feared to live nights like this with her forever. Then the song was over and we were in Hoboken, parked on the cobblestoned street by the train station, the afternoon bright, the city skyline hard and silver against the sky, across the water. I sat and stared out the windshield at the docks.

"Nice place, Hoboken," Jack said, nervous in my silence. "Frank Sinatra came from here. So did Mama. Kind of charming, like. Like Paradise Beach without the paradise."

"It's your voice," I told him. "It's you, Jack, you're backing away. You want bite, you gotta put it there.

58

And if you're afraid that the song's too pretty, change the piano, the middle part, at least, to an organ. Then it'll sound kind of sad, but kind of . . . strong. Like the carousel."

"Yeah?" he said, and then it was his turn to stare and my turn to wait. He rewound the tape and danced it across the dashboard, stuffed it into his pocket, then pulled it out again.

"I think," he said, "I think, maybe, Cood, you're right."

"When did you write it?"

"Couple of weeks ago. Why?"

"Just wondering," I said, but what I wondered was whether I had been part of the snoring in the next room while he was writing it.

"And I think you should do it live before you try to lay it down again. I think that'd help."

"Yeah," he agreed eagerly, and a smile cracked the gloom in his face. "Yeah, we'll have another show. 'Due to popular demand.' I'll do it that way, the way you said, *there*. Right? Thanks, man. I owe you one."

"No, you don't," I said, but he was already out of the car. He knocked on the hood, flashed his grin, and waved, and I wished Macky were there to see him, in that half-scruffy, half-respectable outfit, with those cheap boardwalk sunglasses, knocking on the hood of a fading white Mercedes, because he looked for all the world like a glamorous rock star.

Macky and I had a fight the night Nixon resigned. I told myself I was out of practice, that I would wake up one day and realize I was in love with her and I would trust her. But I didn't trust her. She was a daddy's girl in a high school sweater, and beneath the glow in her eyes when she looked at me, all I could see was seventeen years of a protected, well-ordered life and an innocent faith that remained strong because it had only been bruised and not broken. She was sweet, she was tender, she was crazy about me, but the heart of it was that she knew less about me than the Georgia police did. I fed a fervent hope that I would not have to explain it to her, that she would pick it up in lover's code. But one night, when I was drunk on her kisses and almost asleep, she decided we had to talk.

"I'll bet you were a real quiet kid," she whispered, curling her fingers around my shoulder.

"Yeah, I was pretty quiet."

"Were you unhappy?" she asked solemnly.

"Unhappy. No."

I had been quiet, as Macky had guessed, because they'd expected me to be quiet. Aunt Jane Ellen never went in for much talk, and Uncle Aaron, when he came by for dinner on Sundays and Wednesdays, wanted to discuss parish news with his sister and expected me to shut up and pass the food. They didn't coddle me or punish me, they were neither loving nor harsh. They hardly spoke of my mother in front of me, and when they did, always called her "our sister" or "your mother" and never "Martha Jean." They did not curse her or condemn her or even explain her. They only reminded me that when she died, she would go straight to Hell. I didn't argue, and I didn't answer back. I asked God in my bedtime prayers to spare my mother's soul, and I only did that because they expected me to. I went to school and swept out the church and

60

ran errands for Aunt Jane Ellen, and it was only when I was older, when I went to work for Cal and saw how he lived, with his cars and his old dog and his Bible and his can of baked beans for dinner, that I understood the loneliness, understood that I had been living with them as an outcast. I did not turn to them for comfort when I figured it out, either. I knew that they would have assured me that I was indeed an outcast. It was written that a bastard shall not enter the congregation of the Lord. I was to live by their rules but never to reap their rewards. They told me that I was marked from birth, and at school they told me that I lived in the land of opportunity, but on my secret radio, hidden under my pillow and tuned in at night to the St. Petersburg station across the bay, they told me wildly different things.

At first I thought the Beatles understood, because I heard their words, muffled by my pillow: "I don't belong, yeah *(yeah!)*, 'til I belong to you." But then I found out they were saying, "It *won't* be long, yeah (yeah)," and I realized that they didn't know anything, because it *would* be long, one hell of a long time, before any of the girls in my town looked back at me when I looked them in the eye. They had all been warned against me, because of some long-ago hot night in the back of a pickup truck, when Martha Jean Cutler had surrendered to a temptation that hounded them all, if only they'd had the courage to admit it, with a man who, they say, sang rhythm and blues just like anyone on the radio.

"And when did your mom and dad die?"

"Why do you think they're dead?"

"Well . . . you never talk about them."

61

"I never knew them. They could be alive and kicking for all I know. I hope they're kicking, anyway."

There had been brief snatches of Dylan, although the St. Petersburg disc jockey wasn't very fond of him, but I was grateful for what little there was, because he knew, he wore the same jacket of sarcasm and yearning. He sang at me what I had already concluded, that nice girls weren't all they were cracked up to be, that loneliness was cool, that happy families were made up of fools. Happy families were made up of fools, and I was no fool; I didn't need anybody— no God, no music, no girl, nothing. I had only me and I needed only me. I was tougher than the rest of them and I didn't give a damn about Martha Jean and how she'd had me or why she'd left.

I sat up, since Macky wouldn't let me sleep, and stared at the Elvis Presley movie poster on the wall.

"I was raised by my aunt and uncle, okay? My mother was their sister, but they didn't talk about her much. She left when I was two or three. They never admitted that; they said she left when I was a baby, but I thought I remembered her, remembered *something*, I couldn't say what. Then one night, I was in a bar. And this drunk started talking to me. He knew my mother. He told me what she looked like. Aunt Jane Ellen had got rid of all the pictures, so I didn't know. This drunk said Martha Jean, my mother, had a face all angles, and a long mouth, didn't listen to anybody, damn good dancer, short temper."

"Like you," Macky said, sitting up and trying to touch my face, but I ignored her.

"But she was full of smiles and real happy eyes. My

father, folks thought, was a honky-tonk singer who had passed through Tampa doing a pretty fair imitation of Hank Williams. My mother didn't give a damn what anybody said, the drunk told me. She was proud as hell to have me and was raising me up just fine. Except no one would give her any peace about not being married. So she was gonna move to a big city and raise me up there. But then she had a fight with my aunt about what kind of good Christian home I should be raised in. And then one night she disappeared. She left to try to find my father. The drunk said maybe she got word he was playing somewhere nearby. Anyway, she left."

"And she never came back?"

"No."

"I'm sorry."

I had bought the drunk a fresh beer and left him in the bar and gone out and found an open pawn shop and bought a second-hand acoustic guitar and snuck it past my aunt, who was by that time confined to her bed, her face gray and tired, dying. I left Florida and God behind, and shuffled my way up to Atlanta. I traded in the acoustic for a beat-up Strat when I was inducted into a funky little garage band, whose members adopted me as their leader because I sang the blues better than the rest of them. We played the college club circuit, and I was singing "I Shall Be Released" the first time I saw her, staring glazedly at a glass of beer and surrounded by a group of flashy hippie boys.

I turned to Macky, to bury myself in her and forget, but her caresses were meant as comfort, to give me strength to continue, because after I kissed her she stroked my face and watched me with expectant eyes. "And then what?"

"What?"

"When does that girl come into it?"

"What girl?"

"The one in your Bible."

"You were snooping around in my stuff?"

"It's a *Bible*, Cooder; it didn't look *private*. Then I saw the pictures, you and your band, how cute you were, and then I saw her. Was she your first girl?"

"The first girl I was in love with."

"How old were you?"

"Seventeen."

"How old was she?"

"Twenty."

"Was it real love?"

"Yes."

"Did you know it right away?"

"Yes."

"How did you know?"

"I just knew."

"Did *she* know right away?"

"No. It took her a little longer. Come on, Macky, I don't want to talk about it."

"Did it end badly?" Macky whispered, sympathetic but fascinated. She ran her fingers through my hair and I pulled my head away. "What was her name?"

"It doesn't matter."

"What was her *name*?"

"Maude. Maude Delaney. Maude Delaney."

I could say it a thousand times, now that I had said it once, and I always pictured the way she had said

64

it the first time I asked her: "Maude Delaney. So—?" while I grinned down at her in wild joy and she met my grin with a cautious smile—"what?"

She had eyes the color of wet sand and hair the color of dry sand, dunes of hair falling into her eyes and over her shoulders and across her breasts. She had been three years older than me and ten lovers looser, thousands of dollars richer and a far-out, stop-the-war college education smarter, but I had won. I won because I wanted her, and no one had ever wanted her, not her father, who fed her money and kept himself scarce, not the ten lovers in between her and me, not any of the college boys who fed off her generosity. I had wanted only her, body and soul. We jumped into a strange courtship, both of us poker-faced, both of us bluffing and calling bluffs. I broke through her hippie cool and the numbing power of the rainbow pills she carried in her wallet. She fed me a steady diet of her peculiar brand of self-hatred and I punished her with patience. I remained steadfast throughout the constant state of emergency she tried to twist into our lives. The more she tried to scare me away, the more I wanted her, and the more I wanted her, the more scared she became, and the harder she struck. She screamed at me that she didn't need anybody, didn't need me most of all, some dumb-kid local, and I sang to her from the stage the meanest, saddest blues songs that I knew and felt justified when I saw the tears running down her face.

It took a full year of fighting, and then she surrendered and confessed, and after that there was no turning back; we would never see defeat, no one would take us on. We grew cocky, and my music grew tight and inspired and bold. She finished up college and took a job in a bookstore and moved into a room with me. She sweet-talked people into giving us auditions, charmed them into letting us play gigs. Dark Mark Clark called her "Big Sister" and wrote a song on his harmonica called "Big Sister Blues" that became a shouted request from our audiences. Yeah, we were local heroes there. Maude pushed us like crazy, made up the posters, made the phone calls, lent us the money to make a demo tape and found a studio for us, and we were about to go in and record "Big Sister Blues" for all our grandchildren. The city was sparkling and the night was bright and all we needed was champagne to pour over our heads like we'd just won the World Series, and she took off in her sky-blue Plymouth to go and fetch us some. Then there was nothing left but the ringing phone that ripped into our laughter, then there was nothing left but the flat voice of a stranger saying my name and saying hers, then there was nothing left at all.

"And she's dead," I told Macky.

"I'm sorry."

"Don't say you're sorry."

"What do you want me to say?"

"Nothing."

"You don't want to talk about it?"

"Good, Macky," I said sarcastically.

"Don't you think it helps?"

"No. Talking about it doesn't help. Time doesn't help. Drinking doesn't help. Sweet little girls like you don't help, either."

She started crying and I left the house. I walked the length of the boardwalk and back. When I returned,

I found her wrapped around my pillow, her face dirty from her tears, her knees pulled up to her chin. I wiped her face while she slept on, and in the morning I left for work early and did not wake her up.

I had the day off and spent it in the garage, waxing the Mercedes. Lee's teacher was coming down that night to see the show and collect the car, and the paint job was so neat that it looked wet. Jack stopped by to say hello, then settled in to talk, leaning against Macky's old boyfriend's crippled Buick, which we had hauled into the garage for safekeeping a few days after Macky's arrival. The air outside was a hot yellow haze, and inside the garage a dusty ceiling fan was droning at the same pitch as the chief justice swearing in President Gerald R. Ford.

"Could I borrow your jacket for tonight?"

"My jacket? *My* jacket?"

"I want to look good, man, you know?"

"You nervous?"

"Naw," he said, shaking his head, squinting out at the street. "Well, not about the show. About my sister. She's coming."

I had met Jack's sister a few days before, had greeted her with "Hey, sweetheart," when I slammed into the house and saw her sitting on my mattress reading a rock-and-roll magazine and thought for a quick sun-blinded moment that she was Macky until I saw the easy humor in her face and the keen sparkle in her eye, until she said, "You must be that cowboy Jack told me about." Then I realized that she was Jack's sister, Mary, same age as Macky, same dark hair, but not shy, not wide-eyed, in no need of protection.

"How's she doing, Jack?"

67

"She's good. Well, I don't know. She thinks she's good. My dad's got other ideas. I went home yesterday. Took Cookie home to the folks. It was Mama's birthday. But Dad started in on me and . . . it's been a weird week."

I dipped my rag and nodded. When the band was in New York, Macky and I had our intimacy, but when they were in Paradise Beach, I had my privacy. When Jack was around, Macky wasn't so interested in my history, and I wasn't so cross with her. I felt guilty about Macky; I didn't even know if she knew that Nixon had resigned.

"I saw Macky on the way to work," Jack said suddenly. "She was all upset because when she woke up you were gone and she thinks you're mad at her."

I flipped my rag and cleared my throat and looked up at him, but he showed only a mild interest. He ran an icy bottle of Coke over his face to cool it down, then took a deep gulp.

"She's a sweet kid," he said.

"She is."

"She's crazy about you, you know?"

I looked up at him again and nodded.

"You want a Coke?" he asked.

"Sure."

"I mean," he went on, banging on the machine, "you *must* know. But it's funny. It's like she walked out of a song or something. Like she walked out of 'Be My Baby.' It's so *easy* for her. You know, when I was that age, I wasn't that serious about anything. Except music. But I don't think I could've been that in *love*, or anything. Like Macky. Or my sister."

Jack handed me the Coke and settled back against

the Buick while I continued to polish the hood of the Mercedes.

"Like my sister. That's what my dad and me were fighting about. I was down at my folks'. And I'm sittin' there with Cookie, eatin' birthday cake, and Dad says, 'Look, I want you to talk to your sister,' and I say, 'Okay, I'll talk to her.' So then he yells, 'I MEAN IT, JACK! I WANT YOU TO TALK TO YOUR SISTER!' 'Okay, *okay*,' I say, thinking, Oh, Christ, here we go again. I say, 'What's she done now? She come home too late last night or what?' So my dad keeps yelling— I don't know what's goin' on, but he thinks I do, 'cause Mary and I call each other all the time. But she never tells me about her love life or nothing, anyway. My dad says, 'Your sister is *seventeen years old!* you *hear me*? I know you kids think you can do whatever you want, but you *can't*. I thought I could, too, when I was your age, but I *couldn't*.' I say, like, 'Look, Dad, I'm sorry,' 'cause I don't know what he's talking about and I don't know what else to say, and he says, 'Great. You're *sorry*. Your sister is gonna marry this bum and ruin her life and you're *sorry*.' Now, I don't even know what bum he's talking about, and she hasn't said nothin' to me about gettin' married. So Cookie and I go up to her room and try to find out what the story is. I say, 'Hi, Mary,' and right away she yells, 'Don't you try to talk me out of it, too, Jack! My mind's made up and I'm not gonna argue about it anymore and I don't *care* if you don't come to the wedding!' So I try to calm her down. Jesus, the whole house is in an uproar. So it turns out she's goin' with this guy, he builds houses, he's older than her, he's a real hard worker and a real good guy, and she wants to marry him. I

69

say, 'Hey, Mary, I'm real glad you like him and everything, but maybe you should hold off on getting married and stuff,' and she just says no no no, she knows
what she wants, Mom got married when *she* was
eighteen. And then Cookie tries to talk to her, says
maybe she should take a year off and work or go to
college, *live* a little bit, and Mary just yells that Cookie
always got to do whatever *she* wanted and *I* always
get to do whatever *I* want and this is what *Mary* wants.
So I told her to come down to the show and bring this
wonderful guy with her, and I told Dad to take it easy
on her and I came back here. But hell, I don't know
what to say to this guy tonight. I mean, what would
you do if Macky had a big brother and he came to
talk to you?"

"You mean, if he came and told me to take it easy
because she was too young and not ready to get married?"

"Yeah."

"I'd agree with him."

Jack sighed slowly. "I don't think this guy is gonna
just agree with me, Cooder."

"Well, Mary's different from Macky."

"How do you mean?"

"I mean, Mary's a little more hip, you know? Mary
would never run away from home in her high school
uniform. This guy she wants to marry is probably just
like her. They probably come from the same neighborhood. She probably knows who he is and what he
wants. I mean, Macky's here on vacation and I'm just
part of the vacation."

"I don't think you're part of the vacation," Jack

said. "Naw. Not from what the malt-shop girls say, not from the way she talks about you."

"What does she know? She's just a kid."

"Mary's just a kid."

"But Mary can take care of herself."

"Do you love her?" Jack asked suddenly. "Macky?"

"I don't know. It's not what I had. But I don't think I'll ever get what I had again."

"I know, man, you told me. And I thought about it a lot. And I'll let you in on a little secret. The worst part about Mama's birthday, about that fight with Dad and Mary? We went up there to make an announcement, and with all that yelling going on, we didn't have the heart."

"Announcement?" I repeated.

"Cookie and me," Jack said. "We got engaged."

I wanted to go on a long drive by myself and contemplate the news, but there was no time for it. The wheels of Jack's big night were already in motion, and as soon as he walked away from the garage, Lee came in with his parents and his teacher, Zamenak, to collect the Mercedes. Zamenak was delighted by the job I had done and insisted that we take a test drive.

"It is better than the day I bought it!" he cried, and then he proceeded to tell us about the day he had bought it, about the piano competition he had won that had enabled him to buy it, about the teacher who had diligently prepared him for the competition, about how it was one of the most exciting experiences of his life, about how he hoped that the same experience would happen to Lee one day. I tried not to look bored and Lee tried not to look guilty, and we both tried to hide our frequent glances at our watches, until Lee at last interrupted him gently to tell him he didn't want to be late for the show. Then Lee's teacher drove us to the door of the Outer Limits, and while Lee jumped out of the car and made his getaway, it was up to me to convince Zamenak that his car would not be safe parked there, so we went back to Carl's. There Lee's parents handed me a check for my labor, and I ran home to stuff it into the pages of my Bible. I could live through the winter on that check. But my joy was short-lived; there was no one to share it with. The house was empty. The rest of them had already gone to the show.

I figured that the malt-shop girls already knew about Cookie and Jack—they always knew everything first. But when I got to the Table for the Select Few, they were talking about other things. The Outer Limits was crowded with record-company people, family members, and strangers from New York, and the girls were in a huddle, pointing people out.

"Sorry about last night," I muttered to Macky.

"That's all right," she answered quietly. Her hair was down and she wore a pink ribbon and seashell earrings. She was staring at her hand, which was loosely wrapped around her bottle of beer, which she would take an hour to drink and another hour to play with before ordering her second and last.

"You look real pretty," I added.

"Thank you," she said, her eyes still on her hand.

"Who's that woman hugging Cookie?" Sara asked.

"That's Jack's mother," Trudy answered, and we

all turned to see a slightly plump, kindly woman hold-ing Cookie's shoulders and laughing with Jack's sister. Cookie returned the hug and then turned toward our table.

"Now you know where he gets his smile," Trudy added, and then Cookie was skipping over to us and I stood up. I kissed her and Macky tossed her head and looked away.

"Congratulations," I said, and the malt-shop girls narrowed their eyes and repeated in a chorus, "Con-gratulations?"

Cookie held out her hand to reveal one clear precise diamond on a band of gold. The whole table exploded into cooing and hugs.

"Tell everything."

"There's not much to tell," Cookie said, taking her chair, her face glowing so radiantly that I signaled the waitress for a double shot of whisky.

"How did he propose?" Trudy asked. "Was it really romantic?"

"Well, we've been talking about it for a while. But . . . it was pretty romantic."

"This is so exciting. You two are such a cute couple."

Trudy and Sara and Cindy sighed. Macky glanced at me. I groaned and took my drink from the waitress.

"That's a beautiful ring. Did he pick it out himself?"

"Yes," Cookie said, suddenly sharp. "I wish he hadn't. I told him I didn't need a ring, but he . . . He really can't afford it. He should get a guitar instead. He paid for this out of the advance money. The advance for the album that isn't even finished."

"God," Trudy said. "When are they going to finish that thing?"

"Please," Johnny Streeter said, coming up on Trudy's question. "Don't talk about it. I came over here to get away from it. My father's been screaming at me for the past hour. Except that he *never raises his voice.* Which just makes it worse."

He looked around hopelessly for a chair to pull up, and I provided him with one by pulling Macky off her chair and into my lap. Macky eyed me, half cross, half hopeful, and I kissed her in full apology for the night before. She forgave me with a kiss and a snuggle, and Johnny, much agitated, waved at the waitress and finished off my drink.

"Congratulations," he added dourly, shaking his head at Cookie. "I hope you know what you're letting yourself in for."

"Nice," Sara snapped.

"I hope you're not planning to have kids right away."

"When *are* you getting married?" Trudy asked.

"Oh, I don't know. It's a long way off. There's the album to finish, there's the tour—"

"Are you going on tour with them?"

"No, baby, are you kidding? I'll be in my first year of law school. No, the wedding's a way off, I'd say. We'll wait until things get settled."

"Get *settled*?" Johnny echoed, startled. "When the hell do you think that's gonna be?"

He caught my eye, after searching the table to find that he had no friends there, and I shook my head at him as Macky shifted in my lap and played with my hair.

"Jack said," Cookie went on dreamily, "that we might wait and have the wedding when he gets his first gold record."

"Dad gave Mom a fifty-five T-bird when he got his first gold record," Johnny said, relieving the waitress of two whiskys and handing one to me.

"I'd rather have the car," I said.

"Men," Sara hissed in disgust.

"Girls," Johnny snarled back, "are so *romantic.* The whole world's gotta be in *love* right now. You two"—he pointed, scowling, at Macky and me, then turned to Cookie—"and *you* two, the All-American lovebirds, and Jack's little sister, and Billy and Peggy Sue—"

"Billy and *who*?" Sara and Cindy screeched.

"Oh, haven't you met her yet? She's over there, standing by the pole. That really tall one with the light-brown hair."

Trudy and Sara and Cindy leaned forward.

"She's so skinny."

"She's a model," Johnny told them. "You ought to see her legs. Her name's Marguerite Suzanne Martinvale, but she uses just Marguerite professionally. Billy changed that right away to Peggy Sue, of course. She ought to do panty-hose ads. Great legs. Maybe I should be *her* manager."

"What are you so down about?" Cookie asked. "What's your father been saying?"

"Oh, you know, the usual. I'm too young. I'm undisciplined. I let Jack go over budget like a wild man. . . . Like, last night, when my sister, Linda, told me the president resigned, I thought, Oh, terrific, now maybe there'll be a shuffle upstairs and maybe nobody'll notice that our album's gone over budget. I thought she meant the president of the record company."

75

"God, Johnny's right, look at those legs," Sara whispered. "She looks like a *flamingo*."

"She's a model?" Macky asked, peering at Peggy Sue.

"How long has *she* been in the picture?" Sara whined. "Since when are *we* the last to know everything around here?"

"I'll bring her over," Cookie said, and stood up. "It isn't fair to gawk at her this way."

"He couldn't wait three weeks, until the album's in the can?" Johnny muttered as Cookie walked away. "He has to play Romeo *now*?"

"Is that really gonna get in the way?" I asked.

"Everything gets in the way. Sometimes *I* get in the way. My problem is I remember all the wrong things. My father quizzes me on percentages and royalty rates, and I can never remember. I don't remember how much money he's supposed to get, but I remember how many takes we did on his songs, any song. I remember what a critic said about his voice."

"Oh, what did he say?" Macky cried, perking up.

"He said, 'His voice is urgent and rough, like Dylan's, but not as scathing; deep and low, like Elvis Presley's, but not as mush-mouthed; joyously sexy like Smokey Robinson's, but not as pretty; and does a lot with a little, like Otis Redding, but isn't as forlorn.' "

"I don't think Elvis Presley sounds mush-mouthed," Macky said, and I smiled at her.

"A *real* manager wouldn't remember that shit," Johnny complained, pounding the table. "As long as I remember that kind of stuff, Jack'll still be living in a house with six other people."

76

"Oh, here she comes. *Look*, she's not wearing any makeup."

Cookie ran us through a quick round of introductions, and Johnny surrendered his chair, while Peggy Sue smiled warmly and repeated our names back to us in a surprisingly low and serious voice drenched in a deep Southern accent. Her features were perfect, small and balanced, and Macky leaned so far forward to have a closer look, she nearly fell off my lap.

"So how did you *meet* Billy?" Sara asked immediately. Cookie went to Johnny, who was slouched mournfully against the pillar behind the table.

"Relax, will you? They're not going to the poorhouse because they're a few days over budget," she said.

"I expected you to take their side."

"He must have noticed your legs," Sara was telling Peggy Sue. "He was a track star in high school, you know."

"They made their advance back last time, right? They'll do fine," Cookie insisted.

"Sara's so jealous all the time," Macky whispered, kissing my neck so that shivery currents ran down my spine. "Do you think she's pretty?"

"Just wait 'til he's dropped from the label and there's no milk for your baby. You won't be so cavalier then."

"What baby?"

"What do girls know? Girls have no head for business."

"Johnny, relax," I said. "Peace on earth. Rock and roll is here to stay. Anyway, the show's about to start."

"Oh, it's easy for you to talk," he answered bitterly,

as Macky ruffled my hair and kissed my neck again. "It's all fun and games for you."

"What you need is a little faith," I said.

Macky tugged at my chin and kissed me just as the lights went down and the crowd erupted into its usual chaos of screams and cheers. The malt-shop girls uttered a shrill shriek, and Macky broke off her kiss to look up at Jack.

He was decked out like the Duke of Earl, in skintight ripped jeans, black T-shirt, and my denim jacket with the suede collar and lining, with those mirrored sunglasses and his motorcycle boots. Lee seated himself at the piano and tapped at it experimentally while the crowd quieted down. Billy slid on his wraparound sunglasses and turned from the audience so that he could be seen only in profile. Delrone crushed a fedora over his head and half hid behind Jack, and Eddie, although he was obscured from general view because of his cymbals, was wearing a battered newsboy cap. Lee pulled a pork pie hat out of the piano and placed it on his head with care.

He began with a semiclassical-sounding piece of concerto, full of flourishes and restraints, strong and tingling and quiet.

"Lee's old teacher is here tonight," Jack told the crowd in a hoarse bedroom whisper. "And . . . this is for him." We were all staring at Lee. Everyone in the band was staring at Lee, and Lee hopped and dipped his way through the decades, until he hit concert jazz and began pounding on the keys like an exuberant baby splashing the bath water. He glanced up at Delrone and raised one eyebrow, and he and Delrone struck the same note together.

"And my parents are here tonight," Jack said in the same whisper. "And . . . this is for them."

Delrone and Lee snapped into a wartime big-band skiffle, making all the right sounds with no big band, no leader with a baton, no identically dressed horn section, no sultry virgin singer, just Lee's piano and Delrone's guitar and a half-cocked grin from Jack to his mother. Jack threw back his head and laughed when his mother returned his smile, then turned from the crowd to face Lee while the two of them played the lead melody, on piano and guitar, of "Don't Sit Under the Apple Tree." The crowd laughed and clapped, and then the big band sound dropped out quite suddenly, replaced by the slow tinkling of Lee's piano. Jack turned to Delrone, who removed Jack's sunglasses for him. Delrone then began strumming and Jack turned to the mike, his voice throatier and sexier than ever.

"And my future bride is here tonight, and this . . . is for her."

He went into the song he had played for me on cassette the day I drove him to Hoboken. The shy piano was replaced in the middle section by Jack's urgent guitar, and Jack's voice, sad and strong but spiced with that elusive bite, swept over the crowd like the spray of the sea when the boardwalk has shut down and you and your girl are the last ones walking home late at night. The room was frozen under his spell, and it was impossible to believe, even for those of us who had lived through it, that he had ever had any trouble pinning down the sound that was now at his command.

The gypsy with the flat tire had promised him rock-

and-roll stardom, and his girl, standing trembling and teary-eyed at the pillar where he knew he could find her when he looked up from the mike, had promised him her hand. And in the eyes of most there he was home free, and the bite in his voice was a mystery. But the bite in his voice was the bite of a man who cannot escape the call of the promises he has made to himself in his most bold and private moments, the promises that, except on a night as rare as this, he does not dare give voice to, because he cannot explain how he came to believe that he deserves to see them realized. It was the bite of a man helpless in the hands of hopes he never would have designed for himself, knowing how much damn trouble they would prove to be.

Mine had been a smaller kingdom, where magic was short-lived and hard-won, not summoned with a fingersnap and flashed like a smile, where I had loved Maude as much as Jack loved Cookie, but our love had been a duel and not a waltz. We had lived on no beach and in no paradise. I'd never had Jack's magic, and I knew I never would. It had been a darker kingdom, where we were fighting the Vietnam War and the National Guard and the race riots and our own paranoia and anyone else who would take us on, where we set the beat for our fighting with a mean, raunchy, ass-shaking blues, and Dark Mark Clark wailed away on his harmonica even after the show was over. It had been a sad-eyed, short-tempered kingdom, but I had been king there. I'd had my own turf then. And I had to have it again, or else I might as well have stayed in Virginia, pretending my life was over. The song drifted into a walking bass line, spotlight on Billy.

Eddie began tapping light hissing raindrops on his cymbals and Delrone began strumming in rhythm, and they all looked at each other, peeking out from under their hats and over their shades, Jack donning those reflective mirrored sunglasses again and beginning to strut, volume and rhythm increasing to a fever pitch while the crowd, bewildered and excited and dying to participate, offered whoops of encouragement.

"And *you're* all here tonight," Jack whispered, and was answered by shouts of agreement. "And this . . ."

The band paused and then hit the same chord and went on, playing as though there had been no interruption.

"And *this* is . . ." Jack said, while they paused for a split second and resumed again.

"And this is for . . ."

He paused and leaned back and the band dropped out and he dropped one hand to his hip and let the moment stand, let the suspense hover in the silence until the crowd began to yelp at him and he raised one hand in command for silence, and received the silence, and shouted, "This is for *you!*"

Delrone took the first "Aaaah," and Lee the second, Billy the third, Eddie the fourth, and then Jack screamed a scream that made my heart stand still, and then he tore into "Twist and Shout" with every ounce of energy that was in the room.

In a single flash, the room was drunk with euphoria. I was dancing with Macky when the second fatal chorus began and Jack's overworked guitar made an unholy cracking noise and splintered in his hands. He didn't miss a beat and screamed his way through the chorus, and then dropped the piece of junk his mama had given him to keep him out of trouble at his feet, and the kids at the front threw themselves at the stage, grabbed the guitar and began to tear at it like wild dogs. Jack seized the microphone and went on singing, but the kids were too hungry to own a piece of that precious guitar, and soon there was an explosion of breaking glass at the bar.

There was another crash of glass, a girl's scream, then a chorus of hearty yells, and then a whole family of empty beer bottles sitting on a table lost all hope of ever being recycled. Jack stepped back, blinking in surprise, as a body flew through the air right in front of him.

Then Cookie had Johnny Streeter by the shoulders and was shouting at him, "Get her out of here!" jerking her head at Peggy Sue. She grabbed me and added, "Get *her* out of here, she's underage!" and I took Macky's arm and tucked her head under my arm and led her across the back of the room amidst those who were ducking and those who were leaping into the mad dance and the girls who were shouting at their boyfriends to "*Stop* it!" We arrived at the back door, which led to the alley, and I kicked it open and slammed it shut behind us.

We burst into the warm, beer-drenched air and fell into a pile of damp cardboard boxes next to the dumpster. Macky leaped at me, knocking me off my feet, and as I fell I pulled her down on top of me. She covered my face with eager wet kisses like the licks of an exhilarated puppy. I petted her hair and tried to catch my breath. We could hear the distant rumble of shouts and guitars coming from inside, and from down the street somewhere the irritated howl of a police siren that grew closer and louder and finally stopped in mid scream as I grabbed a fistful of her hair and kissed her as hard as I could. A corps of outraged whistles bleated all at once, followed by loud, half-obscured orders, *"Everybody . . . now . . . move!"* They were answered by loud whines of protest and lusty boos.

Macky wrapped her legs around my waist and forced me deeper into the soggy boxes, until my head hit cement and I pushed her back so I could breathe. She shuffled her hands under my head and flipped back her hair, smiling and frowning in a single flash of her eyes.

"Will they get in trouble?"

"Baby, they're beyond trouble."

"I don't ever ever want to leave them. And I don't ever ever ever want to leave you."

It was August, and sticky. A soft desperation was whistling up the boardwalk, so many romances still unrealized, so many tans still too pale, so close to autumn. We had to be out of our shabby beach house by Labor Day weekend. Billy was cajoling Peggy Sue into wanting a roommate, Cookie was hunting for an apartment that would house Jack, Delrone and Eddie were throwing out junk and looking at want ads. Macky seemed to be waiting for me to decide. The only thing I could decide to do was spend part of my paycheck replacing the four tires on Macky's old boyfriend's Buick. I needed only to adjust a leaking valve on it before it would be ready to drive, ready to drive all the way back to Creve Coeur.

I did not think of her while I changed the tires, not of Macky, the rough-fine texture of her hair, the hard leathery soles of her bare feet scratching up and down my leg at night, the way she lingered over my name, "*Coo*-der," savoring it as if it were a new flavor of ice cream. I thought only of the girl who had to go home, the doctor's daughter, the niece of the debutantes who wanted to give her a debut as well, the girl who had been trained in piano and ballet and the social graces and the finer points of running a house like her father's, a fine white house with a front lawn larger than the beach at Paradise Beach and a back garden sprayed and weeded by some hired hand.

That was where she belonged, and she was lucky to belong there, and I wasn't going to take that away from her. But I didn't tell her that. I didn't even look at her while all the other winter plans flew around our heads. I just held her hand and pretended nothing would ever change.

I came home from fixing the tires and found a note from Macky, on our mattress, telling me that she had gone into the city on a shopping trip with Peggy Sue. Cookie was in the kitchen laughing on the phone with Jack. I went into the bathroom to wash the grease off and was filling the sink with water so I could shave when Cookie popped her head in.

"What're you doing? Oh. Can I watch?"

She squeezed by me and sat on the edge of the tub. "Guess what?"

I saw her face behind me in the mirror and guessed, "The album's finished?"

"Yes!"

"No kidding. Has Hell frozen over, too?"

84

Cookie frowned. "That's not nice. He's . . . well, he's a perfectionist. He wants everything to be as good as it can possibly be."

"Obviously," I said, and when she met my eyes in the mirror I looked away and turned off the faucet. She cleared her throat.

"He's out shopping with Stevie now, to get a new guitar. Poor Jack. There's not a piece of it left, you know. The kids ran off with everything. He's had that guitar ever since he started playing."

I nodded and dipped my razor in the water.

"You wouldn't," Cookie said cautiously, "consider selling him your guitar, would you?"

"No."

"You're pretty attached to it, aren't you?"

"It's just not worth selling."

She leaned forward lazily, so that all her blond hair fell in front of her shoulders, and she turned on the bath water, dropped the plug in and dropped one leg into the tub. Then she threw her head back and looked at me again.

"You never talk much about your band."

"It doesn't exist anymore."

"Do you miss it?"

"It was another life," I said, sliding the razor carefully up my neck.

"Did you write the songs?"

"Well, I wrote some of them. I mean, some of all of them. I just wrote down whatever wouldn't leave my head, you know—a phrase or a riff or a la la la. And if I couldn't go anywhere else with it, I gave it to Dark Mark Clark and he put it all together for me. Or else Maude finished up the words. Really, Maude started

85

the words, 'cause she'd say something to me, and it would never leave. Like she said one time, 'You oughta pray for patience, but it probably wouldn't come quick enough for you.' And that became 'Big Sister Blues.' "

"How do you mean?"

"You know. Blues. I'd go, 'Well, I prayed for patience,' and the band would go 'buh buh'—guitars, horns, everything. Repeat, repeat. Then, 'But it didn't come quick enough for me.' Then a long harmonica solo by Mark. It was, uh, pretty popular down there."

Cookie splashed her foot in the tub and turned the water off.

"Why did you call him Dark Mark Clark?"

"He was a weird breed. I'm not sure. He didn't like to talk about his folks. I'm sure he never had a real easy time of it. He had beautiful skin, though, like vanilla caramels. The kind of skin people suntan to get. He used to tell people he'd just got back from Florida when he met 'em. That's what he said when he met me. 'Oh, yeah?' I says, 'What part?' And then he was stumped, and I still didn't get it. He wasn't white, white like they like their white down South, and he wasn't black, so we called him Dark."

"Why *did* you break up?"

"Well, I don't know, Mary Catherine. Many are called, few are chosen, I guess. I'm no Jack Armstrong."

"You don't have to be."

"Sure would help, though, wouldn't it? Seems like it would help in just about every way."

"Every way?" she repeated suspiciously. "You think it would help, say, with Macky?"

I rinsed off my razor and began splashing water on my face.

86

"You don't like her, do you?" I asked.

"She can't mop the floor or put jimmies on a cone. The other girls think she's pretty dumb. But all the guys seem to think she's real cute."

"She *is* real cute," I said carefully, watching Cookie in the mirror as I toweled off my face. She was staring at her foot, splashing the shallow water impatiently with her toes.

"Real cute, huh?" Cookie said sarcastically. "Real sweet little thing, quiet, docile . . ."

"She's not a screamer, if that's what you mean."

"That's not what I mean!" Cookie almost yelled. She splashed her foot angrily in the bathtub and pulled the plug.

"You could do better," she said. "You could get someone you could talk to. You don't talk to her. I've seen the way you talk to her. What are you gonna do? Take her home after Labor Day? Or marry her? You could do better."

"Well, what do *you* think I should do?" I asked very quietly, sitting on the edge of the tub next to her.

"I don't know. You could . . . stay here. You could work at Carl's, get an apartment by the beach. You could hang out with Trudy and Sara and Cindy."

"And visit you while the All-Americans are on tour?" I asked calmly, sliding closer to her and pressing my hands against the tile wall behind her head, so that she was in my arms but not in my arms, not moving closer and not moving away, staring at me and saying nothing, her face almost grave and almost blank. She nodded, a nod so tiny I wouldn't have seen it if our faces hadn't been so close.

"That's all you see for me," I said. My voice was

87

soft but I saw her eyes widen when she saw that I was angry. "At least Macky dreams about me in technicolor, Mary Catherine. Macky wants me for dinner, at least, and not just dessert."

She leaned away from me, but there was nowhere for her to go except into my hands, and I caught her and pushed her back toward me. Then I took the kiss I had been craving all summer, but it was nothing like I'd imagined it would be. There was something missing that I hadn't even realized I'd grown accustomed to.

"You know, I think that guitar talks to me. It doesn't have long chats or nothing. I don't want you to think I'm some kind of nut. But sometimes, if I'm listening there way down deep, I think I can hear it whisper, kind of whisper an echo. Like someone whispering in the next room. You know? Right when you've stopped punishing it, you know, *nah na na na na naaaaah!* and then there's this *wahahaha* and then this tiny whisper."

"And what's it saying? Your name?"

Jack and I were walking along the highway that ran north of Paradise Beach. It didn't have much of a shoulder, and Jack and I were walking that afternoon in a garden of black-eyed Susans, Queen Anne's lace, purple-flowered weeds, discarded beer cans, Popsicle sticks, and paper that had once covered fast food. He had been practicing with my guitar all morning, and I had the day off from Carl's and was finished with Macky's old boyfriend's Buick and had paced around him until he suggested that we go for a walk.

"Naw, it's just saying . . . I don't know. I can't hear

88

it. It's not really *words*. It's more like . . . whispering. Like, you know . . . like, when you hear two people whispering in the next room."

"Like, when we hear you and Cookie in the next room?"

Jack stood still and stared off down the road for so long that I was afraid I'd made him angry. I was ready to apologize immediately. I'd seen him lose his temper when he was in the heat of recording, but I'd never seen him angry *at* anyone, and I did not want his anger directed at me the first time I witnessed it. But he squinted, ducked his head as though he saw someone coming down the road, then straightened up with a little-boy grin.

"Yeah. Like that. I guess. Or you and Macky," he added. His tone was slightly teasing, but he looked away from me when he said it.

I objected, "We don't do anything with all you guys around."

"I know. I know, man. But you can hear it all the same."

It was baking and buzzing out there. The bugs were swarming around us. I slapped sideways at my forehead. Jack was drenched in sweat, but the gray T-shirt he was wearing was so ripped up and pulled out of shape that sweat seemed to give it a little more class. He just kept walking and shuffling his feet, humming different snatches of songs, checking the sky to see that no clouds gathered to ruin his day.

"Hey. Cookie tells me you're sending Macky home at the end of the summer."

"I don't know where she got that. It's not my place to send her anywhere."

89

"But you mean it's not gonna go past this summer?"

"I don't know."

"That'd be a shame, you know," Jack said, throwing his hands up in the air. He stretched toward the sky, and then looked up at his hands, fingers spread wide. He had the appearance of someone waving up at God to see how He was doing.

"You know, I'm so glad July's over. July was a really bad month for us, all down there in the studio. I don't feel like I ever saw the sun in July. July was not so good, I'd have to say. But the album's done. You know? And I think . . . when I remember this summer, I won't remember July. I think I'll remember June. Billy and me finding Macky outside Carl's. And August. How you two were when we finally got out of the studio. All hugs. And me and Cookie getting engaged. And I think I'll remember right now. You know? July already seems like somebody else did it all."

He dropped his hands, swung his arms, and kept on walking. I peered through the yards of the weather-beaten houses and tried to see the ocean.

"You know?" he said.

"I don't. I don't know, Jack. Maybe that's the difference between us. I think, if I were you, I'd remember July. You know, I'm not saying you *should*. I'm just saying that's probably what I would remember."

"You would. You would, man. I saw that right away. I saw that the first day I met you. I saw July."

"It was May."

"Naw, I'm not talking about the month. Just . . . *July*. You were walking around in the middle of July. You know what I mean?"

90

"No," I said, but I did. He was staring off again, and I stood right next to him and tried to stare at what he saw, but I couldn't see anything but road. He grabbed my arm and pointed, "Look at that!"

"At what?"

"You see that? You see how that looks like water over there? That's so cool. I love that. And then right above it—*there!* Don't that look great, that heat shimmering off the highway? I mean, *don't that heat look great, shimmering off the highway?*"

"Yeah," I said, and suddenly my throat grew so tight that I had to step away from him. I thought I was going to cry, and I never cried unless I was angry. But I was angry then, because the moment was perfect—the look of wonder on Jack's face, the echo of "Twist and Shout" ringing in my ears—the way it was going just after the guitar broke, the sirens screaming and the taste of Macky's kisses in my mouth. And the heat, the heat, the heat shimmering off the highway. I was angry then, because I knew it would disappear just as I reached for it, just like it always disappears, just like the heat never is water.

Jack straightened up with a look of friendly innocence, and I wondered if he really mourned anything except in his songs.

"Listen, Cooder, I want to buy your guitar."

"I'm sorry, Jack—"

"Yeah, I know I'm broke now. I bought that ring and all. But we really ought to get some money from the album this time."

"I'm sorry, Jack. It's not for sale."

"Yeah," he sighed. We began walking again. "Guess there's a lot of memories there. I don't blame you.

Just thought I'd give it a shot. That girl Maude bought it for you, right?"

"No, she didn't buy it for me. I was playing it the first time I saw her."

"Oh, yeah?"

"Yeah. I was up on stage, and I spotted her."

"You're *kidding!*" Jack halted so quickly that his sneakers squeaked. He smiled doubtfully, "You're kidding, right?" And when I shook my head, he lowered his head and laughed. "Oh, man. That *never* happens. Cookie was teasing me one time, 'Oh, yeah, Jack, you're in love with me, sure, until the day you see some cute little thing from the stage.' And I said, 'Honey, for Christ's sake, that's a myth. That *never* happens.' "

"Well, I don't see what's so damn funny about it."

"No, no," Jack said, sobering up hastily. "It's not, like, *funny.*"

"I mean, it could just as well have happened to you. It even *seems* more like something that would happen to you."

"No," he answered, suddenly earnest and staring down the road at the rising heat. "No, I don't think so, man. That's you. I wouldn't. . . . That's you, man, pure you."

Late that afternoon, I parked Macky's old boyfriend's Buick on Seaside Boulevard and met her in front of the malt shop as the boardwalk was shrugging on neon for the night. She kissed me hello and filled me in on the malt-shop-girl news as we walked to the car, then froze when she saw the Buick and flashed me a tragic look.

"You fixed it," she said in the light jaunty tone all

the malt-shop girls used, a hip, any-more-like-you-at-home voice that had its roots in Cookie's sly "Hey, hey."

"Carl wanted me to get it out of the garage." I lied nervously, with an unexpected panic. "It was taking up too much room."

I opened the Buick's door for her, and she stepped in without looking at me or saying anything more. She did not question where we were going, and she sat next to me, silent and still, moving only to remove her apron.

I drove north to a stretch of beach enclosed by a state park, where Jack had shown me how to creep in after dark by crossing the back lot of a gas station and coasting down a dirt road. It was not easy to be stealthy in a Buick, but I wasn't afraid because the cops were patrolling the front gate of the park and the interstate, and the cops who might have caught us were an understanding bunch who excused summertime lovers. I was relaxed enough to keep one hand on Macky's knee during the entire trip. She looked down at my hand as though she had never seen it before, on her knee or anywhere else, and then she looked out the window.

When I parked by the beach and slid my arm around her, she turned her head and kissed all of my fingers with a strong fast passion, then leaned her face into my hand, and I realized that she was crying.

"They all say you're gonna send me home," she said.

"Who's they?"

"Trudy and Sara and Cindy. They say they know from Cookie, and Cookie knows everything."

"Well," I said. I shook her shoulder, but she refused to turn toward me. "It'd probably be best for you, you know."

"Yeah. Best."

"What are you gonna do if you stay out here?" I went on. "Everything's gonna change after Labor Day, and there won't be nothing going on. The guys'll be on tour—"

"What are *you* gonna do?" she interrupted furiously, sitting up out of the safety of my arm. She wiped her tears and glared at me. "*Best.* What makes you think you know what's *best* for me? What do you think's *best* for you?"

"Best for you, Macky, is going back, going to college, going out with nice guys, normal guys, not like me."

"Oh, stop it. You're all just as bad." Her voice was dead quiet, and when it started to rise with tears, she cleared her throat violently and called up the dead tone again. "Either you love me and you want me with you, or you don't love me and you want me to go away. That's all. And I thought you loved me. A little. Not like crazy, not like . . . *her*, but a little. I didn't think anyone could touch me the way you touch me . . . and not love me a little."

"I do."

"Good, I feel much better."

"Sweetheart—"

"Don't tell me it's for my own good. Tell me I'm not good enough. Tell me you want other girls. Don't tell me you're trying to *save* me from something, save me from a big bad guy like you, 'cause it's too late for that. And I'm not going anywhere. I'm staying right here. I'll move in with Peggy Sue and Billy. I'll go in to that agency and try to be a model. I can do that now. Do you understand that? I can do that now, after knowing you . . . and Jack. If you wanted to send me back, you should have done it a long time ago."

"Macky."

" 'Cause I found you once, and I'll look again, only next time it won't be you. Maybe neither one of us will be so lucky next time. Maybe you'll get one of the malt-shop girls. But I want *you* and you're all I want, and if you think anyone else will feel the same way, you're wrong."

Then she did move, slightly, she dropped her hand on my leg and kept it there. I said nothing. I couldn't say anything. It was all flashing through my head like a movie gone mad, Macky stranded in the malt shop because she'd loved Jack's album; picking out my mattress in the beach house because I was new, too; standing soaking wet in the doorway of the house the night after the Fourth of July; sleeping next to me with the teddy-bear nightgown kicked down to her feet; on the phone in the kitchen talking to her father collect, assuring him yes yes Daddy I'm fine, I've never been happier; splashing in the ocean while everyone else baked on the beach, playing in the waves until her skin puckered because she had years of catching up to do on beaches; spending all her malt-shop pay on beach clothes so that she would no longer stand out as a stranger, but standing out in spite of herself; growing pink and remaining silent under the scorn of the malt-shop girls, which was good-naturedly disguised as teasing but remained scorn at the bone of it. Bearing up under it all with every bit of the courage, charity and grace inscribed in her sweater. For-giving eyes and soft soft hair and hard hard legs and a mouth so wise I turned fool when I met it.

"You think that's easy to come by?" she was asking, letting the tears shimmy back into her voice. "Do you?"

I shook my head. I was almost afraid to touch her. It was too late to do the right thing by her; the right thing had already been done; to lose her now would be loss, pure and simple. Then I reached for her and when I did, she folded herself into me as if nothing could be easier and kissed me in a way that let me know that the time I had spent and the care I had taken with her had not been lost, would never be lost, and would not be taken away as long as I kept my head and held on tight.

Jack and Delrone were quarreling in the malt shop because Jack had not been satisfied with any of the guitars he had seen on their shopping trips through the music stores, and Delrone was trying to make him understand the importance of a guitar player's own-ing a guitar. Cookie was closing up shop and cleaning out the soft-ice-cream machines, and Eddie was help-ing her out by serving burgers to the evening's last customers. I was sitting with Billy, who felt obliged to give me a detailed description of Peggy Sue's legs, how long they were and all the tricks they could per-form.

"So what about"—Billy looked left and right, but Macky had left the malt shop five minutes earlier to fetch clean sponges and paper towels—"what about Macky's thighs, Cooder?"

"They're like steel and satin, Billy."

"No, really."

96

"You're not gonna find out, really."

"No, really. I mean, I've seen her in a swimsuit, but I want to know—"

"Cut it out!" Jack ordered irritably, looking up from his cheeseburger.

"Come on, Jack, she's not your sister or nothing."

"She's my sister's age. She's just like my sister."

"I just wanna know, 'cause I'll never find out."

"Damn right you'll never find out," I told him.

Cookie looked over our heads and said, "We're gonna close up soon. You can go next door if you want a burger."

"This is the malt shop, right?"

We all turned around and saw a short, broad-shouldered boy with black hair, heavy eyebrows, and pale, sober eyes. His eyes were skittish; he didn't keep them focused on anything long enough to put across an expression, but the constant motion was hypnotic. Cookie looked down from her sticky struggle with the soft-ice-cream machine. Delrone looked back at Cookie.

"Yeah, it's the malt shop," Cookie said, stepping off her stool. "But we close at nine and—"

"Does this girl work here?" the boy asked, and handed Cookie a photograph. Cookie wiped her hands on her apron, took the photograph, raised her eyes up at me, glanced down again, raised her eyes up at Delrone. Delrone took the photograph, and I peered over his shoulder to look and bit my tongue. It was Macky's high school yearbook picture.

"I think I've seen her on the beach," Jack said cheerfully.

"You think you see everybody on the beach,"

97

Delrone answered calmly, and then turned to the boy with pleasant contempt. "Who are you, son, the FBI?"

"She stole my car."

"Does she look like a car thief to you?" Delrone asked, flipping the photograph at me. Her hair was loose and thick, and she was smiling as if there were no trouble in the world. Billy took the picture from me and said, "She looks like she has thighs like steel and satin."

Delrone snatched it back from him and leaned over to stuff it in the boy's pocket.

"You don't want to lose this, son," Delrone said.

"You didn't tell me if she works here."

"Do you see her working here?"

"Carl told me," the boy said. "Carl the Corvette Specialist told me she works here."

"Well, the boardwalk shops all look alike to Carl, you know. Maybe she works next door," Cookie said. "And they're open 'til nine next door."

"Look," the boy said, becoming tough. "The Jersey police have been on the lookout for that car all summer, and they saw it pull into Paradise Beach early this morning. It's parked outside Carl's. And Carl says it's been in his garage all summer and he thinks Madeline works here."

"If you got the car, what do you need *her* for?" I asked.

"Put her behind bars where she belongs?" Delrone suggested witheringly.

"I have to take her back home!" the boy cried, realizing he was outnumbered and appealing for pity.

"My dad told me not to come home without the car and without her."

They all looked at me. I leaned over to him and almost whispered, "Can I see your hands?"

He squinted at me and backed up, but I grabbed his paws anyway and looked down at them, examining the knuckles and then turning them palms up, remembering Macky's bruises the night after the Fourth of July.

"Nice big hands you got, Jimmy," I said, and his eyes widened when I used his name. "Nice big hands to hit girls with."

"I didn't! She's a liar! I only hit her once!" he whined, trying to pull away, but I dug my fingers in even harder and spoke more softly.

"You take your car, and you get out of the state with it, before I break all your goddamn fingers."

He pulled his hands back in a sudden burst of strength, and hopped away from me. I threw a look at everyone else. Jack, Delrone, Billy, and Eddie were watching him with hard looks fresh from the late show, and Cookie was waving the customers out the door and taking their plates to hurry them along. She raised one eyebrow at me. The customers strolled out without looking back, jangling the bell on the door as they went. Jimmy watched them go, shifted his weight from foot to foot, bit his lip, then put his hands to his hips and took a deep breath.

"I can get the police, you know!"

Our faces remained frozen and mean, except for Delrone's, and Delrone only smiled contemptuously.

"So get 'em."

The bell jangled again, like a sudden laugh, and Macky's voice sang out, "Hi, Jack! Did you find a new guitar yet?"

We sighed to see our scene of tough-guy terrorism evaporate as Jimmy turned, and Macky, upon seeing him, stopped so quickly that she tripped.

Macky plunked down the bag of sponges and paper towels and held out her hand to Cookie.

"My purse, please."

Cookie handed it over and Macky fished through it and pulled out a set of keys. She threw them at Jimmy.

"There. I guess you know where your car's parked."

"Smooth," Delrone said admiringly.

"I'm taking you home," Jimmy told Macky.

"You're not taking me *anywhere!*"

"Don't think I *want* to, you stupid little bitch. I *have* to. I spent my whole *summer* looking for you. My father says I can't come home unless I bring you back."

"I'm not going back. My father says I don't have to go back with you."

"My father won't let me in the *house* until he knows you're all right. *All right!*" he repeated, glancing around at the rest of us. "You look like you've been *fine. I'm* the one who's been running all over this stupid, ugly state."

"You should have thought of that before," Macky said smugly.

"Goddamn it!" he yelled. "You ruined *everything.* You're coming back with me, Madeline. You're coming back 'cause I can get you arrested for grand theft auto and *then* what will your father say?"

"You wouldn't dare. You don't dare *anything.*"

But he dared to slap her again, and he dared to do

100

it in front of all of us. Jack seized Macky and pulled her away from harm, and I was on my feet before I knew it, delivering what Dark Mark Clark had called the "Midnight Special," a punch that started with the fist and kept on swinging around until the elbow hit where the fist had been, a fraction of a second later. Jimmy fell back onto one of the tables, its iron ice-cream chairs already neatly polished and stacked legs up on its top. His body crashed into the table and onto the floor, and the chairs scattered, and then it was so quiet we could hear the freezer humming. I sucked on my bruised knuckles and Delrone strode by me and knelt by Jimmy and touched his neck.

"I haven't had this much fun since that chick's boyfriend went after Billy. Remember that, Billy?"

I turned to Macky, who was watching me with wide wet eyes. I stroked the rising red mark on her cheek.

"Jesus, sweetie. You sure had bad taste before you met me, didn't you?"

"He's not bleeding on my clean floor, is he?" Cookie asked.

"He's not bleeding at all," Delrone said. "He's just out cold."

Delrone straightened up and looked at me.

"Where did you learn that *punch*?"

"Bars."

"Grand theft auto *and* assault, now," Cookie said. "Better get him out of here."

"Where do you think we should take him?" Eddie asked, leaning over the counter to see the body.

"Come on," Jack said, snapping into business as Jimmy began to moan awake. "You guys get on back to the house and throw a few things together and get out of town for a while. Just a night or two. We'll act like we never heard of you. Then you can call us and see how it's going."

Jack went back to the house with us and we packed all of Macky's things so that they wouldn't be there if Jimmy brought the police by the house to look for her. We threw them into the back of my Cougar, along with a few of my clothes and my Bible, and Macky turned to kiss Jack good-bye. Then we saw Billy sprinting up the street.

"Hey, Jack, remember that night at the Outer Limits when the cops came by and the sergeant said that if we caused any more trouble he wouldn't let us play Paradise Beach anymore?"

"So?"

"So that's the cop that Jimmy found to cry to. And the sergeant knows where we live, you know, because of all the noise complaints from last summer, and they're coming, I think, and—"

"Better hurry," Jack snapped to us. "You need some cash, you guys?"

"No, Jack—" Macky and I said together as Jack pulled out his wallet.

"Take it, sweetie," he said, handing a fistful of bills to Macky. "Cookie owes you your paycheck, anyway."

"What are you doing with all *that*?" Billy cried, amazed. "You *never* have any money."

"I thought I was gonna get a guitar with it today."

"*Guitar!*" I repeated, and raced back to the house for my Strat. I picked up my jacket and a few other things off the mattress, then turned down the hall.

I flicked on the light in Jack's bedroom and saw my guitar lying on the bed. The bedroom window was open, and through the blanket Jack had nailed over it to keep out the sun, I could hear Jack rasping directions to Macky on how to get out of town while avoiding major roads and Macky, giddy with excitement, repeating them back to him in a jumble. I reached down and brushed the strings with the tips of my fingers. The guitar answered with a dull, muted sound.

"Cooder!" Jack yelled. "Hurry up!"

Sirens were wailing somewhere down Seaside Boulevard. I touched the guitar one more time. And then I deserted it, left it on the bed while I ran from the room, out the door, across the yard, and into the driver's seat. I started the engine with a scream. The sirens grew louder and Macky kissed Jack, and as I pulled away Jack was waving and shouting words of encouragement I couldn't hear. Macky hung out of the window, waving back and shouting, "Yes! Okay! Take care! Good-bye!" until I pulled her back inside and demanded the directions Jack had given her as an escape route.

I was hugging the wheel until I couldn't hear the sirens any longer, until the blood stopped racing through my ears, until I felt we were safe. Then I leaned back with a long whistle and Macky hugged me.

"You were *such* a *hero*."

"Oh, yeah, I was great. I could have landed us both in jail."

She curled up next to me and said contentedly, "I guess I really shouldn't have stolen his car."

"You didn't steal his car. You borrowed it. Hotwiring a car you've never seen before, *that*'s stealing a car. Now me, *I* stole a car."

"You never told me that."

"Why would I?"

"When did you steal a car?"

"I stole a Corvette in Gainesville and drove it up to Atlanta. I wanted to keep it, but you know how it goes."

"Were you arrested?"

"No. Not for that."

"But you have been arrested?" she asked, perking up. "What were you arrested for?"

"Drunk and disorderly, and trespassing in a cemetery."

She studied me for a moment, then pressed her head against my shoulder.

"That must have been after Maude died."

"Yeah."

We were an hour across the state line in New York, confused as to how we got there and asking for a cheap bed. We settled on the first motel we saw, one that had no color TV, no scenic view, no continental breakfast, no pool, no café, and no pets allowed. We had only a stiff-sheeted double bed with a musty deserted smell, a cold scrubbed bathroom, an orange carpet, a faded chenille bedspread, and a fake oil painting of a plaid-clad fisherman wrestling with a large silver fish. Macky sniffed at the room as I flicked on the light, then she strode toward the bed, unbuttoning her shirt as I pulled the key out of the lock. She was in the bathroom by the time I shut the door, and when I started to follow her in she was already out, dancing past me, scattering her clothes, arriving naked at the

104

bed to dive under the sheet and the chenille bed-spread, punching at the pillow.

I examined the drinking glass wrapped in paper and the rough towels and tiny bars of soap. I washed my face slowly and carefully and then stared at it, as I always did in motel bathrooms, stared at it a good long while to calm myself down and let myself know I was a real guy in a real place, something I used to forget on the road. Only on the road I'd never had a real girl calling for me to come out. I went back into the room. Macky was sitting up in bed, hugging her knees. I walked to the window and pulled back the curtains and stared out at what view we had, the parking lot, and beyond that the small quiet highway that had brought us there. I looked back at Macky. She was watching me with sleepy eyes and a faint serene smile.

"We've got the whole world in our hands," I said flatly, letting the curtain fall. "We've got the whole wide world in our hands."

I'd let sarcasm creep back into my voice, but she smiled and yawned innocently. Her hair was tousled and her eyes watered from the yawn. Her skin was glowing in the dusty yellow light of the room, her eyes were drowsy and happy, and even wrapped in that ratty bedspread, she was beautiful.

"Are we going back to Paradise Beach?" she asked.

"Do you want to?"

"I don't think *you* want to," she said, stretching luxuriously. She relaxed her arms and patted the space beside her on the bed. I sat down next to her and kissed her hair.

"You said there's not much there after Labor Day. The guys'll be gone. And you don't want to work for Carl much longer, do you? You were happiest, like, doing that car for Lee's teacher. You don't like working for other people."

I looked at her in surprise and she yawned again and kissed my cheek. I pushed back her hair and kept my fingers on her face.

"And what do you want to do, honey?"

" 'I only want to be with you,' " she sang, in a convincing, startling imitation of Jack, then she laughed at the look on my face. She kissed my cheek again and reached across me to turn off the light on the bureau. I watched her face hover close to mine and then disappear into darkness, and I grabbed her and held her close, hurting with a sudden humming ache when she pressed her face against me and I could feel her smiling.

"I love you, Macky."

"Oh, Cooder, I love you so much."

The next morning I tried not to worry. I listened to the cars rushing by on the highway outside. I watched the sun trying to fight its way through the heavy ugly curtains; I studied the flecks of dust dancing in the few beams that won the fight. I kissed Macky's shoulder, then her hair. She was clinging to me and sound asleep, and her breathing was deep and slow. I ran my hand from her shoulder to her wrist in a rhythm that matched her breathing. I had spent many mornings that way, between my departure from Atlanta and my arrival in Virginia—on the road, in motel rooms in the morning, listening to the traffic I would soon join, breakfast the first mystery of the day, no particular place to go, one more girl to kiss good-bye. But there was a difference this time.

I'd watched her wake up a little at a time, wake up

hungry, without a trace of worry in her face. We checked out and threw our things back into the car and went looking for breakfast.

We turned west and drove down a hilly, heavily wooded road, one that seemed to lead nowhere, except through pools of sunshine slanting through tall trees and then through tunnels of shadow. We were lost, and had chosen that road only because Macky thought it was pretty, and I made an abrupt turn just to please her. The radio whined country-and-western songs to us, and we were alone on the road, never meeting another car, never even meeting a deer. We had no destination in mind except for a place that would feed us, and we were greeted at every slow curve by more trees, more splashes of sunshine and shafts of shadow, more songs about sorry women and shiftless men and new love on a Saturday night. After nearly an hour we arrived in a small town named Wolf's Ridge and stopped at Mae's Diner, a long silver building with only one pickup in the gravel parking lot.

We were greeted by the smell of baking apples and perking coffee and the friendly "Morning!" and wary eyes of a large gray-haired woman who had to be Mae. We shared the counter with a craggy old man drinking coffee, who glanced at us, pursed his lips, grunted, and returned to his newspaper. Mae poured us steaming cups of coffee and we ordered everything on the menu under "Breakfast." Mae threw eggs and bacon on the grill and bread in the toaster, and served each of us a doughnut. I gulped my coffee and Macky dropped sugar cubes into hers. Then she gasped so loudly that Mae and the old man jumped. Macky clapped her hand over her mouth and raised her eyebrows.

108

"Cooder, your *guitar*."

"What?"

"We *forgot* it."

"Oh, no, baby," I said, picking up my doughnut. "I left it there for Jack."

"You left it there for Jack," she repeated, bewildered, and when I nodded, her eyes melted into a softer curiosity and she said, "But you wouldn't sell it to him."

I shrugged, and thanked Mae as she handed me another doughnut. I swallowed it down as Macky continued staring at me, and eventually she smiled.

"Johnny Streeter's right. You need a manager."

"Johnny Streeter wants to be everyone's manager."

"He wants to be mine, too," Macky said. "He said I should model. He said I could sell ice cream to the Eskimos."

"He's also a flirt."

The old man sighed and drummed the fingers of his knotty hand across the classified ads in the newspaper. Mae patted his hand as she handed us our toast. The old man frowned at her.

"And don't be pattin' my hand."

"Now, Con."

"I ain't given up yet."

"Well, you should," Mae said sharply. "You should give up. You should just get that notion out of your head and sell that place like everybody told you to when Ruthie died. Never shoulda told everybody you were opening the place up again. Nothing's a fact 'til it's a fact."

Mae slapped down two plates of fried eggs and bacon

and we began to eat so quickly that she looked at us again before turning back to the old man.

"You can't do it alone, and nobody's gonna do it with you, so you just give up."

"I ain't givin' up," he repeated stubbornly.

"Just give it up for a little while. Next summer those college boys'll be back again, work on it a little more. You get those young boys to do it. They'll get it done eventually."

"They won't come back. They thought it was fun in the beginning, but then they got bored. You know how kids are. Won't stick to nothin'."

He scowled at us, and Macky froze, her fork halfway up to her mouth.

"Well, you're crazy if you think anybody'll stay up there all winter," Mae said firmly. "Summertime, maybe, but wintertime, no. Nobody from around here. And you know you can't do it. Can't stay up there all winter by yourself. You're too old for that."

"If I'm so old, I'll drop dead before I see it finished, letting kids work on it in the summer only. I got folks want their cabins next summer. Folks remember that place, Mae. I know you think it was a long time ago, but folks remember."

"*I* remember," Mae protested, and then added quietly, "I spent my honeymoon up there. You remember, Con? Just like you and Ruthie. It was a beautiful place then," she said, almost defensively, looking right at Macky.

"What place?" Macky had to ask.

"The old lodge."

"What lodge?"

"Old Crystal Lodge, up on the Ice Caves Mountain. Ya never been up there?"

"We're not from around here," Macky said.

"Aw, it was a beautiful place. Con and Ruthie used to run it. Folks'd rent out those little cottages . . . ten, twelve little cottages . . . all around the lake. Or they'd stay in the lodge if they's only staying a week or so."

Macky nodded blankly.

"Con here wants to open it up again."

"Oh, you closed it down?"

"Closed it down fourteen years ago, when Ruthie died," the old man said, drumming on his newspaper. "Gonna open it up next summer."

"You're *not* gonna open it up next summer," Mae told him patiently.

"Why not?" Macky asked.

"Well, honey, the place is a mess. Nobody's been up there for fourteen years. Con had these college boys up all summer doin' carpentry work on the lodge, but he's still got all those cottages to do. And he's told folks it'll be ready next summer!"

"How are you going to get it ready by next summer?" Macky asked the old man.

"Get a carpenter," the old man said, slapping the classified ads. "Get a young man, do carpentry, I'll do the plumbing, then when the snows hit, young man'll stay up there and finish the cabins. Do all the outside work in autumn, get the heat working, he can do all the inside work in winter. Come spring, come the thaw, I can get back up the mountain and help him finish up."

"Sounds like a nice plan," Macky said, smiling at Mae.

111

Mae snorted and refilled our coffee cups.

" 'Cept the young man he's talkin' about has to stay up there all winter. All winter long. By himself. Can't get up or down that mountain when the snows hit. Up there 'til the thaw. Boy died up there."

"That boy died because he couldn't find the lodge and he didn't have any food," the old man growled. "I'm not sending anyone up there to starve. I'll buy all the food."

"Nobody wants to stay up on a mountain all winter long."

"Ruthie and I did."

"When you's first married. She got pregnant, you came down quick enough."

"When we's first married," the old man echoed dreamily. "It was different then. Before they made cars could get up that hill. Only way to get up that hill was in a pickup. Or hike. Ruthie could always hike."

"Well, she was born up there, she better know how to get up and down," Mae said, watching him carefully.

"She had such good strong legs," the old man said.

"What kind of work do the cottages need?" I asked, breaking the silence that followed.

"Need new floorboards, new porches, new paint. Some of the roofs leak," the old man added, snapping back and folding up his paper. "Some of the doors don't close. It won't be easy work, I ain't saying it'll be easy."

"How much are you thinking of paying this young man?"

"Five hundred a month, free food and lodging." He squinted at me and added, "You know somebody?"

"I might. Can you take us up there for a look?"

"Place started out as a hunting lodge. Ruthie's papa, Old Man Brandt, started it that way. Then he built the cottages around the lake. Got to be a pretty popular place in the twenties. The lake, Ice Crystal Lake, it's fed by a spring up on the Ice Caves Mountain. That's why it's *Ice* Crystal Lake, 'cause it's always cold as the devil. Anyway, word got started that the spring cured things. I don't mean like those Catholic places. No hocus-pocus like that. Just good clean water. Good to drink. Good to swim in. It was the *twenties,*" the old man said again sharply, glaring at Macky as though she hadn't been listening, although, crushed as she was between him and me in the front seat of that bouncy truck, she was intent on his every word. "People had money then. When word got started that the spring was healthy, Old Man Brandt laughed it up. *Anything*, he says, would be healthy to those fast-living city people. Oh, it was popular. Society people came up summers to calm their *nerves*. I gotta say, though, what with the fresh air and the springwater and the good cooking, they left looking a sight better than they looked when they came."

The truck shifted gears with a lurch as the incline began, and we passed a wooden sign with the words "Crystal Lodge" carved into it.

"Anyway, like I say, all those society girls were coming up. Pretty dresses, fast living. Ruthie got it into her head that she wanted that, too. Old Man Brandt

113

pulls me aside . . . I was the caretaker on the place . . . tells me I better marry her quick if I wanted her. Course, I did."

"How long had you known her?" Macky asked.

"Since we's kids. Sent her a valentine in the second grade. Just a matter of time after that. Anyway, so we got married and then there was the Depression. Had the boys. Moved the whole bunch up to live at the lodge. We got by. Lost the boys, both of 'em, in the war. After the war, we got the lodge back on its feet. Different crowd, though. Camping-type folks. Young couples. Honeymooners. Those were good times. I's teaching young Paul, my grandson, how to run the place. But . . . he was always a little wild. Bought a motorcycle. Ruthie didn't want him to have it, but I felt sorry for him, seeing how cooped up he felt. Well, one night he's racing up this road we're on and this huge buck leaped out. Damn things. Can't go slow, going up this hill, or you won't get up, can't go fast or the damn deer'll jump out at you."

Macky squeezed my hand and looked at me, hoping that I would ask what happened to young Paul, but the road we were on was so narrow and winding, and the trees were so thick and menacing, that I knew there was no hope in Con's tale for a teenager on a motorcycle colliding with a buck. I shook my head at her.

"When was that?" she asked.

"Oh, right around the time JFK was sworn in. Ruthie died shortly after. Everybody told me to sell the place, but I couldn't. Couldn't look at it, either. Everybody talked like Mae. They all said, 'Cornelius Vecht, there's no sense in wasting good land or good money.' But

114

so help me, I just let it sit. Let it sit for fourteen years. I knew there'd come a day I'd want it back. Well, here we are."

"Oh, Mr. Vecht," Macky breathed. "It's beautiful."

It was. As soon as I saw the peak of the Ice Caves Mountain, I realized that what we had been driving up for the past half hour was just a slope compared to the stark stern mountain that jumped up behind the smooth lake and reached for the sky. We went into the lodge, a two-story stone building with exposed beams running along the ceiling and a moose head hanging above the downstairs stone fireplace. Con had used it as construction headquarters over the summer, and the dining room table was loaded with boxes of nails and screws, screwdrivers, a power drill, cans of brown paint and clear varnish, clean brushes and rollers, and boxes of shingles. Half of the main hall was filled, floor to rafters, with fresh lumber, and bolts of cloth and cleaning supplies were stored in the porcelain-and-steel kitchen.

"Got to make new curtains," Con said, waving at the bolts of cloth. "You sew, missy?" he asked Macky.

"I do needlepoint," she answered, trying to be helpful.

He coughed and nodded and looked away from us and sat down.

"Maybe you want to walk around?" he said. "Look at the cabins?"

We strolled around Ice Crystal Lake, along paths clogged with fallen branches and rotting leaves, surveying the cabins and noting the loose doorknobs, the sagging porches, the broken windows, the fallen rafters, the holes in the floors.

"Oh, Cooder, it's so sad," Macky said.

"This place?"

"No. I like this place. The story he told on the way up. He worked so hard and everybody kept dying."

"I can't believe he wants to start over. He's almost seventy years old and he wants to start over."

We were at cabin seven, the one farthest from the lodge, and we could see Con through a window clear across the lake. We sat down on the porch step; the scene before us was a perfect postcard honeymoon retreat, the forest bright and rustling, the air fragrant with musty wood, clean lake water and apples. Macky leaned into me and I kissed her hair.

"Can you see the newlyweds arriving in their Ford V-8s?" I asked her. "Spending too much time inside their cabins, coming down to the lodge for dinner, and not looking or talking to anyone else? And then the other couples, the couples who came here as newlyweds and now have their little kids with them, handing each other fried chicken down that long dining room table? And Ruthie in the kitchen, and Con running the rowboats and doing repairs and scolding the little kids and not letting anyone go swimming alone? Can you see it? The war's over, and Con's always wanted to run this place, and both their sons died in the war but they have their grandson and everyone in the world is getting married and having babies? And the radio might be on, and sometimes maybe they're playing Elvis Presley but most of the time they're not, most of the time they're playing big-band things with big old orchestras and girl singers crooning away . . ."

116

I paused, and we listened to the chirps and rustles in the forest and the splashes in the lake.

"And he wants it back," Macky said softly. "He really believes . . . believes . . . if only . . ."

"Yeah. If only. 'Even so faith, if it hath not works, is dead, being alone.' "

Macky pressed her forehead against my neck and kissed my throat, my neck, my mouth, until I pulled her into my lap.

"Oh, Cooder. I'm so glad we found this place," she said. "It'll be just the two of us up here all winter, just the two of us. And we'll bring it back for him."

Perhaps it was because there seemed to be nothing better immediately in store for us, nothing except a one-room apartment in an alien town and day jobs in a garage for me and a restaurant for her. Perhaps it was because we had lived all summer off the generosity of the All-Americans and we felt as though we ought to pay back our debt with generosity to a stranger. Perhaps it was a sermon of my uncle's, the text of which I couldn't recall but the spirit of which was something along the lines of doing good when a chance to do good is held out to you, that hovered in the back of my mind. Perhaps it was that there was truth in what Macky had said to me that night on the beach in the state park when I finally woke up to the fact that she was a precious gift I would be damned for throwing away, because all she wanted was to be with me. Maybe that was true, I told myself, because she was so young and so warmhearted, she did not yet lie, she hadn't had me long enough to begin to

117

want something more. Perhaps it was because, as we joined hands and walked back along the soft paths of the woods and around the cabins to the lodge, the air was so pure and promising. And perhaps it was the combined hope and pride in Con's eyes when he met us on the porch at our return, but we shook hands on it, for five hundred a month and free food and lodging and the rest of the world a mountain away.

Con was with us all through autumn, helping me on the roofs and the porch work and showing me what I would need to do indoors and how to operate the heaters for the cabins. Macky, as soon as she realized that the free food was not going to arrive in the form of TV dinners, took my car down during the afternoons to Mae's diner to learn wilderness cooking first-hand. Mae understood that Macky was totally ignorant on the finer points of homemaking, but she did not pass the word along to Con, who left a generous amount of fresh game on the dining-room table one afternoon. Macky's discovery of the gift produced a scream we heard all the way down at cabin four, where we were repairing the porch. Con shuffled up to the lodge to see what was amiss. He was gone so long that I put down my hammer and started up. When I arrived, Con was coming out the front door, chuckling and scowling.

"Ain't she never skinned a rabbit before?"

"Uh, no," I said, glancing past him with pity. I stepped around him and looked in the door to see Macky up to her wrists in blood and fur. "Need some help, honey?"

"I'm fine, Cooder," she answered in a voice as pale as her face, and Con pulled me away, whispering that it was always best to leave the skittery ones to themselves the first time.

"Eh, well, you married her in a hurry, didn't you?" Con sighed as we walked back to the cabin. "Guess she'll learn everything soon enough. She's a nice little gal. Awful sweet. Pretty as you'd want her, and dainty little hands. Ruthie, now, Ruthie was never what you'd call a beauty, but she sure could cook. Cooked for fifty people without batting an eye."

Con nodded and wiped his bloody hands on his handkerchief.

"Did she tell you we were married?"

"Ain't you married?"

"What did she tell you?"

"She says you ran off together. She says you got married the night before I saw you-all at Mae's. She says you had to sneak off, 'cause her father was a doctor and a Catholic and your daddy was a preacher and a Baptist, and the two of them wouldn't hear of the two of you. So you two ran off, she says, and got married. Ain't that what happened?"

"Well, yeah," I said. "Except we, uh . . . we didn't have time to get married. Couldn't find anyone that night. We were going to get married that next day, but then we ran into you."

"Well. There's a preacher in town. I'd be happy to stand for you."

"I don't take much stock in preachers."

"I thought your daddy was one."

"Of sorts."

"Well," he said, his eyes both smiling and disapproving, "I guess you won't be joining the congregation."

"No, sir. But thanks."

The following Sunday we sat in one of the rowboats, floating around the lake, too lazy and tired to do anything more. We had made a provisions trip the day before out to the nearest shopping mall, two hours away. I cashed the check I had gotten from Lee's parents for the work I did on the Mercedes. We bought magazines and automotive manuals and a radio, hats and gloves and sweaters and robes and socks, canned fruit and cookies and chocolate, whisky for Saturday nights, champagne for Christmas, sketch paper for Macky, who liked to draw the forest animals, and an acoustic guitar, at her insistence—she wanted to hear me play and she wanted me to teach her.

Macky was sketching the mountain and me. She had a rag wrapped around her head to keep her hair out of her face, and she wore one of Con's old plaid shirts. She'd never looked prettier.

"How come you told Con we were married?" I asked.

" 'Cause he asked me how come I didn't have a ring. When I was pulling the ears off those poor dead bunnies." She raised her eyes up to the mountains, then lowered them to her sketch, then looked at me. "He asked me why I didn't have a ring, and that story just came out. Didn't he believe it?"

"Oh, he believed it all right. Are you really Catholic?"

"Mmm? No. Episcopalian."

"What do *they* do?"

"What do you mean?"

"How do they practice?"

"Practice?"

"In *church*."

120

"I never went to church. When Mommy was alive, I went to Sunday school, but after she died we just stopped going."

"What did you do in Sunday school?"

"We drew little sheep and cut angels out of construction paper. Stuff like that."

I sat up, leaned my elbows against the seat and squinted at her.

"Are you serious?"

"Yeah." She looked up and nodded. "Why? What did you do?"

"They never told you about sin?"

"Well . . . they told us to be good."

"They never told you about *Hell*?"

"Maybe they did. I don't remember."

"Were you baptized?"

"I was christened. Is that the same thing? I was a little baby, and I had this beautiful gown with all this lace on it, and they sprinkled water on my forehead. Right here."

She scooped up a fistful of water and flicked her fingers at my face and giggled, but when she saw that I did not even crack a smile, she leaned forward and wiped my face off.

"Why? Were you baptized?"

"You get your whole body wet when you're baptized. They took me down to the river and held me under and when I came up again I was supposed to be reborn."

"They'd throw a little baby into the river?"

"I wasn't a little baby. I'd just turned eleven. You have to be old enough to know what's going on. You have to be old enough to accept Jesus Christ as your saviour. They don't do it all for you when you're a baby."

"Well," Macky said, setting aside her sketch and moving closer. "What makes you decide to accept?"

"I don't know how most folks decided. It must've been different with them. I was just beginning to understand my place with them. The Bible said, 'A bastard shall not enter the congregation of the Lord.' But anybody could accept Jesus, they said. I thought it'd make them all stop treating me like a bastard. I thought maybe I'd just stay down there in the river and when I came up I'd feel different. But I didn't. I felt just the same, and they treated me just the same. Then I got home and washed all that river water off of me and I was supposed to stay in my room and contemplate God, but I couldn't contemplate nothing, I was so goddamned mad because I felt just the same and it was all out of my hands. I couldn't contemplate, and sure as hell I couldn't pray, so I turned on my radio. It was playing 'Duke of Earl' and then I just put my head down and started crying. You know? 'Cause the Duke of Earl, the way he was singing it, he sounded like it hadn't worked for him in the river, either, but it didn't matter. 'Nothing can stop me now, 'cause I'm the Duke of Earl.' I don't know why it made me cry, except maybe I couldn't figure out how he *got* to be the Duke of Earl. Maybe he left his town or something. I don't know. *I* left town, anyway."

"Poor Cooder."

"Ah."

"Why were they so mean to you?"

"That's just the way some folks are."

"I love you," she said, in a voice she had never

122

before used to say those words, an even voice, pure and easy, with a steady gaze that made me look away.

"Yeah," I said, and I couldn't turn my eyes to her. "Well, I was wondering, when you told Con we were married, if that meant something. Like, maybe, if that meant you'd like to get married. I mean, to me."

"Is that a proposal?"

"Well, yeah."

"Oh, Cooder!" she cried, leaping at me and rocking the boat. "That's the worst proposal I've ever heard!"

"Oh, yeah?" I said, catching her. "How many proposals have you had?"

"None. And there won't be any after this, ever, so I want you to say it right."

"Will you marry me, Macky?"

"Yes. Of course. Don't you know that?"

We worked on as the leaves fell off the trees and the branches grew blacker against a sky that grew less blue and more gray. We pulled the rowboat in and tied it back up. We finished the last roof in November, our hammer sounds echoing clear and hard across the lake and into the woods. Macky painted the cabins, baked pies, roamed the woods, and worked her way through the attic, unearthing Con and Ruthie's wedding pictures and dozens of snapshots of people who had visited the lodge, young couples sitting on the porches of their cabins, labeled on the back "Eddie and Sue, 1952," "Bob and Diane, 1954," "Jim and Lorraine, 1955." As the nights grew colder, we had our dinner and then huddled in our room in the big quilt-covered four-poster bed while the fire burned and Macky read to me from the adventure novels she

had found in the attic, or I read my automotive manuals and tried to teach her about cars. I kept the fire
burning high and Macky brushed out her hair in front
of it, every night, in long slow strokes and then rubbed
cold cream over my chapped hands.

On nights when I was not too tired, she pressed me
to teach her guitar chords and tell her stories about
what I had done before I met her. On nights when the
work of the day had worn me out, I lay with my head
in her lap. She massaged my face and neck with the
tips of her fingers while she told me about her well-
mannered lonesome days in her big empty house that
she shared with her father who was never home, the
nice green lawns and the Saturday piano lessons and
the proper prettiness of her cousins' weddings, the
white satin that whispered to her like a warning on
those spring afternoons. She told me how, looking at
those weddings, she saw her days of freedom numbered as carefully as everything else was numbered
for her, numbered like the one and two and three of
the elegant waltzes her piano teacher assigned to her.
She told me how, staring from her window down to
the garden at night, she had heard on her radio tales
of the kind of crazy love she thought she would never
have, because she was a good girl who did what she
was told and she had to be content with hearing about
what other people did and comparing it to what she
did and wondering if there would ever be a middle
ground for her, until the day that scruffy boy saw her
modeling girls' juniorwear in the department store
and waited to talk to her.

He was like no boy she had ever met; her aunts had
made sure of that. They fought her on it, but for the

124

first time she fought back; she had a boyfriend, and maybe he was conceited and maybe he was rough, but he had a car and a record collection. And he introduced her to the record that turned her head, a record better than any she had heard on the radio, one that told stories of wild girls and heartless boys and nights that went on until the day cut them off, a record sung in a hoarse bluesy voice crying over heartbreak and loneliness, a rowdy yelling voice chanting about careless love affairs and careful dance steps in the middle of some downtown where no one had a last name and no one asked for one. She was so desperate to see that world that she couldn't help but listen when that bragging boy began sketching out the plans that led her astray, that led her to Paradise Beach.

Con appeared one morning wrapped in his thick plaid coat with two more boxes of food and blankets, and remained on the porch after we had dragged them inside.

"Storm's coming. Be here in two three days. Right before Christmas. Looks to be a mean one. Coming down from Canada. Stay inside until it stops altogether. No sense shoveling snow that's gonna get all covered up again next night. Should last about a week, all that snow. No telling how long it'll take me to get it off that mountain road. We got a tractor, but still, don't expect to see me for a couple more weeks. But you should be able to get out to the cabins in 'bout a week. Well, we got a lot done. Place should be back on its feet by summer. Place should be ready to open up again."

He nodded at the cabins. Macky began shivering

next to me and I slid an arm around her. Con looked back at me.

"I'm grateful to you," he said.

I nodded and tightened my grip on Macky's shoulder.

"We're grateful to you, too, Mr. Vecht," Macky blurted. "It's so beautiful up here. We feel like we're on our honeymoon."

"Eh, it's a good place for a honeymoon. Keep your feet dry. I'll get back up this little old hill as soon as the plows clear. Have a Merry Christmas."

"You too, Mr. Vecht," Macky said, and hugged him.

He pulled himself away, embarrassed, and thrust a small package into her hand.

"That's for Christmas," he said. "Don't open it 'til then. Good-bye."

The wind came first, screaming the blues and forcing the trees into an unhappy dance. I carried loads of wood up to the bedroom and built the fire into such a steady roar that Macky had only to wear her flimsiest nightgown while she plucked at the guitar or read adventure novels. Then the sleet came, attacking the window with a steady volley of pecking. I kept the shutters locked and the curtains drawn and the fires burning, and Macky cuddled next to me for warmth at night, and I held her close and thought of nothing but nature. Soon we lost the radio reception in a storm of static and we were left with no voices but our own, and Macky shoved the guitar at me one night in demand for music while she kept guard over the whisky bottle.

"I never drank whisky before I met you," she told

126

me, sipping it from a wineglass while I strummed the guitar as I sat in the chair by the fire, looking over at her on the bed. She sucked on her fingers.

"You sure learned a lot of important things from me, huh? Whisky, sex, the basic rock-and-roll chords. Really does me proud."

"The basic rock-and-roll chords *hurt*," she said, pulling her fingers out of her mouth. "I have blisters."

"Everybody gets blisters."

"Did you? Does Jack?"

"Sure. No guts, no glory."

She gave me a whisky-sweet smile, pulled the quilt around her and came over to sit at my feet. I stroked her hair.

"No. Keep playing."

I kissed the top of her head and kept playing.

"You never sing to me," she said.

"You're lucky."

"If I give you more whisky, will you sing?"

"No telling what I might do if you give me more whisky."

She filled my glass, and when I reached for it she kissed my hand, rubbed her face across my fingers, and purred, "You won't sing me a love song?"

"I don't know any."

"You must know one. You must have written a love song for Maude."

"No. I never did."

"You never wrote her a love song?"

"I wrote her songs, yeah, but not love songs."

"What did you write songs about?"

"Well, we were a blues band, Macky. It wasn't poetry, like Jack's stuff. They were mostly about . . . pain.

127

Things we didn't have. And greed. Things we wanted."

"What kind of things you didn't have?"

"Money. A place to belong. Peace of mind. Control."

"Why did you stop?"

"I lost something," I said, and strummed aimlessly. "I lost the picture in my head of the person I was singing to."

"Maude."

"No. Not her. Just . . . some kid. Some kid driving along with his windows down, me on the radio. I lost that. Then I lost my voice. Because I lost that image. I didn't know who I was singing to, and then I didn't know what I was singing about, and then I didn't know what I was singing *for*. I didn't have the . . . you know . . ."

"What? The *what*?" Macky demanded. I set down the guitar, stared into the fire, and shifted away from her. She felt the shift and touched me with gentle hands. When that failed to move me, she climbed into my lap, and even then she had to turn my head with both her hands to force me to see the faith and trust in her eyes. "You can't find the word 'cause there is no word. There's nothing that you don't have, Cooder."

The sleet stopped and instead we had snow, big flakes that reminded Macky of the ones she used to cut out of paper in Sunday school. We opened the shutters to watch it fall, and it fell for three days, covering the black arms of the trees and the haughty face of the mountain and covering the ice-hard top of the lake so that it no longer looked like the lake but like part of the blanketed land around it. We had snow and nothing else—nothing but the cold, the smokey piney smell of wood crackling in the fireplace, the tingling scent of new snow, the chocolaty steam of the cocoa Macky carried up from the kitchen, nothing but silence and kisses and the warmth of the bed we left less and less often, nothing but whispers and murmurs and more silence still.

Macky remembered Con's present on Christmas morning, and she peeled away the paper while I combed out her hair, wet from the bath. She pulled out two gold rings and a note from Con: "These were mine and Ruthie's. You take them and be happy with them. Merry Christmas, Cornelius Vecht." I slid Ruthie's ring on Macky's finger, but Macky's hand was too small and she had to wear it on her middle finger. She slid Con's ring on my finger and it fit just fine.

And I was suddenly calm, after all those giddy nights of love in front of the fire, all those nights when she was so precious to me in one choking moment that I wanted to kill us both so I'd never have to watch her leave me, all those quiet nights when I told myself I didn't deserve her and then said a quick prayer to ward off bad luck. Of course I deserved her, I'd always deserved her, I'd suffered without her, I had her now, and, knowing me, any day now she wouldn't be enough. "You take them and be happy with them," Con had written, and I knew we would try, but it wouldn't be easy.

All the comfort you can borrow
All the lies that you destroy
All I've ever wanted
In the eyes of that one boy.

129

It was a bitter little ditty Maude had written for me after one of those cataclysmic fights that forever alters the current of a love affair; it was a verse I was reinterpreting to fit the love I shared with Macky, because Maude had originally written, "All the *lies* that you can borrow/All the *comfort* you destroy," and that did not apply to us.

I cleared the paths between the cabins when the snow stopped falling, after the New Year. Aside from the marks of my shovel and a few animal tracks, the land was undisturbed, the cottages were restored and cozy, and the place looked like a town on a Christmas card: "How still we see thee lie."

Macky helped me clear the paths. I saw that the work tired her and told her to let up and go inside, but she wanted to stay with me. Then she caught a cold, which turned into a fever. I forced her to stay in bed and gave her baths and prepared broths for her and held her until she shivered into sleep. Each day I returned from my work on the cabins to find her sullen and moody and desperate for entertainment.

She hinted that my reluctance to sing to her the songs I used to know was a failure of love on my part.

I argued that I did not remember them and that blues singing required a blues band. But she saw that for the lie it was. Once sung, the blues are not forgotten. And the only accompaniment they require is a heart angry and betrayed.

But an angry and betrayed heart could be put to other uses, I realized. It could be put into work. It could be put into restoring what had once been, or what had never been, to rebuilding, in the present, a tangible thing out of the memory the heart held of the past. The voice of the blues could mourn, like a eulogy, a loss that cannot be recovered. But hands inspired by the blues could set themselves to the business of recovering, of mending, of healing.

I stood on the porch of cabin seven, watching the lodge and humming Maude's song. I thought of my uncle, the Reverend Aaron Cutler, who had preached against the blues not so much because the music was obsessed with sins of the flesh but more because they lured men into bitterness and away from the pious duty of action. I thought of Dark Mark Clark and how he'd argued with me to keep the band together when I couldn't hear the music anymore. And I thought of Robert Johnson.

There was a legend about Robert Johnson, king of the Delta blues singers, who lived and died before my mother was born, perhaps my father, too. Coming from nowhere, he hung around the master blues players, pestering them to teach him a few licks on his guitar. What he knew of his guitar was so little that they ignored him, told him to give it up. He dropped out of the scene and was not heard from for no one remembers how long; then he returned to be the best there ever was.

"Now I shouldn't say this to a preacher's boy," said the man who told me the story, the same old drunk who had told me what my mother had looked like and who my father had probably been. "Preacher's boy like you would like to think he prayed and all. Began to believe in Jesus and believe in himself. Was ruh-

131

deemed or somethin'. But they all say he sold his soul to the Devil."

When I drove out of Atlanta, with my Strat and my band, my only home, and Maude, my only love, all behind me, I vowed to avenge myself for my losses by making a pact to become the best player there had ever been. Two thousand miles later, I realized I had no hope of selling my soul to the Devil. I had sat on a bed in a motel too sleazy and forlorn to be part of a national chain, and reckoned that if the Devil had had any interest in my soul, he would have bought it long ago. I'd had too many bad dreams and sour mornings, too many shots of whisky in too many bars, too many anonymous girls who didn't deserve my abuse, too many cuts on my hands from punching out mirrors and blisters on my fingers from trying to chase down my talent, to go on believing that the Devil was hurrying up out of Hell to fetch my soul. I figured it out then about God, that He was not out to get me. He just wasn't interested. He held for me no more strong a dislike than that of a girl who, no thank you, won't let you buy her a drink. And the Devil must have figured that a soul not worth wrassling over was a soul not worth bargaining for. Maybe many were called, maybe few were chosen, but there still remained many who were ignored, left to their own devices, willing to surrender to the first thing that had enough passion to sustain them. I was one of those.

I walked from the front porch to the back, and installed a new back door in cabin seven, singing a hymn we sang in Uncle Aaron's church. Then I returned to the lodge and made a tray for Macky, broth and toast and tea with honey, and took it up to her.

"I heard you singing in the cabin," she complained, as I felt her moist forehead. "But you won't sing for me."

"How could you hear me singing in the cabin?"

"I went downstairs and stood at the door and your voice carried all the way."

"Shouldn't be standing in the cold like that."

"It felt so nice and cool."

"You're not gonna get any better standing in the freezing air. I'll pour you a bath."

"And put new sheets on the bed. And the radio's coming in now, but it's really faint. I think it needs new batteries."

She padded after me down the hall, coughing mightily. I frowned at her and she scowled back and slid into the tub.

"I'll be all right," she said. "You could open the window for just a little while and let the fire die down. It's so *stuffy* in there."

I went into the bedroom and opened the window a crack and put new batteries in the radio and turned it on. The weatherman predicted more snow. I groaned and set the radio on the dresser, picked up the whisky, the jar of honey, and a cup, and returned to the bathroom. Macky watched me with deep suspicion as I poured a little whisky and honey into the cup and began to stir them together.

"What is *that*?"

"It's good for a cough."

"Is this another one of your weird country remedies?"

"A girl named Emily Ann taught me this."

"Were you in love with her?"

133

"I don't even remember what she looked like. Just her name and her recipe. Here. Drink it down."

She sipped and grimaced and sipped and grimaced and gulped it all down and plunged her face into the bathwater to get the mixture off her lips. She came back up and poured shampoo into her hair.

"How come you don't remember what she looked like?"

"There were so many that year."

"What year?"

"I'll tell you about it some time."

"How many were there *that year*?"

"I'll go change the sheets, sweetheart."

I shut the window and checked the fire and pulled the blankets off the bed. The radio was playing a surf song. Macky came in after me a few minutes later and stood by the fire, brushing her hair.

"What was that song you were singing in the cabin?"

"Just a hymn."

"What was it called?"

" 'Give me Jesus.' "

"It sounded so pretty, just your voice in the woods."

"All right, Macky," I said, sighing in defeat as I gave a final tug to the pillowcase. I sang as I folded up the old sheets and gathered the dirty glasses onto the tray.

"Take the world, but give me Jesus
All its joys are but a name
But His love abideth ever
Through eternal years the same. . . ."

It was in steady three-four waltz time, which made it a good song to work to, a song that went *da* da da *da* da da with words that I remembered because I always remembered words, lyrics, and passages and the names of girls long after their faces disappeared.

"Oh, the height and depth of mercy!
Oh, the length and breadth of love . . ."

Macky stopped combing her hair and stared at the fire. I took off my shirt and threw it into a pile of dirty linen. I tossed the quilt over Macky's shoulder and pulled back the covers on the bed.

"Oh, the fullness of redemption,
Pledge of endless life above."

I threw my boots into the corner on the last word. She raised her head when I was through, her eyes so bright I thought she might be feverish again.

"God, I wish I was like you."

"What?"

"I do. I wish I could stand the way you stand. I wish I could be just like you."

"You couldn't be," I said slowly, still surprised.

"Why?"

"Who would I love, then?"

"Me. You'd still love me," she said, advancing on me. "Because if I was more like you, I'd love you more. And if I loved you more you'd love me more."

"Is that how it works?" I asked, wrapping the quilt, which she'd left to dangle over her shoulder, around her. She smiled up at me and I kissed her and she grabbed both my ears.

"That's how it worked before," she said.

Macky's cough cleared up at the same time the skies cleared up, and then the thaws came, and then the rain, and the lodge and all the cabins were soaked in rain and surrounded by mud. The carpentry work was all completed and there was nothing left to do but hang the curtains Macky had figured out how to make, and pack away the supplies we had not used into the cellar and wrap them all up so they would remain dry, and scrub out the lodge for the guests who would fill it in the summer.

I swept out the chimneys and scrubbed the floors and Macky aired out the upstairs rooms and washed the sheets and blankets and unpacked the boxes in the attic. She unearthed more sweaters and curios and photographs of people with no names and 78-rpm phonograph records of such hits as "I Found a Million-Dollar Baby in a Five-and-Ten-Cent Store" and "They Can't Take That Away from Me" that we danced to in the lodge hall after I learned how to bully the ancient phonograph into working. We made up the steps with the help of our memories of the dance hall scenes between soldiers and USO girls in the movies from World War II that we saw on late-night television. And we shared the floor with the ghosts of the honeymoon couples who were in the photographs in the attic. Macky brought the photographs downstairs and pinned them to the mantelpiece so we could make up stories about the people in them.

We had spring fever and cabin fever and solitary fever and a fever of nostalgia for times we had never known. After dinner we sat on the porch and watched the sun dip behind the mountain while Macky read to me the last of the adventure novels she had found in the attic, the exploits of Davy Dash, Boy Detective, a plucky young lad who solved mysteries with his

quick wits, his father's roadster, and his two pals—
the school bookworm and the school football star.
They were in high school for ten straight novels; they
were tied up in gangsters' dens and marooned on is-
lands and trapped in caves and stranded in deserts
and thrown down stairs and held at gunpoint and
called troublemakers and punks more times than I
had been called a sinner, but they always got out all
right and got their homework done on time, and the
only suffering Davy Dash went through was at the
hands of his sweetheart, Mary, who was always being
stood up for dates at the drugstore because Davy was
down in some cellar being menaced by a gangster.
Finally, they all graduated from high school and went
on to State University, and Mary had her own mys-
tery-solving adventure, which pleased Macky a little,
but by that time we had both grown to hate the whole
bunch of them so much that we made up our own
ending, where Mary ran off with one of the gangsters
and destroyed Davy's love for her so thoroughly that
he turned to a life of crime himself. Macky sighed and
let the last adventure fall to the floor of the porch and
settled her head on my shoulder while we creaked
back and forth on the porch swing.

"Episode Sixteen," she said lazily. "Cooder and
Macky marooned in the mud on the Ice Caves Mountain."

With nothing left to read, we were back to Macky's
music lessons. She had progressed so far that I could
leave her alone while she taught herself new tricks.
From where I stood, applying another coat to the porch
steps and railings just to use up the paint and keep

my hands busy, I could call out corrections to her. When I corrected her too often, she switched to an easier song and sang it straight through, every verse and chorus, in an effort, usually successful, to teach me to keep my mouth shut.

One evening she was singing a jazzed-up, sweetened-down version of the song Maude had written for me. She picked out the chords in little ripples of notes.

" 'All I've ever wanted,' " she sang. " 'In the eyes of that one boy . . .' Okay. What's wrong?"

"Nothing."

"You were scowling. You don't like the way I sing it."

"No, it's fine."

"What *is* it?" she snapped.

"Well . . . it *is* a blues song, Macky. I mean, you're singing it real pretty and everything. But it's supposed to sound kind of sad and nasty and, maybe, mocking?"

She threw the guitar aside abruptly and grabbed the radio.

"I'm sorry," I said. "Macky, keep playing."

She said nothing. The radio crackled with static and the muffled, blurped voices of the stations she passed over.

"I'm *sorry*," I said again, setting down my paintbrush. "Honey, don't listen to me. I'm no expert."

"Oh no?" she said. She did not look up. She turned the volume up on the radio, so that the static grew louder. "I want you to think about something, Cooder. Maybe when I sing 'All I've ever wanted in the eyes of that one boy,' I don't *want* it to sound sad and nasty and mocking. Maybe I don't *feel* that way about the eyes of that one boy. Okay? Think about that."

138

"Honey . . ."

Music burst forth from the radio, cutting me off. Macky raised her head, her eyes back to the way I liked to see them. I jumped over to join her on he porch swing. It was Jack on the radio, and he was singing the song he had written for Cookie while we lay asleep in the other room.

It was last summer, it was all the romance that had hovered in the air that summer like a humid haze, and it was a romance so real that it had to be Jack's, so unexpected it had to be Billy's, so necessary it had to be mine, so fleeting and bittersweet it had to be romance itself. There was the girl, a girl who was your best friend and a girl who was a vision you saw when you stayed too long at the Outer Limits, a girl like Cookie, a girl like Macky, a girl like Trudy or Sara or Cindy, a girl like Peggy Sue, a girl like the one who slapped Eddie's face, a girl like all the other girls who didn't matter at all. The girl was nobody, but singing about the girl was everything.

I could see Jack, pleading and casual, his eyes cloudy with longing, then running his hand over his mouth, wiping the expression off his face. I could hear in his voice what I'd seen in him all summer—how completely he needed it and how completely it didn't matter so much after all. The girl and the need for the girl were captured in the song as they could never be captured in real life, and Jack knew that that was the important thing.

He had changed some of the words since we had heard it last, performed at the show-turned-riot at the Outer Limits. He had replaced part of the piano with an organ, but the melody was the same. The bite in

139

his voice was perfect and raw. He had laid down the track the way he wanted it, and listening to it we could remember his struggle through the recording sessions in July; that romance, that struggle, that July, had been seized and recorded, a myth made of a time we could now never deny. Then the song shimmered out like the last notes of the old carousel at midnight when it closed down.

I turned off the radio. Macky pressed her head into my chest, and I held her close.

"I want to see him again," she said.

"We'll see him again."

"I wonder if they're married yet," she said, and I said nothing. She put her hands around my neck and kissed me. "I'd like them to come to our wedding. I want them all to come. I miss them."

"We'll see them again."

"I had this dream last night that we were living up here like we are now, except in the dream we were living up here *forever*, and no one ever came up to see us. And it was so scary. I don't mean I'm not happy here. I love you, and I love you more than I ever did on the beach, but I miss the beach. I even miss the malt-shop girls. All I wanted last summer was to fit in and have the right look and for you and me to look so neat and be so happy that they would never dare tease me about you. All I wanted was to have you all to myself and to have you love me and now I have it and I don't know, I don't believe in God the way you do, but maybe it's a sin to want more."

She toyed with my hair and looked at me with such grave, wise eyes that I felt like a small boy.

140

"And that's why I don't want you telling me how to sing those words, Cooder."

A week later, Con had still not come, but we were packing up anyway, because I had declared that as soon as the mountain road drained a little more mud and a little more rain, we would make our way down in my car. We were still in bed one morning when we heard a ruckus on the mountain road, and we dressed and hurried out to see a tractor pulling Con's pickup into the clearing in front of the lodge. We cheered, and two lanky farm boys jumped off the tractor and took a bow, and then Mae got out of the pickup and stood in front of us on the steps. She looked around at all the cabins and followed us into the lodge. Macky peered back over her shoulder, but the three of them were all who had come. Mae admired all the work we had done. She gazed at the photographs of the honeymooners on the mantelpiece, clucked over the few couples that she still remembered, and strolled across the dance floor.

"Oh," she sighed, when she stood again at the front door, looking across the porch to the lake and the cabins and the mountain. "What a fine job you kids did. It looks beautiful. It would have made him so proud."

Macky's hand was on my arm. She gave me a sudden biting squeeze and then relaxed her grip. Mae looked at her steadily, then gave us both a wan smile.

"When did he die?" Macky asked.

"During the blizzard. Right after New Year's. Heart attack, and the ambulance couldn't get through the

141

snow. He'd been out shoveling it. Damn fool thing to do, at his age, but he never would believe he was as old as he was."

We stopped at Con's grave before we left town. He was buried next to Ruthie and the boys. Mae had settled with us in cash and insisted that we keep Con and Ruthie's rings on our fingers and told us to please go through the lodge and take anything that we took a shine to. She had no plans to open the lodge for the summer but, she said, then again, she might, and we were always welcome back. Macky took the quilt from our bed and some of Ruthie's sweaters that she had always worn when we sat on the porch together, and the photograph of the honeymoon couple "Eddie and Sue, 1952" because she said Eddie looked like me, and I took the phonograph records because I didn't want to see them thrown out and a few of Con's tools that I had grown too comfortable with to leave behind.

"Maybe we should say a prayer?" Macky asked softly as we stood shivering in the graveyard.

"I don't know any."

"You don't know any prayers from your uncle?"

"I never learned his prayers."

"You want me to say one?" she asked, and I nodded.

She bowed her head and said a nice prayer, talking to God in a polite, respectful tone, as if He were one of her high school teachers, about what a kind man Con had been, and how he had never been bitter over his misfortunes and how good it was that Con was now with his wife and children and how she hoped God would let him see the fine work we had done on

Crystal Lodge and the cabins because it was a dream of his and we were glad to have known him; a good, simple prayer that didn't mess around and one that I could never have said myself in a million years, although I amen-ed it quick enough when she was through. Then we walked carefully through the mud back to the car and got in and started the drive down to New York City.

We walked into Frank's Place on Washington Street in Hoboken that afternoon. We were still in our mountain clothes and had driven down that morning from Wolf's Ridge. All I originally had in mind was a shave and a haircut and a weekend on the town, but as soon as we reached civilization, Macky made me stop at a record store and buy Jack's new album. The address of Johnny Streeter's office was printed on the bottom of the inside jacket, and Macky insisted that I call the office and find out where Jack was before we traveled any farther. Johnny Streeter's secretary told me that Johnny had been looking for me the longest time, and that he was now with the band at Frank's Place.

The walls of the bar were covered with photographs of Frank Sinatra, the jukebox was playing Frank Sinatra, and the patrons were middle-aged, heavyset men who began muttering to each other when they got a look at Macky. I didn't see the band, or anyone young enough to know the band, and I wanted to take Macky out of there, but then a man came up from the back room wearing a three-piece black suit, a black fedora pulled over his eyes. He ordered two whiskys and a beer, then looked over his shoulder, smirked at our shaggy appearance, and said, "Woodstock ended six years ago, kids."

"Stevie!" Macky shrieked, and hugged him, knocking off his hat. He replaced it with diffident care, as though he were crowning himself, and kissed her on the forehead. I went over to shake his hand.

"Delrone," I said.

"Cutlas," he said. "You look like Daniel Boone."

"You look like hell," I answered. He was pale and too thin, and he carried about him an air of gloom that was only heightened by the black suit. "Who died?"

"The boy I was. My innocent youth. Killed on the tour."

Delrone picked up his drink and motioned for us to pick up the ones he had ordered for us, then tilted his head to the back room. "Come on."

He took us to the end of the bar and opened a door, revealing a pool table, another jukebox, more pictures of Frank Sinatra, two tables, a rickety upright piano, Johnny Streeter, Peggy Sue, Lee, Billy, and Eddie. We were met with a great roar of greetings, and Macky flew around hugging and kissing everyone. Johnny Streeter was seated at a table with Peggy Sue, and when he saw me he shouted, *"Sit!"*

Macky, who had interrupted a game between Billy and Eddie, stood at the pool table laughing with them,

145

telling them, Yes, I had treated her well during the winter; Yes, we just got into town; Yes, she had missed them, while they fingered her hair and turned her around and told her what a beauty she had become.

I sat down in the middle of an argument between Peggy Sue and Johnny. Peggy Sue had agreed to let Johnny be her manager, and he had, I gathered, just let her down in some way. They were both agitated and welcomed the diversion of my arrival, although my story seemed to disappoint them. From the way Macky and I looked, from the way we had appeared so abruptly, they seemed to expect a tale of adventure, and instead I was giving them poetry. I described the mountain, the lake, the blizzard, the mud, until their bemused smiles began to make me feel like a child in the middle of the night describing a fantastic dream to his sleepy parents. Peggy Sue glanced from me to Macky.

"*She* looks wonderful," Peggy Sue said. She looked back at me with a wistful smile and I smiled back, realizing that it didn't matter if Wolf's Ridge sounded like a dream to them. They'd only wanted us back happy and healthy. Peggy Sue pulled on her hair and looked back at Macky, her smile now troubled, adding, "*She* certainly looks fresh and innocent and virginal."

"Peggy Sue didn't get a job she wanted," Johnny Streeter explained. "They said she looked too sophisticated. They want more of a sweet-young-thing type. It's for a perfume. Crescent Moon. It smells awful."

"It's not the perfume I care about. It's the photographer. Daniel's very hot right now. Everyone wants to work with him. I'd do anything to work with him and he says I'm too *old*."

"He said *sophisticated*," Johnny corrected. "He said he'd love to use you when he needs your look. But he's very picky about this rancid perfume. He hasn't found anyone. He doesn't want a girl who looks too professional. He wants someone like Macky."

"No," Macky was saying ten minutes later. "I mean, I'd love to do a test some time. But not right now."

"No time like the present," Johnny Streeter said.

"I don't have any makeup. I haven't had a haircut in months."

"They do your hair and makeup, anyway."

"Won't you be upset?" Macky asked Peggy Sue. "I mean, what if he actually likes me?"

"She won't be upset," Johnny answered. "Daniel's been looking for a girl for weeks, and if I deliver the one he wants, he'll remember me next time he needs a girl. We'll have Peg take you. Smile real pretty."

Johnny and Peggy Sue turned from Macky to negotiate a plan of action. Johnny would make the appointments by phone and Peggy would take Macky and talk her through them. Johnny ran to the phone. Peggy ran for her purse and car keys. Macky turned to me.

"Isn't it funny? I ran away from home a year ago just for this. Just hoping for this."

"And to see Paradise Beach," I added.

"And to see Paradise Beach," she repeated. She brushed her lips across mine and stepped back. "Do I really look all right?"

I took her hands and found her trembling.

"Don't worry, baby. They'll love you."

"Yes," she answered with a sudden show of calm. "Yes, okay, they will. I'll make them."

Then Peggy Sue swept her off and I stared after them, wishing I could follow and see how she posed, until I saw Delrone and Billy watching me.

"Where is—" I started to ask.

"He's at his sister's wedding," Billy said.

"How is—" I began again, but was interrupted by the return of Johnny Streeter, who snatched my beer from my hand and finished it in one gulp.

"Models," he sighed. "Why did I ever let myself get mixed up with this?"

"You thought it would be a diversion," Billy reminded him, looking up from the pool game. "And you wanted to hang around my girl."

"Some diversion," Johnny said. "She gives me more trouble than Jack."

"So how *is* Jack?" I asked, glad to finally get the question in. I was met with a heavy silence; Billy and Eddie became extremely absorbed in the clicking of their pool balls, Lee plinked at the piano, Delrone became fascinated with my empty shot glass and Johnny kept his eyes fixed on a photo of Sinatra.

"Well," Johnny said at last. "He'll be glad to see you, I think."

"And Cookie?" I pressed on, mystified, and then they all looked at me with wise and melancholy smiles.

The evening fizzled out soon after that. Lee shook my hand and left for Manhattan, and Eddie smiled and said, "Not my business, you know, man?" in answer to the shocked question that was on my face, before he headed for the apartment in Weehawken he shared with a red-haired waitress. Johnny, Billy, Delrone, and I drove my car from Frank's Place to the Hoboken brownstone where Jack occupied the top flat. Billy and Peggy Sue lived just below him. During the drive, through their shrugs and coughs and drawn-out stammers, I pulled the story out of them. Cookie and Jack were not going to be married, and in fact she had left him and never wanted to see him again.

"I broke the tour in two to make it easier on the guys," Johnny Streeter said. "The South and the West in the fall, the Midwest and the East in the spring."

"The South loved us," Billy said. "But the West was tough. We finished that leg of the tour in December and came back for a rest. Jack and Cookie were great, then. At least, it looked very nice and Merry Christmas-y. Then around March we went back out."

While the All-Americans were touring through the spring and winning the hearts of new fans (but "not, you know, breaking any records" in attendance or record sales), while the All-Americans had been struggling to bring Paradise Beach to dozens of other cities in the country, somewhere in that haze of opening numbers and standing ovations and encores and parties and hotel rooms and homesick phone calls and strange friendly girls who thought they were all awful cute, somewhere in that crowded scene, one night in Boston, Cookie had come up to visit, and after that they had not seen her again. There had been people in Jack's room when Cookie arrived after the show—Eddie and Delrone with some girls—and Cookie had requested that they leave, so they moved next door to Delrone's room and Delrone had been busy with them until the wee hours of the night. The next thing Delrone heard was a drum solo of thumping crashes, furniture being thrown, the wall being kicked.

"So I came out of my room. I thought someone was *murdering* him. And he was coming out of *his* room at the same time. I said, 'Jack?' but he didn't hear me, he just went on by."

"Scared *me* to death," Johnny grumbled. "Didn't come back 'til six the next night. Missed the sound check. He *never* misses a sound check."

"This is it," Billy said, indicating the brownstone.

I parked the car and waited. We listened to the engine's dying clicks.

"Well?"

"Well," Delrone went on, his hands tight fists in his pockets. "We went on that night. And he wouldn't look at us. He *always* looks at us. I mean, we never do the same show twice, we gotta look at him for *cues*. But that night, he was Elvis and we were the Jordannaires, man. Then he does that song, that pretty song, that one he wrote for her."

Billy and Johnny took my luggage and went into the building.

"It's not a popular topic," Delrone said. "And we've been through it so many times."

"He did the song," I said.

"Yeah, he did the song. He did the song like someone killed his whole family, like the killer was working on him next. He was *screaming*, kid. Hunched over. Then on his knees. Lee, hell, he got all worked up, broke a key. And me, I'm crying. I thought maybe Cookie had a serious disease. I thought maybe Jack'd gone crazy. Billy sees me, *he* starts crying. The kids loved it, though. They yelled for more. I go over to

150

Jack, and he turns and says, 'Let's give 'em something to remember,' something like that, and we tore into it. I think we must've played every song we ever knew. The show went on for five hours. No party that night. For the rest of the tour, we never did that song again."

The rest of the tour had consisted of three weeks, and the tour had been over for three weeks. A fight could last six weeks, especially between two like them. Cookie would probably return.

"You think so, huh?" Delrone bit one corner of his mouth and shook his head. "Take a look at what he calls home."

There were two bedrooms, each containing a dresser and a bed. I knew which one was Jack's by the mess of his clothes on the floor and my old Strat lying across the bed. The other bedroom, with a view of the neon Park sign of the parking garage across the street, had been used by his sister until her marriage. It now echoed with her absence. The main room, a living room with a semidetached kitchen, held a couch, a stereo on a set of utility shelves, one table, two chairs, and a dozen coffee cups. The room was so large and stark that our voices bounced off the bare, white-washed walls. The walls had once been as heavily adorned as the walls of the house at Paradise Beach, with photos, posters, calendars, playful notes between Jack and Cookie. Cookie had taken everything with her, everything except her ring. Peggy Sue had watched her pack.

"What does Peggy say about it? I mean, what happened? It doesn't make any sense. Doesn't anyone know what *happened*?"

151

"We think," Johnny said lamely, "maybe Cookie suspected Jack of cheating on her."

"Cookie wouldn't come through here like Sherman's March to the Sea because of a *suspicion*."

"Well, Jack's not talking. He's not thinking about the next album. He's not doing anything. I hope you can talk sense to him."

"Me?"

"I've got two big problems on my hands, Cooder. Jack and this damn '55 T-bird. And you can help me with both of them."

"I don't know about Jack," I said. "What's wrong with the T-bird?"

In 1955, John Streeter, Sr., after ten dedicated years with his record company, achieved his first rock-and-roll milestone when a doo-wop group he had signed to the label, Kenny Lark and the Sparrows, earned a gold record with their hit single "Blue Marie." In celebration, he presented his wife Marjorie with a gleaming new '55 Thunderbird, with a bored-out, two-hundred-horsepower V-8 engine, power steering, power brakes, in the fashionable turquoise of the day. Marjorie loved fast cars and fast music, and escaped daily from the life she otherwise managed very well as suburban housewife and mother. John knew about his wife's hot-rod afternoon trips, when she would leave her home and her caution behind and zoom around on the two-lane roads beyond the shopping malls, blasting away any fragment of the "bad nerves" that plagued the wives of John's colleagues. The Streeter children blossomed under Marjorie's serenity, never guessing that their mother led a secret life as an over-aged dragster until that terrible year when Dylan went

152

electric and John's frequent absences from home, as he stayed late at the office holding meetings about the electric folk trend, strained Marjorie's nerves so that her drives grew longer and more reckless.

A truck outside Cooperstown did her in. The T-bird suffered a crushed left door, a badly damaged chassis, and a shattered headlight. Marjorie was thrown from the car and suffered a fractured jaw, three broken ribs, a broken arm, and numerous bruises. John Streeter handed his workload to his eager assistants and returned home to tend his wife. The T-bird was dragged home and cursed and buried in the second garage among the children's discarded sleds and Schwinns and ski equipment, and then it was forgotten when John bought Marjorie a hardtop Corvette to celebrate her recovery.

John Streeter planned to retire that summer, after thirty years with the record company. His twenty-fifth anniversary with Marjorie would take place in June, and July would mark the twentieth anniversary of the year "Blue Marie" went gold. Marjorie and the record company planned to restore the "Blue Marie" T-bird and present it to John as a gift. But the few mechanics who were willing to touch the car refused any guarantee in the way of deadlines or results. The Streeters needed the car completed by the first week of August, in time for the retirement party.

"That gives me three months to find the parts," I said. "If they can be found. And do the repair work. And find a garage."

"It's sitting in DeMassi's Repairs and Realignments of Hoboken, two blocks away," Johnny said. "We had it towed down here. DeMassi's strictly a sedan man,

153

but he'd be happy to rent out space to you. If you didn't show up, we were gonna see if Carl the Corvette Specialist knew someone. But we were really waiting for you to show up."

"I don't know—there's not much time."

"*Cooder,*" Johnny Streeter said, sliding his arm around my shoulders in a persuasive, managerial way, "you can do it. I've seen the way you work. In the business, we call it a *gift.*"

Jack's cupboard was so bare that I felt compelled to go shopping for kitchen utensils and food, and I postponed my long-coveted night on the town to clear the dust out of the place. I was rewarded Sunday morning when Macky brought me a full Wolf's Ridge-style breakfast in bed. I had spent Saturday looking at the T-bird, talking to DeMassi, and composing a letter to the Classic Car Club of New Jersey, begging them for information about parts and supplies. Macky had spent the day in New York, doing test shots with Daniel, the ritzy fashion photographer Peggy Sue was trying to impress. We had returned to Jack's last evening too tired to have fun, but cheered by the thought of what was in store.

"They're going to let me know next week," Macky said. "But I think I've got it."

"Of course you've got it," I said, and she kissed me and we clinked coffee cups in a toast to our newfound destinies.

We heard a shuffle in the hall and a key in the lock, and Macky whispered, "Jack!" and jumped for her robe. She ran from the room as I searched for my clothes. I heard Macky giggle and Jack rasp, "Oh,

154

man!" and then a drawn-out silence. I walked into the
room to see them still hugging, Jack hanging on to
her as though he feared she would disappear. He was
wearing the suit he had worn to his sister's wedding,
and he looked as though he had slept in it—or not
slept in it. He raised his head and gave me a half-
sardonic smile more suitable to Delrone. Then he dis-
engaged himself from Macky and walked toward me,
meeting my eyes with a shrug of resignation and ad-
miration, and I knew by that shrug that he had always
known how I felt about Cookie. Maybe he had never
known that there was a low-smoking fire between us,
but he had known by the way I looked at her that I
wanted her for my own; he had known that then and
he knew it now, but also he knew that I had found
someone else. I offered my hand and he gave me a fast
hard hug and then stepped back.

"How ya been?"

"Good. Real good," I answered, studying him. He
was so cheerless and haggard that I didn't have the
heart to return the question. "Long wedding, huh?"

"Long *night.*"

"You want some coffee? Breakfast?" Macky asked,
skipping to the stove.

"Yeah, that smells good."

He eyed the room and then me, and gave me a
jaunty, weary grin as he sat down at the table and
took a cup of coffee from Macky.

"I smelled it coming up. You know, I thought . . ."

He trailed off. I opened my mouth but could think
of nothing to say. I drummed my fingers on the table
and tried not to look at the walls, wishing that we
had thought of something to put up—a calendar, one

155

of Macky's test shots, anything to break that bare monotony—and wishing that we had brought something to him besides a request to put us up again.

"Jack, I'm sorry—" I started to say, but he cut me off.

"Yeah. You missed all the fun."

He picked up the fork Macky had set before him and stabbed the table with it, nervously, absently.

"Johnny Streeter's been looking for you. Did he tell you about the T-bird?"

Jack nodded as I listed the problems involved in restoring the T-bird. He was glad to hear I was going to take a shot at it. He owed everything to John Streeter, he said, and then he lapsed into silence. Macky tried to cheer him by telling him about signing with Peggy Sue's modeling agency.

"So you're gonna be a model, too, huh? Well, you're sure pretty enough. Where'd you go to get so pretty? Why'd you stay away so long?"

Macky put his plate on the table and I stood up to let her sit with him and paced the room while she told him about our stay in Wolf's Ridge and our return to Hoboken. Jack listened with the clouded eyes and hesitant appreciation of a man just returned from the war. Macky grew more solicitous, serving him, and more compassionate, speaking to him, until she was nearly spoon-feeding him and telling him the story of the Three Bears.

"Yeah, we just got in Friday," I threw in. "Johnny said it'd be all right if we stayed here 'til you got back. We'll get out of your hair as soon as—"

"You're not in my hair, man," Jack said, turning from Macky to me. "It was good to find you here. You

156

can stay as long as you want. I don't want the place empty. I didn't want to come home, you know."

Macky put her hand over his and smiled, then raised her eyes to me and frowned, a graceful, charitable frown that left me no choice but to try to chase away any doubts I had about living off Jack again.

I asked Marjorie Streeter for a photograph of the car when it was new. She sent me a fading color photograph of the T-bird in all its turquoise glory, parked in front of the dark-green lawn of the Streeter's old Scarsdale mansion, back before they had moved to their present fifty-acre keep-away spread. In the photo, Marjorie was sitting at the wheel in a shrimp-pink dress, waving one gloved hand. She looked handsome, kind, and mischievous. In a quick hot minute I wished I could have been her son, knowing that if I *were* her son, I would risk life and limb to make her proud. I dismissed that thought immediately, but I was still determined to make her proud, make them all proud.

"Good luck," the secretary of the Classic Car Club of New Jersey wrote. "A car like that deserves it. If you succeed in restoring the Thunderbird, please let us know, and send a photo so we can include you in our newsletter. If not, we salute you for the attempt and encourage you to register your name with us. I am enclosing a list of parts dealers and junk-heap owners who might be of some use to you." I called every name on the list and finally received a vague but hope-inspiring reply from a dealer in South Newark who thought that maybe, yeah, he might have seen a '55 Thunderbird somewhere around the lot, no engine, but exterior looked good. I took the risk and drove to Newark and found the T-bird, left door perfectly intact. The insides were, as the man had remembered, rusted to hell, so he sold it to me cheap, and I had it towed back to Hoboken. I left it in the alley behind DeMassi's and ran home to find Macky waiting, euphoric. Daniel had decided to sign her as the Crescent Moon girl.

"He says I'm pretty," Macky told me, as I soaped the grease off my face.

"You know you're pretty."

"Not just *pretty*," Macky said impatiently, shoving me out of the way so she could study her face in the mirror. "*Lots* of girls are pretty. He says I have the right look, and good features, and I photograph well. And he says . . . Cooder, he says I've got *style*."

"Style."

"They don't like my eyes because they're dark and they like blue eyes. And my nose is a little too long. But they think I have adaptable features. And . . . oh, Cooder!—you know how much they get *paid*? Now we can get our own little place, and maybe you can get a garage. He wants to use me right away, Daniel does. Peggy Sue says I should do whatever he says."

"Whatever he says," I echoed, walking into the bedroom and peeling off my jeans.

Macky followed me, shut the door behind her, and peered into the bedroom mirror. "I have to get my hair cut, and my eyebrows plucked, and go to a consultant," she said. She shrugged out of her blouse and unsnapped her jeans. I clicked off the lamp and saw her, by the intermittent orange light across the street, turn from the mirror and crawl up my feet and over my legs and under the covers. But then she said musingly, "They said they liked my look. I know I'm not like Peggy Sue, I don't have a perfect face. They said it was my *look*. Peggy says they're always eager to see new girls because the new girls have this bright attitude, and the girls who've been modeling for a while, sometimes they lose that, they start to look bored. They like my look, but Cooder, that look is you. I mean, I wouldn't have that look if it weren't for you. I just think of you when I'm with them. They say 'Give us sexy' and 'Give us cool,' and I think of you and I do it."

I got out of bed and turned the light on and pulled the covers off her. She held her hand up against the light and asked, "What're you doing?"

"I just want to see you one more time."

"C'mere, you silly thing."

They said she had style. They said they liked her look. But I knew they would change her look and dictate her style. I knew that was true that very night as we lay together in bed and she exhausted herself and me with her whispers and her baby-hand caresses and kisses around my neck, and I held her tight and returned her kisses and watched her eyes close and listened to her voice fall into sighs and felt her chest rise and fall with the ready rhythm of sleep while she posed in dreamland in front of busily clicking cameras, surrounded by praise. I saw the neon illuminate the thick long hair that covered all of her pillow and half of mine, and I plunged my face into the hair and breathed in deep, because I knew it would soon be gone.

And when she returned from her next New York trip, it was. They must have had some mercy in their souls, because they left it long. But they hacked it into layers and curls and tresses of different lengths that skirted away from her face and fell down her back like a waterfall; all she needed was a crystal ball and a caravan.

I returned home night after night covered in grease and sweat to find her in front of the dresser, staring and posing in the mirror, trying on the new makeup she brought home every day, trying on different attitudes, testing different moods, devising ways to camouflage great flaws in her face that I never saw in the first place, bringing out new girls I had never seen before and then dismissing them with a handful of cold cream.

She won the job as the model for Crescent Moon, a fruity cologne that smelled like the kind of orange-and-lime-laden cocktail you order for a girl who doesn't drink much. In the photo, Macky sat at a vanity table, wearing only her stockings and her slip, with her shoes near the chair, a slash of dark rouge on each cheek and dark lipstick on her mouth, splashing Crescent Moon cologne on her shoulders and staring into the mirror with the look of a girl going to her first prom, a girl keeping her date waiting downstairs while she toys with the idea of giving in to more than a kiss that night. She had done her job well, and everyone was pleased with her. But a small success, she told me, is worse than none at all. She was anxious about her next job. The cosmetics and the charades in front of the mirror went on and on. Her confidence that she could make them love her was replaced by insecurity as she tried to chase down that crazy jumpy thing called style.

160

I never knew what girl would be waiting for me when I got home. Sometimes she was a shady lady from a black-and-white murder movie, in a seductive mood and ready to try her seduction out on me, raising one plucked eyebrow, tossing back her lacquered curls, lowering the strap of her slip, bathing in the venetian-slit blinking of the neon Park sign across the street, purring and mocking. Sometimes she was a schoolgirl with a childish smirk, giggling up at me as though I had caught her in her mother's wardrobe, turning from the mirror that hung over a dresser swamped with tubes and bottles and sticks and powders, more coy and teasing than she had ever been in the last days of her innocence. But most of the time she was simply a tired model, and sometimes a tired, weeping model.

"A bumpkin," she sniffed one evening while I searched Jack's cabinets for a can of soup. "A country *bumpkin*."

"You know you're not a bumpkin, Macky. You can't even skin a rabbit."

"It's not *funny*."

"Of course it's funny. I don't know why you let those girls upset you so much."

"She said it in front of a whole roomful of people."

"She's jealous."

"That's easy to say. They're all so sure of themselves. Half the time I don't know who to be."

"Be yourself," I said, still rummaging.

"You're not even listening," she said. "All you ever think about is that T-bird. You don't even take this seriously."

I turned from the cabinets and went to her.

"I take it seriously," I said. "But you take it *too* seriously. You're driving yourself crazy."

"You don't know what it's like."

"I know what *I* like. And I like what I see."

"Well. You're prejudiced."

"I sure am."

She smiled reluctantly and I kissed the poor nose that in a few short weeks had become too long, the cheeks that had become too full, the forehead that had been shrouded with curly bangs.

"Come on," I said. "I'm starving. I'll buy you dinner."

She shook her head and pulled away.

"No, I can't. I'm fat."

I had to share her most of the time now. She spent most of her days in Manhattan, and many of her evenings with Peggy Sue, discussing what she had done that day and what she would do the next, contracts, portfolios, agents, accounts. At night, through my sleep, I could feel her tossing and murmuring, just as I could sense Jack outside the door, pacing in the living room or throwing crumpled sheets of paper at the fickle Stratocaster that had once been mine. The mornings found them both red-eyed and restless, and breakfasts, when we shared them, were sullen events. I tried to comfort them, but I was new at the job of cheering up and I had to ration a certain amount of inspiration for myself.

Because I had my work, too. I was toiling for long hours over the T-bird in Mike DeMassi's garage with the juvenile delinquent teenage assistant mechanic he had found to work for me—a friendly kid named Rilla with an endearing smile and a criminal record—

spending all those afternoons up to my elbows in engine parts and grease because I wanted to have a moment brought back. It was a moment I had never known, but one I could picture clearly. Marjorie Streeter holds the brand-new keys to the T-bird in her gloved hand and stuffs them eagerly into the ignition to spark that fine fine engine into action and clicks on the radio and turns the volume all the way up so that "Blue Marie" by Kenny Lark and the Sparrows—that sad sweet doo-wopping slow-dancing ballad that her husband had recognized as a hit when it was still a street-corner ditty, then turned into the number-one song in the country—blasts across the lawns. "Blue Marie" blasts across the Scarsdale lawns on one of those thoroughly sunny days that only grows more and more yellow as the years go by; it grows bright as the colors on the Polaroid fade. Even though that moment had taken place when I was so little that Aunt Jane Ellen had to say my prayers for me at bedtime while she pulled my thumb out of my mouth, even though that sunshine moment was no more mine than the memory of the days of Con and Ruthie's lodge, I had to resurrect it. It was the work I had set out for myself.

It became clear soon enough that what we had dreamed of getting back to, when we were stranded in the mud at Old Crystal Lodge, was already gone, even at the time we were dreaming it. There were no more All-American carefree nights. There were no more beach girls, there was no more beach. The boys were down to business. And when they weren't working, Delrone had his pool games at Frank's Place, Lee had his Juilliard friends, Billy had rockabilly and Peggy Sue, Eddie had his red-haired waitress in Weehawken.

I had my work and I had my assistant, the kid Rilla, with his grin and his horror stories of life "back there" in the juvenile correction center and his broad repertoire of stupid American folk songs, which he whistled all the livelong day. Rilla had spent his entire sixteenth year paying for the crime of driving a stolen car without a license. He loved cars, and he always drove them, no matter who owned them, and he had been driving a jet-black Jaguar on the night that he was caught. His father was a mystery and his mother no memory to him, and he had been living with foster parents who tried to speak on his behalf, but they couldn't try too hard, because they had kids of their own to worry about. But he was a level-headed kid with a pretty-boy face and eerily innocent eyes. He had long arms and clever hands and hair cut short, so it wouldn't get pulled in fights, and no chip on his shoulder. One foster mommy had left a permanent scar on his face, and another had sent him to bed without supper as punishment so often that he developed anemia and a severe vitamin deficiency. He was then moved to his only "real nice *nice*" family, where foster dad fussed at him about his homework and foster mom praised him sweetly for minding the three younger children so well, but he was with them only a short time before he was sent "back there," where he was forced to share a cell with a teenage rapist who enjoyed bragging in rich detail about what he had done to his girls. But Rilla bore no grudge against the world for anything that he had suffered, and figured that his only two disadvantages were his name, Morris Rilla, and his felonious weakness for the automobile.

164

Delrone took a liking to Rilla because, for all his gangster attitudes and accessories, he had never before met an "actual criminal," and Jack found Rilla's presence soothing, partly because Rilla knew all fifty-odd verses of the song "Clementine" and mostly because Rilla was the only available pool partner who wasn't edgy with desire to know about Cookie. Jack's heartbreak was an enigma without any clues, a mystery he did not want probed. On those nights when I took Rilla by Frank's Place on my way home, Jack greeted me with a wry smile and then avoided my gaze while he asked Rilla to sing or told us rambling, pointless stories about how different shows had gone in those far-away cities during the fall, or mentioned occasionally, and briefly, the progress of the recording sessions in Manhattan. But he wouldn't answer a direct question about the recording, or the songs; he wouldn't answer a direct question about anything.

There were times I wanted to grab him by the collar and shake the story out of him, but most of the time he was too forlorn and coiled up, most of the time I was too tired and put off to try. The room at Frank's, with its chipped tile floor and ugly gray curtains obscuring a window too dirty to let in the light, was as dismal as a church basement, and the three of them couldn't understand why I lingered there when I had the Crescent Moon girl waiting at home. They didn't realize that I couldn't escape the atmosphere of tension and expectation merely by changing rooms.

Then there was only a month left until the big celebration party for John Streeter. The T-bird was realigned, reupholstered, fine on the mechanics, but ugly as sin on the outside. I needed to paint it, to find a

165

blue similar to the shade of fifties turquoise for "Blue Marie." The Streeters invited Macky and me for dinner to plan how to best present the T-bird to John. The house was a palace, and Marjorie moved through it like a busy queen, lively and gracious, with a fluid energetic command. It was easy to see, as we sat down to dinner with his fast-talking mother and his chattering sister, where Johnny had acquired his ability to barrel through any conversation the band might be trying to have around him. But this time, he sat back and ate while his mother grilled me about the car and his younger sister, Linda, who was Macky's age and had Marjorie's handsome wholesome looks, kept turning to me to cry, "I can't *believe* you're fixing up that old car! How did you ever do it? And you say it's almost *done*?"

Macky was dressed in a low-cut blouse, hair down and earrings long, and she appraised the dining room critically and watched Linda Streeter with an expression that was at best cold. Linda's hair was braided back, her face clean and undecorated, and she was dressed in tennis whites. Aside from her high-pitched voice and avalanche of questions and silly exclamations, I could not understand what it was about Linda that bothered Macky. But Macky was bothered; she gave the girl curt answers and tight frigid smiles. I tried to compensate for Macky's haughtiness with extra courtesy to Marjorie, but that seemed to annoy Macky even more, and Johnny finally looked up and mimed, "What's with her?" to me. I shrugged helplessly. He smiled and shrugged back. And Marjorie, deciding that the subject of the T-bird was upsetting to Macky, politely announced in a bright, change-the-topic voice

166

that there was so much *packing* going on these days,
what with John retiring and Linda going off to college.

Macky flinched at the mention of college, then
straightened up and told Linda that she had gone to
Creve Coeur Girls' Academy in St. Louis, had Linda
heard of it? Linda was sorry, but she hadn't. Did that
mean Macky was going to college? Linda was going
to Radcliffe. Macky was not going to college; she was
a professional working model. Oh, that sounded so
exciting, was it exciting? Yes, yes it was, very exciting,
very glamorous, wearing all the latest clothes. Yes, it
sounded very exciting, Linda cried merrily, although
Linda didn't really know anything about modeling, it
was just a bunch of pretty pictures to her, and Macky
was certainly lucky to be pretty enough to be photographed and everything. Linda sure wasn't—well,
Daddy wouldn't allow her to live that kind of life,
anyway—but Linda sure didn't have that kind of talent. Oh, but she had *other* talents, Marjorie cut in with
the defensive pride of a mother. Linda played the piano
beautifully—why, that nice boy who played with Jack,
the one who had gone to Juilliard with Johnny, that
boy Lee with the lovely manners, he had said that
Linda played *beautifully*, wasn't that so, Johnny? Yes,
Mom, Johnny said, watching me as I watched Macky
with a growing fear as Macky said with a thin smile
that Lee's praise certainly did mean a lot, but unless
Macky was mistaken, Radcliffe wasn't exactly a top
music school, or was she wrong? Oh no, but Linda
wasn't going to pursue music *professionally*. . . .

I was about to leap across the table to prevent Macky
from responding when Johnny knocked his glass of
wine into the oyster casserole, apologized to his mother,

167

and thanked the maid when she arrived to mop it up. He leaned back in his chair and drawled, "So what, Cooder, are you gonna take the car down to Carl's to have it painted?"

"Carl? The Corvette Specialist?"

"Sure, why not, Cookie went around after you and Macky left town to explain what had happened, and she said he wasn't mad at all that you ran out on him, he was just sorry to see you go. I'm sure he'd let you have the space."

"I hadn't thought of that."

"You think you'll find that awful color of *blue*?" Linda squealed.

"That was a very popular color in our day, Linda," Marjorie said.

"Oh, Mommy, it's *aqua!*"

"Actually, I might have some trouble finding that color, ma'am, I—" I stopped cold when I saw Macky glare at me, a violent splash of what looked like real hatred.

"Oh, that's all right. Whatever blue you think best."

"Do you know all about all cars?" Linda asked.

"I know a lot about most American cars. Fifty-five T-birds are good cars to know about because they're . . . one of the best ever made."

"Well, Daddy's famous for his good taste!"

We had drinks in the drawing room. Linda wasn't allowed to drink, so Marjorie prodded her into playing "something soft, dear" on the Steinway baby grand. Macky wouldn't drink because of the calories, and she slumped in the easy chair and pulled on one of her curls, glowering at a board of ivory chess men. Johnny offered me bourbon, and it was my best friend in the room at the moment, a faint amber smoke rising from the ice. I sipped it with gratitude while Marjorie mused on the presentation of the T-bird on John's big day.

"I'd love to *really* surprise him, but I suppose the best thing to do would be to simply park it on the lawn and show it to him before the guests arrive. There's no other way to do it without making a spectacle."

"Cooder could drive it up early and we could push it out onto the lawn near the tent," Johnny said.

"If you don't mind coming early," Marjorie said.

"No, ma'am, that's all right with me."

"Daddy'll be so pleased," Linda said.

Macky said nothing all the way home. I spoke to her a few times and then gave up, rolled down the windows, turned up the radio, and tried to pretend we were out for a cruise and enjoying ourselves. When we arrived home she still said nothing; she only yanked off her earrings and stripped naked and threw her clothes into a corner and strolled across the living room toward the bathroom. I grabbed her robe and followed her in and threw it at her.

"Jesus, Macky, you can't parade around here like that. Jack could walk in."

"I don't care," she said listlessly, dabbing white cream all over her face.

"Maybe you don't care, but I do."

"Oh. You care?"

"Yeah, I care. Hell, Jack could—"

"I didn't really think, after tonight, that you cared what *anyone* thought of me."

I sat down and braced myself and waited. She said

nothing. I watched her throw water all over her face at least a dozen times before I said warily, "Okay. What do you mean?"

"I mean, all night everyone was treating me like a slut, and you just sat there saying 'Yes, ma'am' and 'No, ma'am' and never saying a word for me."

"Who was treating you like a slut?"

"That Linda."

"She was not."

"That Linda . . . lording it over me because she went to a good school and her father's so rich. My school was just as good as hers, and I *know* I made better grades than she did. And what's *she* got to be so snotty about, her father's got all that money from rock and *roll. My* father's a *doctor*, at least he *does* something. Sure, we didn't have sixteen *rooms* and a cook and a maid."

"So what?"

"So *what*? She was shoving it all down my *throat*, all that college business."

"She wasn't shoving it down your throat. And even if she was, you got her back good enough with all that shit about modeling."

"What *shit*?" she asked angrily.

"All that shit about how exciting and glamorous it is."

"You don't know anything about it."

"I know how you come home every night, all tired out and cranky as hell because people have been moving you around all day like a dress-up doll, and if I even look at you too hard you get all jittery—"

"It's what I *want*!"

"Then *do* it and don't complain about it!"

"I'm not complaining, I'm just *saying*—" she lowered her towel and leaned on the sink "—I'm just *saying* it's so *hard* sometimes. Dragging in from Hoboken every day. *Hoboken!* All the other girls live in Manhattan and . . . and they have people taking *care* of them. They have it so *easy*. And tonight I was just thinking, when I saw that house, I used to have that. I used to have it so easy."

She finished in a whisper. She had it so easy once and she left it in search of something a better man might have been able to give her by now. We had the whole wide world in our hands. But now we were back living with Jack and working harder than we ever had, with nothing as yet to call our own. I would rather have her yelling; I would rather see her angry than see her subdued by the despair and envy I thought I had put behind me. The thought that I had, instead, passed it along to her brought home a mighty guilt that defeated my impulse to comfort her. If I wasn't a good provider, it wasn't my fault; she was to blame for her choice of me.

"You can always go back to it," I told her brusquely.

"You mean quit?"

"If you want."

"I *don't*."

"Then don't."

"Is that all you have to say?"

"What do you want me to say?"

"It's not that *simple*. I never *belong* anywhere. I didn't fit in at home. I didn't fit in at the beach. Or at the Streeters' tonight. I don't fit in with those Manhattan girls. Maybe you don't care. Maybe you don't think what I do is worth trying for. But I can't give it up, the way you did. I can't just walk away."

I repeated very softly, very softly and with care, "Give it up, the way I did?"

"I just want a *chance*," she said, her head still bowed, as intent upon the sink as if it were an altar. "I deserve a chance. *You* had your chance."

"And I gave it up?" I said, in a voice so hard and velvety that I scared both of us. I felt a mean quivering clutch in my gut, like I'd swallowed a whole bowl of cold fire and it was just settling down inside of me. I'd been her hero, her tough strong cowboy, but I had stumbled, I had let myself love her. In spite of my caution, I had let her in on it, let her see all the weakness and the doubt, a little at a time, when I held her too close or told her too much or stared at her too long with too much hope in my eyes. I never should have trusted her, never should have expected her to understand. I should have known better. Her faith in me was just a string of pretty words with nothing behind them.

"Cooder—"

"Gave it up? Gave up my chance? My chance for *what*? My chance to be *Jack*? You don't know, you weren't there, you have no right to talk about it. I wasn't gonna *be* Jack, Macky, *ever*. I thought you knew what you had here."

"I do—"

"And it's not good enough, is it? I don't take care of you. You don't *belong* anywhere. Funny, but I kind of thought you *belonged* with me."

She held her arms out to me, her eyes wide, her

172

fingers shaking. I pushed her away. She flicked away a tear and reached for her robe, but I snatched it from her, snatched it so roughly that I ripped it in half. I pivoted away from her to save her from my reach. She ran after me and seized my arm.

"Cooder—I didn't mean—try to understand—"

"There's something *you* have to understand." I grabbed both her wrists in my hand. "Do you know the difference between giving something up and just kidding yourself?"

"What?"

She was breathless, and trembling, and it was unfair for me to leave her naked, but I didn't care. She tried to fight my grip, but I jerked her closer to me and held on tighter.

"Do you love me, sweetheart?"

"What?" she whispered.

I didn't want to hear her whats. I shook her a little. She winced but said nothing, and for one strange second I was proud of her for not complaining that I was hurting her.

"Do you know the difference between giving something up and just kidding yourself?" I asked again, and did not let go.

"What? I love you, yes, you know . . . Cooder, you *know* I love you."

"But what if you found out I didn't love you now? What if I didn't love the way you look now, the way you *are*. What if you found out I want you back the way you *were*? Would you stay with me? And all this running around trying to be a star . . . would you *give it up*?"

Her hands were limp in mine and I let them go.

She was crying hard without making any noise. I stormed into the living room and she followed me and fell on the couch and hugged her knees close to her chest and let herself cry.

"And if you gave it up," I finished slowly, "would you call yourself a failure? Like me?"

"I never called you a failure."

"What did you mean, then? I must be a *fool* to give up my great big glorious chance? Or maybe I just didn't have the guts to try!"

"I never *said* that!" she shouted. "I don't think that about you. *You're* the one who acts like everything is second-best."

"Like *what*?"

"Like *me*. All you ever do is wish I were different. Smarter. Stronger. All you ever do is wish I were *her*."

"Who?"

"Maude!"

"*Maude?*"

"All you ever do is wish I were Maude."

"Maude? I never even *think* about Maude anymore. I love you more than I *ever* loved her. I love you so much it makes me sick."

She dropped her head to her knees and held it with her hands, and I walked out.

I had my keys in my pocket, and I went out to my car in the street and drove out of Hoboken and headed for the highway. I had to clear my head, because being in the room with her was putting me into a frenzy. If I went back to her now I would hurt her, smack her pretty face the way my Uncle Aaron had smacked me when I took the name of the Lord in vain in front of him two days after my baptism. But why would I do that to her? Poor baby. But no, she wasn't a baby, and she didn't mother me the way some girls had, and she wasn't a sister to me the way she was a sister to the All-Americans. She was my lover. She was the lover I had always wanted, and it was only the work that had come between us, and the grim dedication to the work that had seized all three of us in that apartment, until the very bareness of the walls conveyed the hard bleak price of duty. She had learned it from Jack and me, that the good things come after the work has been done. She was only doing what she had been told. There was no good reason to be running away from her in search of a bar where the light was low and the music muffled and the company indifferent. No good reason at all.

I knew the kind of bar I wanted. It was the kind of bar where there was a baseball game on the television, with the sound low but not off, and the jukebox buzzing so that you could only hear the song playing if it was one that you liked, and mostly men in the place, men with young women back home who knew where they were and would let them be unless it got to be too late, and then the men would finish the last gulp and head for home. By this hour of the night, the arguments about sports and gossip about women would have died down, and the conversation would only be mumbles and nods when I walked in. At this late hour, Frank's Place was that kind of bar, but I couldn't go there because I knew who would be there, and Jack was the last man I wanted to see, Jack with his failed love affair sunk deep into his face and his eyes filled with a grudging kind of jealousy whenever I caught him watching me—jealousy because I had given up

175

what he was working for, and I had what he had sacrificed. I didn't want to think about his sacrifice or my failure; I didn't want to think at all, I only wanted to drink among strangers. I knew the kind of bar I wanted, and it was in Paradise Beach.

But by the time I got there, the television baseball game was in the bottom of the ninth and the jukebox was not playing and Carl the Corvette Specialist, who had introduced me to the place, had gone home. I nursed a whisky and water and tried not to think about Macky and thought about her anyway. I stood up to read the menu on the jukebox and then I heard someone call my name. I looked up and saw a girl leaning against the cigarette machine and smiling at me. In the dim light I could see only wide hips and blue jeans, a peasant blouse and beach-battered blond hair, and a smile.

"It's Trudy," she said.

"Trudy," I said, and stepped closer to her. "I didn't recognize you out of uniform."

"Oh," she said, tapping her pack of cigarettes against her wrist. "That's not my uniform anymore. I work at the Outer Limits now."

"Oh, yeah?"

"Yeah. It's not as much fun since you guys left. What are you doing down here? You back in town?"

"No, I just came down here to see Carl. You . . . you want a drink or something?"

"Oh," she looked past me. "Are you alone?"

"Yeah."

"You got your car with you?"

"Yeah."

"Well, if you're alone, and you got your car with

you, you can give me a ride back to my place. I got whisky back there. You still drink whisky, don't you?"

Everyone said she was Lee's girl, but I never saw anything more than a smile between them in public. She hadn't been around with Lee at Frank's Place, but then, none of them had. They were more or less exiled, according to Delrone, who kept Cindy around on the sly, because seeing the malt-shop girls agitated Jack. Trudy didn't mention Lee now, and I didn't mention Macky. I told her about the car I was doing for John Streeter and how I planned to use Carl's paint compressor, and she seemed pleased that I would be down in Paradise Beach again, and she told me that she had spent last winter at a local college and would be going back again in the fall, and then we were stumbling through her hallway and she was playing with her keys and then she fell into a dark room and giggled breathlessly, "It's kind of a mess!" and turned the lights on.

It was a complete mess: towels and shirts all over the couch, jeans all over the stereo, panties all over the television, T-shirts and textbooks all over the floor. The closet doors were wide open and more clothes were trying to fight their way past them into the room. She turned to the wall that served as a kitchen—a refrigerator next to a counter next to a stovetop—and pulled a bottle of whisky out of her cabinet. I looked at the posters on the wall. There was a framed photograph on her dresser, and I strolled over while she dropped ice into the glasses. Her dresser was covered with more makeup than Macky's was, along with hair things and books of matches and little silver-colored plastic tokens redeemable at the Penny Arcade on the boardwalk for prizes like Kewpie dolls and souvenir mugs. There was a jar of change, the kind waitresses always had, stuffed with silver coins and dollar bills. I moved it out of the way to see the photograph. It was of Jack and Delrone and Lee and Billy and Cookie standing on the boardwalk, and it must have been taken the summer before I met them all, because Jack's hair was longer and Cookie's hair was shorter and they looked like a bunch of kids on the boardwalk in the summertime.

"Here you go," Trudy said from behind me, and I turned and took the whisky from her. I studied her while she sipped hers, studied her soft round features and that dried-out blond hair.

"You've got freckles all over," I said.

"I had freckles last summer," she said lightly, pushing some of her clothes off the couch. "I've always had freckles. All over."

She straightened up and looked at me.

"Too messy for you?"

"No, it's . . . nice."

"Homey?"

"Uh, yeah."

"Then you can make yourself at home, you know."

She pushed her jeans off the stereo while I settled uneasily on the couch. I looked around while she flipped through her records, and rested my eyes on a blue dress that was hanging on a knob on the closet door, a crisp blue dress that looked as though it had never been worn.

"That's a nice dress."

She looked up, followed the line of my eyes, nodded and blew dust off the record she had pulled out.

"Oh, that dress. I keep meaning to take it back."

"How come?"

"Well," she said, leaning over the turntable and lowering the needle onto the record, "I bought it for Cookie's wedding. And I keep meaning to take it back, 'cause it wasn't cheap, and I guess you know I never had to use it. But I can't bring myself to do it."

"Why?" I asked. Strings and guitars filled the room, and she lowered the volume and turned to me. "You think you'll use it after all?"

"No. Cookie's got her mind pretty well made up."

"Jack's in pretty bad shape."

"Well, Cookie's not exactly tap dancing herself."

"You still talk to Cookie?"

"I still talk to everyone. Or, everyone still talks to me. Calls me up in the middle of the night and fills me in. Guess I'm the midnight confessor. Like that song. Right? There was a song like that, wasn't there?"

"How's Cookie doing?"

"She's all right. Law school, you know, and she's working real hard now that she . . ." Trudy stopped and tilted her head curiously, her smile suddenly different.

"Now that she what?" I asked.

"You still have a crush on her."

"Who said I had a crush on her?"

"Oh, come on."

"What do you mean, crush? Crush is high school."

"You had a crush. On her. We all had crushes on each other."

"Yeah? So who did you have a crush on?"

"Who do you think?"

"Jack," I sighed.

179

"Idiot."

"Who?"

"You."

"Me?"

"Yeah, and I've got freckles all over."

She rattled her ice and watched the cubes bounce around. I set down my glass and felt all at once every drop of bourbon and every drop of whisky I'd had that night, burning and humming and spinning inside.

"Well," I said. My words were slow but my pulse was racing and my logic was running three paces behind. "You never . . . did . . . anything or . . ."

"That's what crushes are like."

She sounded very calm and kept her eyes on the ice cubes. I was so confused by her silence and so tantalized by her confession and so out of practice that I had to call back the boy from Atlanta to handle it. He'd been a cool one, that boy, and he knew all the right lines. At least, I remembered him that way.

"You could do something now, Trudy. You could—"

"It's *my* crush," she said sharply, setting her glass down hard. "Don't you start ordering me around."

"Sorry, I—"

But by that time she was moving, knocking the shirts off the television set and turning the set on, turning the sound all the way down, turning off the overhead lights and the light in the kitchen, so that there was no light in the room except for the silently clamoring black-and-white shadow of the television.

"The couch folds out into a bed," she said, and pulled off her blouse.

I stood up and told the boy in Atlanta to go back to his graveyard, I couldn't use him anymore. I walked

180

over to her. She started to move away but I put one hand on her shoulder and the other under her chin and tilted her face up. She seemed almost puzzled, as though she didn't know what I was doing in her room. But she leaped into it like it was one of last summer's volleyball games, breathless and careless. And faithless, I realized later and knew even then; we were both so faithless.

I couldn't find the turquoise for the T-bird, so I had to settle for a grayish industrial blue. Rilla whistled "Little Liza Jane" while we applied the first coat one afternoon at Carl's. We studied the car, when we were through, from the outside to avoid the fumes. The blue was the shade of slightly faded jeans. Rilla stepped back and shook his head when I told him so.

"Naw, it looks like the color blue of the shirts we had to wear back there. But it's nice. It's nice, right? I like it. Looks good."

"Anything looks good on a T-bird. So that's our color. Couple more coats. Then we'll finish it off with two clear acrylic coats and it'll be so shiny it'll look wet."

"And then what?" Rilla said.

"And then we'll be done."

"And then what?" he asked again.

"And then, I don't know. See if I can get some money together. See if I can get a garage started. See what happens."

We headed for the malt shop for lunch while Rilla whistled on in his pleasant way. He stuffed his hands in his jeans pockets and looked around him happily. Then he glanced at me, bit his lip, cleared his throat,

181

coughed, then, when he was sure he had my attention, spoke.

"You know that glass factory down by the river in Hoboken?" he said. "Couple blocks down from Frank's Place? There's a garage for sale there. Kind of cheap. I mean, it's not in real good shape, it'd probably cost you something to fix it up, but Jack said that wouldn't bother you. He said you were a prime one for fixing things up."

"Jack said?"

"We were walking by there. He's the one made me go in and ask the price."

"What were you doing walking by there?"

"Just walking. Jack was getting restless at Frank's, so he asked me if I wanted to take a walk."

"What did you talk about?"

"You know. Things."

"What things."

"Just things. I asked him how he met you. About when you lived down here in Paradise Beach." Rilla gazed down the street with a smile and stretched his arms up high. The heat wasn't shimmering off the highway, it wasn't hot enough for that yet, but there was a shimmering in my eyes, and when I saw that smile on Rilla, I collared him.

"What else did he talk about? Cookie?"

"Naw, nothing about girls. I don't know. He told me how the album was doing a little."

"He told *you* about the album? *You*?"

"Well, why not?" Rilla asked, his expression first wounded, then settling into the punk petulance he had learned in jail. "I've got ears, don't I? I'm not dumb."

"Where was *I*?"

182

"How should I know? Probably down here with that chick."

"What chick?"

"That blond chick you're fooling around with."

"Who says I'm fooling around with her?"

"I saw you making out in the parking lot of Angie's Clams."

"Jesus Christ."

"Macky know?"

"Shut up."

"Sorry."

"Of course Macky doesn't know."

"Doesn't she notice when you don't go home?"

"She's staying in Peggy Sue's apartment in New York. I told her we were having a painting marathon down here."

"And she thinks you're sleeping in the garage like me?"

"I guess that's what she thinks," I snapped. "I don't really know what she thinks about anything."

She had forgiven me for the tiny bruise on her left wrist. She had forgiven me for leaving her alone all night. She had forgiven me with a sad smile when I returned the next morning to find her sitting on the couch exactly as I'd left her, as though she hadn't moved since I left, except to put on Jack's robe. I had knelt before her and kissed her bruised wrist and carried her into the bedroom with the silly hope that I could restore our understanding if I could restore our tenderness. We knew how to bring back our tenderness, because it was part of our passion. But we couldn't bring back our understanding, because we needed time and we needed patience and we needed privacy. Her

183

patience was spent waiting for the blue jeans people to decide if she could be on their new squad of girls. Our privacy was crowded with all the other girls she was trying to become, and with Jack, even when he wasn't home. All we had left was one brief hour in bed before we went to sleep. And for the past two weeks, even that one hour alone had been taken away, since she was spending her nights in Manhattan and I was spending mine in Paradise Beach. After I'm through with this car, I told myself, and after she's photographed wearing those goddamned blue jeans, we'll make it up to each other and everything will change.

"Rilla saw us making out."
"Where?"
"In the parking lot of Angie's Clams."
"Oooh, Angie's Clams. I could go for some Angie's Clams right now."

There were plenty of snacks there already. The room was always the same for me. I let Rilla go prowl the boardwalk once the sun went down, worked until around midnight, left the garage when Rilla returned to sleep on Carl's floor, and I headed for Trudy's, where the room would be dark except for the television's glow, and soul music would be on the stereo, and Trudy would have the convertible couch folded out into a bed, and she would be sitting on it, counting the change from her apron pocket. I arrived with the food—the Oreos, the ham and Swiss cheese slices, the rye bread, the Fritos, the Seven-Up, the bourbon. Twice during the two weeks we spent together, we went out, once for pizza and once for Angie's Clams. Trudy was

184

a boardwalk junk-food gourmet, and she taught me on the night we were seen by Rilla that the best way to eat Angie's fried clams was to hold the fried clam in your mouth until it cooled, strip off the breading with your tongue, chew the breading down, bite the bare clam in half, and swallow. There was also a particular, dainty way to eat pizza slices, and Oreos and ridged potato chips. The silent television was always tuned to Midnight Mystery Theatre. The music was always records of soul groups with five or more members. The rest was up to me.

Everything between us was like junk food, a quick rush of a sugar high, a savoring sucking of salt. She wanted me because I was a craving she had never satisfied, and I wanted her because she had found me that night in the bar and looked at me without demands, without expectations, without love, only with the most basic kind of interest. She brought on the same blindness as a good whisky drunk, only not the same loneliness, except for the few hollow seconds that would flash up every time at the end of it, like a tunnel in the middle of a highway.

Then one night when the last coat of acrylic was drying and I was getting my last few crumbs of Trudy, the phone rang. I tried to make her ignore it, but she pushed my head away and found the receiver under one of her T-shirts.

"Hello," she said brightly as I sat up grumpily and reached for the Seven-Up she had not finished. "Oh, *hi*, sweetheart. How are you? Is it? Is it really? Oh, Lee, I'm so glad. This one was on time, wasn't it? Only two days late. How's it sound, is it great? Is it? Oh, I can't wait to hear it . . . oh, yeah. The mix. Well, *you're* free, at least. Oh, I've missed you. Oh, yes yes yes, come down. When can you be here?"

She sounded so sincere when she said she missed him that I looked at her again, set down my soda, and looked for my shirt. I bent down over the bed and pawed at the floor while she whispered into the phone. I found my shirt and sat up again as she said, "Okay. Come down soon. Come down tomorrow. Can you come down tomorrow? Or I'll come up. Oh, I don't care about the tape, I just want to see you." Another short giggle. "Yeah, that too. Listen, you get some sleep, sweetheart, you haven't had any all summer. Okay. See you tomorrow . . . me, too. Bye."

"Lee," she told me when she hung up.

"I guess so."

"The album's finished."

"Oh, yeah?"

"Well, they still have to do the mix. But Lee doesn't do that. It drove him crazy last time. That's Jack's job."

"Great. Is it, like, real heavy between you guys?"

"What's heavy?"

"I don't know. Were you together all winter?"

"Well . . . he was on tour some of the winter. I spent Christmas with him."

"I mean, are you, you know, in love with him?"

"What's in love?"

"Well, I guess you're not, then."

"Well," she said, a little frosty, "I guess that's kind of between him and me, right?"

"Does he think you love him?"

"He knows how I feel."

186

"Well, I mean, he calls you right when the album's done."

"What's it to you, anyway?"

"Well, is there some trouble between you or something? What am I *doing* here, anyway? Are you mad at him? Or were you just lonely? Or . . ."

"I think you'd better watch where you're stepping," she said sternly. "If you know what I mean. Look. Lee and I have an understanding. We're not hurrying into anything. Someday, maybe, it'll get to the point where we have more than that, but I told him, as long as he's touring with the band, forget it. I'm not gonna let what happened to Cookie happen to me."

"What happened to Cookie?"

"God, she was so loyal and naive. So stupid."

"Cookie's not stupid."

"Oh, come on. Sara warned her and *warned* her. I mean, I know Sara's a little bitch, but she's a possessive little bitch when it comes to the band, and when she saw that girl with Jack all the time, she started calling Cookie and telling her, 'You know, this girl has followed Jack from Cleveland to Cincinnati to Chicago to Kansas City, and there doesn't seem to be any sign that she's gonna let up.' "

"What are you talking about?"

"During the *tour*," Trudy said, sitting up. She pulled a T-shirt over her head and began to brush crumbs out of the bed. "Sara always follows the boys around when they go on tour, all over the country. She follows them around, washes their clothes, stuff like that. I don't know why. They're nice to her *then*. 'Cause she's a familiar face. Anyway, she knows what they're all

187

up to, and usually she keeps her mouth shut, and that's fine with me, 'cause I don't *want* to know what Lee's doing when he's on the road. But she had to break down and tell Cookie about this girl—her name was, like, Joanne or something—following Jack around, and Jack letting her. And Cookie didn't believe it!"

"I don't believe it, either," I said.

"Well, Cookie didn't believe it!" Trudy repeated, annoyed. "So she waits until they're in Boston and she goes to pay him a surprise visit and Joanne or whatever was still there. And I guess you know what happened after that."

"No."

"You don't?"

"No."

"Didn't Jack tell you?"

"No. He hasn't said a word to anyone about any of it."

"You didn't know any of this?"

"No."

"Wow."

"Well, what happened?"

"Oh, well, I don't know, but I don't think it was real pretty. But Cookie . . . she just couldn't *believe* that Jack would cheat on her!"

"Well, why should she believe it?"

"Because it was true!"

"Well, Jesus, it's not her fault she trusted him and he broke her trust. But still . . ."

"Still what?"

"There's gotta be more to it than that."

188

"There always is. Well, she knew all along that it would be rough going with Jack. You *guys*, I tell ya . . ."

"Poor Cookie."

"For Christ's sake, Cooder," Trudy said indignantly. "You could just as well say 'Poor Macky.'"

It was the first time either of us had mentioned Macky. I stared gloomily at the television.

"I do say 'Poor Macky.'"

"You're really nutso crazy about her, aren't you?" Trudy asked, looking at me with a new, pitying interest.

I nodded.

"Then what *are* you doing here?"

I shook my head.

"Lee told me," Trudy said, touching my arm, "that Macky did that ad. For the perfume? That one where she's in a slip or something? He was telling me on the phone that they have it pinned up in the studio where they were recording. You know, she seemed like such a little girl to me last summer. I could never figure out what you saw in her. Now I guess everybody sees it. I guess she grew up real quick."

"She's not growing up, she's getting wise," I said. "It's these friends of Peggy Sue's. She's getting wise real fast, and now she thinks she's wise to everything. Wise to me. So she doesn't need me."

"Well, you're being a little hard on her."

"Why do you say that!" I shouted. "Why does it have to be *my* fault?"

Trudy was on her feet now, pulling on her jeans. She picked up our empty glasses and carried them to the sink.

189

"I think I'd better go," I said.

"Yeah," Trudy said. "That's probably a good idea."

I came home with roses. It was late when I got in, and I wasn't sure if she would be there, if she would be awake, or what good the roses would do me. But I brought them anyway and stopped at the kitchen for a vase. Of course there was no vase, so I filled a bowl with water and took it and the roses into the bedroom. Macky was in bed. I set the roses in the water, put the bowl on the dresser and took off my shoes as quietly as I could. I heard her sniff into the pillow. I whispered her name and she raised her head and whispered back, "How's the car coming?"

"Almost done."

I sat down on the bed and handed her one rose and she sat up, her breathing rapid like a cat's, her head bent, her fingers kneading at the blanket. I leaned forward and lifted her chin and saw her face, dirty with tears, in the blinking orange light.

"What's the matter?"

She wiped her eyes with the sheet.

"Oh, nothing," she said, her voice thick with the next splash of tears. She took a long unsteady breath.

"What is it? Did the blue jeans people turn you down?"

"No," she said, and her voice broke then, and I scooped her up and held her close. I stroked her hair and rocked her. "Oh Cooder, I missed you."

"I know, baby, I know. I missed you, too. I won't stay down there anymore. There's only the polish left. I can do that here. I'll be here every night."

190

"Then can we go somewhere when the car's finished?"

"Sure, sweetheart." I brushed at her tears and kissed her. "I was thinking we could do that. Take a little trip."

"And then what? Can we move? Can we just move away from here?"

"Where do you want to go?"

"Just . . . *away*."

"Well, honey, what if you get the blue jeans job?"

Her face collapsed and she grasped a fistful of the quilt. She shook her head.

"And there's a garage," I went on. "Down by the river. I'm thinking of buying it. I've looked at it with Rilla. It's a nice place—well, it's a dump, but I'll fix it up and it'll *be* a nice place. It'll be mine. You know, Macky? Just mine."

She nodded and began to cry again and shook me off when I tried to hold her.

"What *is* it, sweetie?" I asked gently, gentle because of guilt and guilty because of her troubled eyes. "We'll get our own place, too. Is that what you want? What do you want?"

"Oh, I don't know. It's good for you, your own garage. It's just . . . oh, garages and blue jeans and albums being mixed and I *just* . . . I just want to go somewhere. Just run off, like we did before. We can make out all right. We did before."

"You don't *want* to just make out all right. Jesus, Macky, you went crazy at the Streeters' because of all the things you didn't have. Now we're just getting started, you can't throw it away just to 'go somewhere.' "

191

"The people in Jack's songs do!" she shouted with sudden violence.

"But Jack doesn't, does he?"

"Somebody must. It *must* be out there for someone, or why would he write about it?"

"Because it's not there. Not all the time. Not often enough. Not enough people do it. It's a dream, that's all. It's like you in those pictures. You don't really look like that."

"I don't really look like that."

"And that's not really you."

Her eyes filled again and I reached for her. Jack coughed in the other bedroom and rattled his closet door, and she stiffened, threw back the quilt, and stood up. She walked to the window. The strap of her damp, wrinkled silk nightgown fell from her shoulder to her elbow. The orange light soaked her face.

"That's not really me," she repeated, her voice small and quivering. "Is that why you don't want me anymore?"

"I still want you," I said, but I felt that chill hand in my gut.

"Do you?"

"I'm sorry I haven't been here. Is that what's bothering you? It's just the work . . ."

"The work," she said.

"I told you I'll be back here from now on."

"Yes. You told me."

"And you know I love you. C'mere. You want me to show you?"

"I don't want you to show me."

"You want me to tell you?"

"I want to know."

*   *   *

Then at last came the day of the Streeters' party. She was beautiful that day; even on that day when everyone looked beautiful, she was the most beautiful of all. The denim blue T-bird, glistening with its carefully applied coats of paint and acrylic and wax, was the center of attention for all the record company guests, but she was the center of attention for me. Her hair was piled up high, with a few curls spilling down, and her dress was cut low, with her shoulders showing, and she was glowing with the glory of having been picked for certain the day before as one of the new blue jeans girls. I watched her floating through and smiling at the guests, shying away from meeting my eyes or standing near me, and I cursed myself. She was as fidgety and high-strung as a thoroughbred, and Jack was as tense and elusive as he had been all summer, and the T-bird, the cause of my isolation from both of them, was bringing me the showers of praise I thought I wanted. But the praise meant almost nothing without them to share it with, and I couldn't get next to either of them.

The record company people who had helped to pay for the repair work followed me around all afternoon to deliver their compliments and tell me that they considered their money well spent, and a movie producer was trying to engage my interest in providing him with a herd of vintage cars for some nostalgic rock-and-roll film, and I answered him absently and tried to edge closer to Macky. But she was as persistent in avoiding me as I was in pursuing her, and my day of good reckoning was spoiled by fear. It was more than fear that she knew about Trudy and me. There

193

was no accusation in her eyes. But there was disappointment. I knew something had happened to her during all that time I had spent away from her, maybe something in New York, maybe something with the model people and the photographers, maybe a lingering sense of not belonging, not belonging still, and not belonging even to me since I wasn't there to comfort her, to talk to her, or rescue her.

"She looks darlin', doesn't she?" Peggy Sue asked, coming up beside me. "I tell you, they're all just goin' crazy about her. Daniel just loves her. The blue jeans people are thinkin' about doin' one of their shoots out in the desert, in New Mexico, and they're thinkin' about pickin' her to be the one to go."

"She didn't tell me that."

"Didn't she?"

"No. She hasn't said a thing about it."

"It's a lot of pressure when you get a big account like that. And you can't let it show, 'cause it shows in your face. I'm glad you're back up here with her, though," Peggy Sue added, and I could have sworn her voice became slightly knowing. "She really needed you all that time you were down in Paradise Beach."

"Couldn't be helped," I answered briefly.

"Oh, well. You look very nice yourself. I like that suit. I wish Jack'd worn a suit. Can you believe the way he's dressed? Didn't anyone tell him this was *formal*?"

"I think Delrone did."

"You know his trouble? His trouble is everyone lets him get away with everything."

Peggy Sue wandered off, and I wandered back to-

194

ward the punch bowl, and was snared by John Streeter, Sr., the guest of honor, who was talking to a group of record company people. Streeter grabbed my arm as I walked by and didn't look at me, but kept right on with his speech.

"The thing about him that impressed me so much was that when he first came to me, nobody was making that kind of music. And yet, everyone had made it once before. It was a synthesis of everything that had gone before him that he loved as a boy. All the old rock and roll, the meat-and-potatoes rock and roll, and the rhythm and blues, all that. All that old stuff, but it didn't sound old, coming from him. His mother knew what she was doing when she named him after the All-American Boy."

The hand he was not grasping me with held an ice-filled glass, and he took a long sip from it. He was a tall, well-shaped man with silver hair and firm tanned skin, with a sharp range of wrinkles stamped over his temples and a tiny network of red veins crisscrossing his eyes.

"And who were *you* signing at the time?" he demanded. He dragged me in, swinging me at the circled group, keeping his hold on my arm, watching me as though I, too, had signed foolish acts to the record company. "Big British bands with one-syllable names and ten-minute solos. Things that only got college airplay."

"Well, John," one of them said. "Jack Armstrong hasn't exactly been living in the Top Ten, himself."

"He will. He'll get there. He's an American classic. He is to music what this boy is to cars," Streeter said, shaking me, and I found myself blushing and grinning like a child. "Taking what was old and making it new and vital again."

"At least he gets his work in on time," one of them said, meaning me, and as Streeter dropped my arm to step in and defend Jack, I made my escape and found the punch bowl.

Lee and Trudy were standing over it, saying nothing. Lee had his hand on her shoulder and his fingers on her neck, and he was looking at her with a great deal of satisfaction. He smiled up at me when I saw them, as though no intrusion in the world would cause them any serious disturbance.

"Hey, Cooder. Nice suit."

"Oh, that *is* a nice suit," Trudy said. "You look so good."

"Thanks."

"Have you seen Jack? One of the guests thought he was you."

"How come?"

"I guess he thought Jack was dressed like a mechanic. He said 'Nice work on the car,' and Jack said 'Yeah,' and the guy said 'How did you do it?' and Jack said 'Oh, I prayed.' "

Trudy smiled at me and winked, and tugged at my lapel as they walked by me, and I didn't see them again until the party moved inside and everyone began dancing to the music that John Streeter had made possible for us over the years by signing groups to the label. They began with his postwar big-band selections, and Macky refused to dance, so I danced with Trudy, and then with Peggy Sue, and then with Linda Streeter, and then went back to Macky.

"You will dance with me during 'Blue Marie,' won't you?" I asked.

"Why?"

"I'd like you to."

"Why?"

"Sentimental."

"Why are you sentimental?"

"Macky, what the hell's the matter with you?"

"Nothing," she whispered furiously. "Don't you dare yell at me here. Just leave me alone."

"Darling," I said helplessly. "I'm not *yelling* at you."

She snatched her hand away and hurried out of the room. I sought out Jack and found him next to Delrone, who was wearing a black suit and tie and a white fedora, and looked as if he were going to rob a bank on his way home from the party. Jack, as everyone had noticed, had not dressed for the occasion, but was wearing blue jeans that were all in one piece and a clean white shirt, making cleanliness his token gesture of respect.

"Do you know what's wrong with Macky?"

His eyes turned strange and sullen, and he snapped, "Why the hell should I know what's wrong with Macky?"

Delrone raised an eyebrow at Jack's sour tone, and when Jack saw that, he strode away. Delrone transferred the raised eyebrow to me.

"What's wrong with *him*?" I asked.

"Why the hell should I know what's wrong with him?" Delrone answered, but with some humor. He threw down a shot of whisky. "I've given up trying to figure that out."

But she was there for me when they played "Blue

197

Marie," her curls beginning to fall down in the sticky air of the evening, her pale-blue dress shimmering in the evening light, her eyes hidden from me when she pressed her face into my lapels, her hands around my neck. She raised herself on tiptoe to kiss my neck, and I held her very close.

Marie (ma mow Marie)
Someday you won't be blue (ma mow Marie)
Someday I'll make it all
Come true (ma ma ma ma)
For me (for me)
And you (for Marie, for Muh-reeee)

I kissed her forehead and crooked my finger under her chin to raise her mouth. I knew she was crying. I had learned to read the moves she made to try to hide her tears. I moved my finger up to her cheek.

"Do you love me?"

I nodded and kissed her forehead again. I pulled her in tight and she wiped her face clumsily on my shirt. Our dancing grew less graceful. Kenny Lark and the Sparrows hit their doo-wop chorus—"Muh-*reee* (oooooo-weeee, *ooooo-weeee*), listen to me (lis-*un* to *meeeee*)"—and she lifted her face and I thought she wanted to be kissed and bent my head, and then I heard her ask, "Have you been faithful to me?"

My feet kept moving without my instruction. I was sure that I had heard her wrong. I had never betrayed her in my heart, so it couldn't possibly show. I loved her more than ever; my guilt couldn't be showing, I was too cool for that; it was the secret guilt, the guilt that was mine alone, like the guilt about Jesus and Aunt Jane Ellen, and Dark Mark Clark, it was private, it was mine; I could never share it, and I could never tell. That was the way I did it, that was the way a man walked. I had given her patience and love since my return. She had given me tears and fits, carried on like one possessed by an evil spirit, and I had answered her calmly. I had played my part perfectly, and it was easy to do it because I loved her and that was what showed, not my guilt, and I didn't want to hurt her with the confession of my sin when I could keep the sin to myself with all the others I would have to deal with some day. She couldn't know. It wasn't fair. She couldn't know.

"What, darling?"

"Have you been faithful to me?"

"*What?*"

"*Cooder.*"

And then I knew it wasn't happening. There was no baby-blue dress. There was no record of the late Kenny Lark and the fabulous Sparrows playing in any small converted ballroom. I was not hearing the master tape of "Blue Marie." There was no Blue Marie T-bird covered with the fingerprints of admiring party guests sitting out on the lawn near the party tent. The car wasn't even finished yet. I was still in Paradise Beach, sound asleep between rounds with Trudy, and Trudy was watching a horror movie and it was the sound-track of that movie that was creeping into this bad dream. I was being punished in my nightmare for my stupidity and my lust, and when I woke up I would return to Hoboken and marry Macky immediately and never look at another woman for any reason. I would repent as soon as I woke up. Only wake me up, get those swollen eyes of hers off me, and wake me up.

"Macky—"

"Oh, Cooder. *Damn* it."

She was backing away from me, colliding with couples swaying to Kenny Lark and the Sparrows, couples blissful in their melody and fidelity.

"Macky—"

"It's *all* ruined—"

"Macky, *listen!*"

But I had to shout it, because she had pushed herself too far across the room, and my shout was a cue for her to turn on her heel and run. And then she was gone, and all eyes were upon me, and I was alone.

I got a ride home with Billy and Peggy Sue because Macky took my car when she disappeared from the Streeters' party, leaving me stranded. Billy and Peggy were cuddly and cheerful and they were considerate enough not to try to draw me into their cheer, but they annoyed me all the same. I thanked them at the door to their apartment and went up another flight of stairs and walked into our place. There were dishes on the table and dishes in the sink and Jack's discarded clothes scattered over the floor and the couch. There was a fine layer of dust on the furniture. The light was on in the bathroom. There was no one home. In the quiet I could hear Billy and Peggy Sue talking in the apartment downstairs, and I flipped on Jack's stereo and looked through his records.

It was very late, and I didn't want a drink. I'd been drinking steadily since Macky left me on the dance floor and Delrone had walked over to me at the end of "Blue Marie" to hand me a shot of bourbon like the ones he'd been feeding himself all night. I discovered very quickly that I was without my wheels and that I would have to remain, drinking alone and suffering public sympathy and feigned indifference, until Billy and Peggy Sue exhausted their good time and decided to go home. Jack had disappeared around the time that the twilight turned to black, and I hadn't seen him for the rest of the night.

I picked up the lacquer disk of Jack's new album and put it on the turntable. Jack had brought it home just that afternoon, and neither Macky nor I had heard it yet, although Macky had heard most of the material at a small club in Philadelphia where Jack had played one night while I was painting in Carl's garage. Macky had gone to see him and told me that he was more magical than ever, that his moves were slicker and smoother and sexier. I had answered that he was probably sexier onstage because he had nowhere else to be sexy, and she had responded with reproachful silence, then added in his defense that the crowd loved him. That was no news. The crowd always loved him. He had the gift, and he shared it with them, he passed it around, he let them borrow it for the evening, but in the end he was the one who would go home with the gift, and they would only have the memory.

The song I was listening to, the title track, was called "Night of the Hunter." It was about two lovers alone in a house that wasn't theirs, two lovers on the lam, finally together and safe for a night. Outside, they could hear the action on the street, the cars rushing by in brief blasts of radio and shouting, the teenage life the runaway lovers had just abandoned. The song was one long yearning. The soothing strums of Delrone's guitar gave way to the bitten whine of Jack's guitar just as Jack's voice, edgily triumphant as he sang the verses, revved up to desperation when he reached the chorus: "No one left now for you and me to trust/On the night of the hunter, baby, they'll be looking for *us*."

It was a song that expressed the hell that the three of us had been through that summer, our conflict between duty and desire. It was full of bitterness over the things we had left behind and full of determination to make good on what we had settled for. It was about Cookie and Jack, and about Macky and me, and I didn't want to hear it. I didn't want to be in his songs anymore.

I lifted the needle off the record and didn't listen to the end. I could guess the end. He deserved reward for his sacrifices, and I deserved reward for mine, but as long as I lived in his shadow, I would not get mine. Macky was right. We had to get away from them. Macky was not home with me. She was out somewhere, out to be away from me, she was probably even fighting fire with fire. Or maybe it wasn't fighting. Maybe it was only surrendering.

I poured three fingers of whisky, despite all I had had to drink that night, and put on a Supremes record. She was with someone else. I was sure of it now. Who was it, I wondered, and how was she doing it, how was she *touching* him. Was she doing it to him the way she did it to me? She would be kneeling over him, her knees hugging his hips, staring down at him with those eyes so dark in the dark that the night came through them, while she touched his mouth with the tips of her fingers. She would touch him lightly, lightly, nothing would ever again touch him so lightly, and it would tickle in a way that would make him want to bite his lip, bite her finger, bite her everywhere. It would make him want her so much that he would begin to shake when she took the finger away and bent down to him in slow motion, her eyes never leaving his, even when it hurt him to keep looking, her hair spilling forward inch by inch until, when her face was right next to his, they were harbored from heaven and earth by the walls of dark hair on both sides. And then she would kiss him, she would kiss him gently and briefly and pull away, do it again and pull away, pulling back each time to study him with eyes that held no hint of a tease, building up his hunger—and then she would give him everything he wanted.

But maybe she was just letting him touch her, maybe she was lying there letting him do it to her, because she'd wanted so much all summer to be pretty and he, whoever he was, had admired her without conditions. He had to be only a man who was not me—a man who would make love to her without the complications of love—a treat, an indulgence, as Trudy had been for me. He had to be that only, if there was any justice in the world, only a man, any man, who would make her feel pretty and desired.

No, I had to be missing something. Macky loved the complications of love; it was all she had lived for ever since we met. Making love without the complications of love was not something she did, for fun or for revenge or for any of the stupid reasons I did it. It wasn't Macky's style.

203

Of course, I didn't know anything about Macky's style; she had told me so in the midst of so many impatient, circular arguments at the end of so many working days. "I do know *something* about style, Macky," I had said. "That doesn't do *me* any good," she had snapped. "I'm not a *car*." I knew damn well she wasn't a car. If she were a car I would have spent more time with her the past three months.

Diana Ross and the Supremes were singing "Stop! In the Name of Love." Macky didn't love him, any more than she loved her new haircut. He was something new. That was all. I hoped to God she would come home soon and when she did we would Stop! in the name of love . . . stop being so stupid about each other.

And every Stop! I was punctuating by throwing one of the dirty drinking glasses in the sink to the floor and watching it shatter. There was such jagged comfort in the sound of breaking glass. There was so much blind faith battling with dread. There was an outraged knocking at the door.

I kicked my way through the broken glass and opened to Peggy Sue in a sexy, almost transparent, nightie. She really did have great legs. I stared at them, remembering how Billy had described them to me in loving, lecherous detail the night that Jimmy had come into the malt shop to try to take Macky back, the night that Macky and I had fled Paradise Beach and stumbled into a season of joy so removed from us now that it seemed more like fable than history. Peggy Sue growled, pulling my attention from her legs to the wild anger on her face.

"What are you *doin'*? I got a nine-o'clock call in the

morning and I *need*—my *God*," she went on, pushing by me and skirting away from the pile of broken glass. She pointed and tossed her long mane of hair. "Are you breaking them on *purpose*?"

"Did you see her leave with someone at the party?"

"*What?*"

She gave me innocent eyes, but that meant nothing to me. Macky looked innocent, too. At least, she had looked innocent until Peggy Sue got her claws into her and told her that she had the right look.

"Macky," I said. "Did she leave with someone?"

"How should I know?"

"Some friend of yours? Did you set it up? Is it some guy all the models have to sleep with to get their careers started?"

She gave me a hard, stinging slap on the side of my head. I jumped away from her and landed in the broken glass. She tossed her hair again and headed for the door.

"Sweep that up," she told me. "And keep it quiet. I don't want to hear another sound out of you. I got a nine-o'clock call."

I turned off the stereo and swept up the glass. I poured myself another drink and sat on the couch to wait for Macky. Through the window I could see the city taunting me with the smug electric beauty of its skyline. It made me even lonelier to see the city, so I drew the shade and turned on the radio to hear another human voice. But by that time the light outside began to pale and all I could hear was the faint whispering in my head. Maybe she didn't just want to be pretty, I told myself, as my eyes closed. Maybe I didn't know what she wanted at all.

I slept through the church bells, but when I woke up I knew it was Sunday by the dusty, stale smell of it. Jack was snoring in his room, and in ours, Macky was curled tight like a fist in the bed, her pale-blue dress on the floor. I threw my wrinkled suit on top of her discarded dress. I showered and made coffee. I arranged the cups and the pot on a tray and brought it in and placed it on the bed. I reached over to shake her shoulder and found that she was already half awake. She looked at me without expression and pushed the pillows so that she could lean against them as she sat up.

I poured the coffee. Black. She had stopped using sugar, and the only sweet that would have satisfied me was the chocolate I always craved on wailing mornings like this. She still had on her makeup from the night before, a powdered rose rouge sinking into her skin, the paint around her eyes making her look like a sullen sleepy cat weary of being petted. I stroked her cheek and she pulled her face out of reach and with her eyes closed sipped her coffee as if it were sacramental wine.

"Do you remember," she asked, "when you asked me if I knew the difference between giving something up and just kidding myself?"

"Yes."

Her mouth twisted, but there was no amusement there. I should have left her to sleep. I cursed myself quickly, Damn you, you dumb cracker, you should have left her to sleep, instead of sitting there feeding her coffee before she even has time to miss you. You could have waited for her to call you and then you could have gone in and begged her for forgiveness. But maybe she wouldn't have called you. She doesn't look like she would have called you. She looks like her mind was made up long ago, but how long ago you don't know and you don't know because you were tempted and you slipped and fell.

Oh, that's in a sermon somewhere, too, the idea of falling in a slippery place, the idea of the foolishness of ever believing that your efforts would be rewarded because your intentions were good, that mere hope would save you from defeat. "How are they brought into desolation as in a moment?" Uncle Aaron had yelled, the certainty of doom in his voice. Do you know the difference between giving something up and just kidding yourself?

"Well, I do," Macky said.

"Were you in love, or were you just cheating?"

"I'm not finished."

"Because *I* can answer that. *I* was just cheating. I was just cheating. But you were in love, weren't you? I can tell. You were, weren't you?"

"It's not that simple."

"Weren't you?"

"I cared for him very much."

"Jesus."

"It's not him, it's me."

"You mean," I said, "it's not me, it's him."

She pressed her fingers against her head, then pressed them against her mouth.

"Just trust me on this. I'm so confused, Cooder. I'm so *exhausted*. I just don't want to argue anymore."

"You're confused. Well, it must be confusing for a little girl like you, trying to handle two men and a busy career and all."

"Don't call me a little girl. I'm not a little girl."

We were in a twenty-four-hour, family-style, turquoise and plastic-wood restaurant off the highway. Jack had needed the apartment to himself to listen to the lacquer disk of the "Night of the Hunter" album, and he wanted it quiet. It hadn't been quiet for a week, not since Macky told me she was leaving me to be the New World Jeans girl in far-away, exotic locations. She was going to stand her own ground, in New Mexico among the rocks and sky, and in Ireland among the grass and hills, stand with her face hard and independent. She said she had to get away from what she had been calling home to see if it *was* home. She said she had to get away from me to see if she wanted me enough to come back.

I'd confessed all my sins to her, but I got no redemption in return. She'd confessed hers, and hers turned out to be worse than mine. She'd been cheating on me, too, but she would not give me any details. After two days, I stopped trying to wrench the name of my rival from her. I didn't need a name. I didn't want to know. My dread painted a picture clear enough to feed panic. I'd told her to go, go and never come back, and I'd pulled her clothes from the closet. I'd told her that she had to give me better reasons or I'd tie her to the bed and watch her try to go. I'd sworn up and down that it didn't matter a damn that she'd been with someone else. I swore that it didn't matter as long as she would stay, that I would dismiss it as

209

long as she promised to come back, but she knew better than to believe me and she didn't give me any kind of sign.

Jack hovered in the background of our fights, slamming out the door for short fitful walks and to escape the noise of our dueling, slamming his way back in, shoving the furniture aside, throwing the dirty coffee cups into the sink, turning on the stereo, letting us know he was home.

It didn't matter that he was home, not to me. I would have argued my way through an invasion of foreign troops, would have tried, even as they axed the door down, to extract from her some kind of promise, some words of hope. I begged and bullied; I wouldn't let up until she was lying on her back with cold washcloths on her eyes, until she was drained and shivering and moaning, "Please just stop. Please just let it alone," so desolate that I had to do it, had to leave her alone, had to go out into the living room, where I collided with Jack. We paced and stood still and stared at different sections of the wall until one of us cracked and headed out the door.

One night when I was heading for the door, I turned right around and went back for Macky, dragged her out to the car and drove her to the twenty-four-hour restaurant so that we could argue without an audience. The food in the place was so cold and greasy that I wouldn't have been able to eat what I'd ordered even if I'd had an appetite. I banged a spoon against my bottle of beer, even though I knew the clatter was making her nervous. She had a cup of black coffee in front of her, and her hands were trembling.

"I'm just . . . *confused*," she repeated, as if her behavior so far had been a model of logic and clarity. "The only thing I know is that I can't stay here. You never have time for me when you're working, anyway, and that garage'll take up *all* your time. I'm tired. You want me to just sit around and wait for a pat on the head, but I have work, too. You don't want me to want what I want."

"What *do* you want?" I asked. "New Mexico? Ireland? Okay, they seem like good places to think. You can go and think in the desert. You can go and think on a sheep farm. Then you can come back and I'll have everything going. I'll have the garage. I'll have a place for us. Why can't you just say you'll come back? Why do you have to be the mystery girl?"

"I'm not sure what I'm going to do after Ireland," she said, and snatched the spoon away from me. "I might get more work over there. I hope I do. Then I want to fly home and see my daddy."

"See your daddy."

"Don't make fun of me."

"Tell me not to call you a little girl and then fly home to see your daddy."

"Shut up. It's your fault. You don't want me to grow up. You don't want me to grow up, and then you sneer at me for being a little girl."

"Why does growing up have to mean cheating on me and leaving me?"

"What would you do with me if I stayed? You have your garage."

"Damn the damn garage."

"No. You *want* it."

"Not more than you."

"That's not true. And even if it *is* true," she went

on quickly, "even if you could make that true, what would it mean?"

"What do you mean, what would it mean? I'd pay more attention to you, ask you about your work, do all that stuff you said I wasn't doing. I'd quit work early, come home, and throw you in bed so you wouldn't go looking for it somewhere else."

"And how long before you'd hate me?"

"I hate you right now!"

She answered me with a sad, eerily wise smile and said nothing. A lock of hair fell over her shoulder and across her face. The urge to grab it and kiss it and the urge to grab it and yank it out of her head hit me both at the same time.

"I don't want you like that," she said.

"Looks like you don't want me at all. Do you want *him*?"

"No. I don't want anybody."

"Then go and don't come back," I snarled.

She smiled in that same way. "And you wonder why I'm confused? You love me, you hate me. Come back, don't come back."

"Me, *him*," I threw in, pretending to be helpful, narrowing my eyes at her and trying to remember how sweet she had looked in braids.

"There's more to it than that," she said.

"There always is," I said. "What was it? Didn't I make you feel pretty enough? Wasn't I good enough?"

"What was it about *Trudy*?" she flashed back in a shout. She caught an uneasy look from the teenage waitress who didn't want to witness a fight on the night shift. Macky leaned forward and dropped her voice so low she was nearly hissing. "You think you're

212

the only one hurt here? You always think you're the only one who feels *anything*."

Two days later she was packing and packing and packing. I cleared two dozen coffee cups off the kitchen table, washed them out, cleaned up the rest of Jack's mess of a kitchen, and listened to Jack's muffled conversation from the next room, where he was on the phone talking to Johnny Streeter. Johnny was calling him every day now that the album was finished and the tour was about to begin; Johnny's father had told him to break Jack big this time around or quit the business. I listened for sounds from Macky. I hoped that she'd at least ask me if I knew where she'd put something. But all I heard was drawers opening and closing, the closet door squeaking, and little sighs of exasperation. I went in and sat on the bed.

"What time is your plane leaving?"

"I told you. Ten o'clock."

"Why do you have to leave in the middle of the night?"

"You don't have to take me to the airport. Jack said he'd—"

"Guess again, sweetheart."

"Then you can *both* take me. I'm not gonna argue about it."

"Why are you packing *now*? You think you have ten hours worth of packing here?"

"I'm having lunch later with Peggy Sue and Daniel."

"Great. Give Daniel my best, huh?"

"Hey," Jack said from the doorway, and we both turned and scowled at him. "Uh, Johnny wants me to tell you that his father got the bank to approve your loan. He says the guy at the garage is just waiting for you to sign."

It was a shabby-looking building, sitting on a corner, a block from the river, across the street from a glass factory. Next door to it was a vacant lot filled with rubble. The most striking drawback of the inside of the place was its filth and disrepair, but I reckoned that it didn't look much worse than the cabins at Wolf's Ridge had when I first started repairing them, and at least in the garage the fixtures were in good shape. The place had high ceilings, ample work space, a dirty office just off the main floor, and a rambling series of upstairs rooms that were divided by frosted glass doors, including a bathroom and a cubbyhole that had once served as a kitchen. From the long front upstairs room, I could, by standing on my toes, see the Manhattan skyline over the roof of the glass factory. I figured that I could take one of the upstairs rooms to live in, give the other to Rilla, and worry about the rest of the space when I needed it. I'd have my hands full until then.

The whole place would have to be hosed down and disinfected. The realtor denied that there were rats, but that building, a block from the river and next to a vacant lot, had to be rat heaven. Rilla walked around playing with the doorknobs and sighing over the mess, while I sat in the office with the realtor and signed my name a thousand times.

John Streeter, Sr., when I'd told him of my plan to open my own business, had offered to help me with a mortgage loan, and threw a personal loan of his own into the deal. I had asked him for help at the first

214

opportunity I could find, while his joy in the Blue Marie T-bird was still fresh, before his first burst of postretirement nervous energy died down, before he realized that he hardly knew me at all.

The realtor handed me my copies of the agreements, shook my hand and handed me the keys. I placed my copies carefully in the broken-down desk, and tried to clean the office window with my handkerchief. Rilla skipped in as the realtor was leaving.

"You need my signature on anything?" he cried.

"No."

"Can I have the back room?"

"Yes."

"The whole back room? All to myself. This'll be my first . . . home." Rilla paused and repeated the word. "Home. We're gonna make this place shine, Cooder. We're gonna make it glow. We'll get curtains, we'll get paint. It'll be the prettiest place you ever saw! What's wrong? Oh. She's leaving today, huh?"

We had a drink to celebrate the birth of Cooder's Custom Cars. I was poor company for Rilla, but he was too excited to care. I tried to share in his cheer, tried to find some solace in the fact that I was partly responsible for it, but I was defeated by pity, for him and for me and for the whole world.

I took my time returning to Macky. I walked so slowly that I could have read words off the cobblestones had anything been written there. She was packed and dressed and cooing on the phone. She was wearing a black sequined T-shirt and a black silk gypsylike jacket that fell down to her knees, and tight black New World Jeans. She wore half a dozen thin gold bracelets, which jangled as she moved the phone from ear

215

to ear, her voice rising and dipping with chipper false enthusiasm, the voice she employed to talk to people in her business. "Ooooh, yes. Oooh, *no*. You're *kidding*. Well, I don't *believe* it!" I poured out a shot of bourbon and sat on the couch staring her down until she made a flustered apology about the time to the silly girl on the other end of the phone and hung up.

"Don't *look* that way!" she ordered.

"How the hell am I supposed to look?"

"I feel terrible already."

"Yeah, you look like you feel terrible."

"Well, I'm all in black, aren't I?" she laughed, trying to jest, which made the pit in my stomach sink to a lower level of fire, and I glared at her. She sighed, "Oh, Cooder," and added, "Did you get the garage?"

Not answering, I went into the bedroom, fell on the bed, and tried to breathe like a normal man. My hands were shaking. My hands had never shaken so much before. They had never shaken at all. They had been calm, talented hands, steady like a surgeon's. Doctor of the automobile with those hands, magic hands; with those hands I had driven her to love me. I couldn't drive her anywhere now, except away. She wanted no part of me.

I heard her heels click across the living room floor. She closed the door behind her with extreme gentleness. She sat on the bed. She ran her fingers through my hair in tiny strokes. Even at such a slight touch, I felt my eyes stinging.

"I'm sorry. God, Macky, I'm so sorry."

"Cooder—"

"God, don't. Don't say anything."

I felt her hand stop and start to pull away. I reached

216

up and grabbed it. We held on. After a moment, she continued stroking my hair with her other hand.

"Cooder, I've got something for you."

I felt the weight on the bed shift, then felt her lean back to me. I opened my eyes. She handed me a check for five thousand dollars. I handed it back.

"I got the garage. I don't need it."

"You need something to live on."

"What are *you* gonna live on?"

"New World Jeans is paying my expenses."

"I don't want it."

"Maybe Rilla does," she said kindly. "You have to put him on salary. Maybe the garage does. You have to clean it up, paint it. It's a mess, that place."

"How do you know?"

"I went down and looked at it."

"I didn't think you cared about it."

"Oh, I care. I care too much."

I loved her then the way you love a girl across the room whose eyes, meeting yours for the first time, promise you all kinds of trouble. This was someone new. All those glamorous girls who had played dress-up in front of the mirror all summer had melted together, made a new Macky from the best pieces of all of them, the same way Jack had melted together all the faceless men who were the early rock-and-roll heroes and made them into himself. I wanted her in a way that made me desperate and shy. It was far too late for me to introduce myself and ask her for a dance. We lay on the bed, holding hands and remaining silent. We stayed like that until Jack came back.

He carried her suitcase and I carried her flight bag and she carried her portfolio. Our spirits were so limp that the noise of the car radio seemed like an assault, and we turned it off and drove to the airport without accompaniment. Once Jack asked her the flight number and departure time of her plane. Thirty minutes later, I asked her the same thing. We all tried to pay for parking and bickered over it.

When we got to the gate, she said, "Good-bye, Jack," and kissed him, and he said, "So long, Mack." She said, "Good-bye, Cooder," and kissed me, and I said, "Good-bye, baby," and kept my eyes closed as she pulled out of my arms, hoping that when I opened them I would find that she had changed her mind. It was exactly the same good-bye for both of us, exactly the same kiss. Jack nudged me and I opened my eyes to see her walking away. We watched her and waited for her to turn around and wave good-bye. She'd seen enough movies to know to do that, but she didn't do that, she just disappeared with the crowd onto the plane. We went back inside and looked at the airport waiting room.

I was disgusted that after a year of love and a month of discord and two weeks of outright strife, we could find ourselves parted with such a simple, ordinary scene. I'd expected her to break down in the airport and—but I didn't know and what. Confess? She already had, far too much. Apologize? For what? Even in my anger and grief, I had the sense to see that there was no reason for her to be sorry, no reason that I hadn't put there myself. Promise that she would come back? A promise wouldn't make me believe that she was coming back any more than I believed it already. What I believed already was not so much that she would have to come back as that I couldn't face it if she didn't.

Still, I had wanted more beauty in our good-bye. I'd wanted better colors than the orange and brown of the airport lounge, wanted a better kiss than the ordinary type she gave Jack, wanted a better soundtrack than the voice of a stewardess chanting flight numbers. It had taken less than a minute to pull us apart. I deserved more than a minute. I deserved at least three minutes, like any good golden oldie.

Jack said, "Let's go to Frank's, shoot some pool."

I wasn't in the mood for games, but we went. I wanted to stay up all night, so that when I hit the sheets I would crumble into sleep immediately. By the time Jack racked up the balls, it was well past midnight. The owner of Frank's let Jack and the All-Americans keep the back room open as long as they locked up when they left, and Jack favored the place because the owner hadn't changed the jukebox in seven years. The jukebox was staked out entirely by former Jersey kids—Sinatra, of course, and Lesley Gore and Connie Francis and some obscure noisy garage bands. Jack would join them, the owner promised, as soon as the All-Americans arrived at the Top Ten.

Lesley Gore was singing "That's the Way Boys Are." I chalked my cue to the beat. I saw Jack frowning at me, and I realized that I had chalked my way through two choruses. I wiped my hands on my jeans, nonchalant, trying to pretend I was always a careful chalker. Jack continued watching me as he rattled the change in his pocket, ready to prime the jukebox for happy songs, hoping, I suppose, that they would help to make it better. They didn't help. Nothing helped.

"Break," I said, and Jack broke and didn't sink anything.

I took my turn and sank two solids. I glanced up, but Jack wasn't looking. I moved to the other side of the table and called my shots, one to the corner, one to the side. I called another shot, missed, straightened up and turned to him. He still wasn't looking. He was studying Macky's Crescent Moon photograph, which Billy had taped to the wall between a head shot of Peggy Sue and a framed movie still of Sinatra. I'd seen guys study her picture before. Rilla had stared at it with such intensity that he jumped when I tapped his shoulder to regain his attention. Eddie winked at it and wiped his mouth whenever he knew I was watching him, just to get on my nerves. Lee had told Trudy that the band taped the photo on the wall of their recording studio. Macky looked gorgeous in that slip, and the black-and-white photograph was full of the kind of light and shadow that fired Jack's imagination. He wasn't admiring the picture, though. And he wasn't distracting himself with Rilla's type of fantasy or Eddie's type of leer. He had taken his interest a step further, I suddenly knew, he had taken it a step too far.

"Jack," I said. He turned. His face was straight but his eyes shimmered with the trouble that was on his mind.

"Your shot," I said.

"Yeah," he answered, without much enthusiasm. "Hey. Listen. Five bucks a game."

"I didn't think you gambled, Jack," I said, trying to sound nonchalant. "I thought you were a good boy."

220

"Maybe I'm not so good. Yeah? Huh? Maybe I'm not what—"

My head snapped up, and he stopped as if I'd slammed my hand over his mouth.

"Not what, Jack?"

"Not what you think."

"What *do* I think?" I tried to keep my voice level, but it still growled. He dropped his eyes and began bouncing the pool cue off his wrist. "I think you're my friend, Jack. I think we know what that means here."

He took a shot, missed, and turned away from the table with a sigh.

"Listen, Cood. I want to tell you something."

"Go ahead," I said, so sick and sad and curious that I sounded coaxing.

He sighed again, and then a change came over him. I could see it even though his back was to me. He shrugged off his slouch. He ran his hand through his hair. He began pacing in a brisk, rhythmic gait that puzzled me until I recognized it as his stage saunter, the one that took him from Eddie and Lee to Delrone and Billy and into the hearts of the girls in the audience.

"You know that song 'Night of the Hunter'? The one that you like?"

"The title track of your album, Jack?" I asked, but my sarcasm couldn't break him; he was sinking deeper into his haze.

"You know, I was watching that movie this spring, the night before my sister got married, and she was out having a bachelor girls' party or something, and my dad and I were up watching it. And then when I

221

came home, you and Mack were there. And a couple days later, Mack was, like, talking about these guys, telling you this story about these guys that used to drag race by her house in St. Louis on this narrow road that went through her neighborhood. And you weren't listening to her 'cause there was this song on the radio. That song by Little Feat, the one that goes, 'I've seen the bright lights of Memphis, and the Commodore Hotel.' And I could tell you were thinking about your band. But I don't think Mack could. Then you went off to work on the T-bird and Mack got all prettied up and went into the city to the modeling people. And I sit down with my guitar—your guitar—like, alone at last. Right? Nobody but me. Cookie's gone, my sister's gone, you two are there, but you're not *there*, not like you were last summer. Well, that's good, right? I got work to do. Gotta get the damn album to hang together. Gotta get the guys to stop looking at me that way when I walk into the studio. Gotta be a *genius*, man, gotta do something that'll make it up, be a consolation prize."

"Consolation prize," I tried to repeat, but my voice was so thick with gravel that I had to swallow three gulps of beer just to clear it.

"And I'm thinking about you two and I'm thinking about this movie. It's about these two kids. They're, like, petty criminals. He's the kid in one gang of criminals, and she's, like, the daughter of a criminal or something. They meet under a billboard at night. There's a billboard in the beginning of it, anyway. They're real innocent kids. They try to be real tough like the criminals they're living with, but it doesn't work. What they really want, but they don't know it

222

yet, is to make a break from all that and just be with each other. Because they're not criminals down to the core. You know, all the way down. They've just been raised that way. With hard-core people. They've just been, like, soaked in the criminal culture . . . yeah, that's it. Soaked in the criminal culture."

He stood for a moment, satisfied with the phrase, nodding at the neon beer sign behind me, and I began to chalk my cue nervously. I leaned against the jukebox and kept my eyes on him.

"They're real pure, these kids. They fall in love in this tough kind of way, but they're real pure. And then they do something, I forget what, and they're on the lam. The cops are after them, the criminals are after them. They have this real nice night in a motel and then the kid, the guy, gets caught. He gets taken away, I think, or else he gets shot. Anyway, the girl's crying by the end. My sister came home then, so I missed the exact end. But it stayed with me, kind of . . . you know, these kids. If they could have just been in love and lived that way, been happy together and everything, but they thought they had to be something else. And so I wrote that song, 'Night of the hunter, honey, they'll be looking for us.' You know, 'cause these two kids, they think they have to be a name. And they end up getting hurt trying to do it. 'Cause they're already a name to each other. And they don't think that's enough. But it is. It is. You really know that when you don't have it. But you . . . these kids don't know it. They think they have to be a name. You know? 'Cause they've been soaked . . ."

He trailed off just as the last song on the jukebox faded out and the machine began clicking for more

223

coins. There was blue chalk all over my fingers. I wiped it off on to my already dust-smeared jeans and pulled change out of my pocket. I met Jack's eyes and he looked away swiftly as though we'd indeed had money on the games and he didn't have the funds to pay me.

"Well, that's a real nice story, Jack," I said finally, my back to him as I read the menu on the jukebox. "Except that's not what the movie *Night of the Hunter* is about."

"What's that?"

"No. The movie *Night of the Hunter* is about these two kids, and they're being chased—"

"Yeah, that's what I said, these two kids—"

"No, these are *kids*. About eight years old. They're being chased by Robert Mitchum. He's a crazy preacher. He's got 'Love' tattooed across the knuckles of one hand and 'Hate' tattooed across the other hand. And he keeps singing 'Leaning on the Everlasting Arms,' this old hymn, while he's stalking these kids. They trust him at first. Then they figure out he isn't a preacher at all."

I punched out numbers at random and turned around. Jack was looking quite grave.

"He wants to kill them. They've got some money that he wants. That's *Night of the Hunter*."

"Well, there was something about night in the title."

"Uh-huh. Is that it?"

"What?"

"Is that what you wanted to tell me?"

"Yeah."

He rolled a ball down the length of the table, watching its journey with all his heart and soul. I made no move. My fingers were too cold to touch my cue. No wonder Macky didn't know if she was in love or just cheating. In his world, there were the people who helped him make his music and the people who made up his audience. *He* was the one soaked in the culture, I realized, so soaked in his criminal culture that he couldn't step outside of it long enough to be honest with me. He wasn't honest with Macky either, I knew; he must have hurt her far worse than he hurt me. But hurting her was hurting me, and she was now too far away to comfort. Then my temper floored it; I didn't think about the consequences, I only wanted to hurt him back.

"You remember last summer, in Paradise," I said, hard as steel. "You asked about Maude's dying, about whether you ever get another one like that. I said I'd tell you about it sometime. 'Cause I got another one like that. Better, even. Better because—"

"I don't want to hear it now, man," he said quickly, and with that my disappointment was sealed up tight, sunk all the way down to the bone.

I moved out the next morning.

I pulled into the garage with all my belongings in the backseat of the car. Rilla met me at the bottom of the stairs, rubbing his shoulder.

"Where's my *bed*?" he demanded.

"What bed? Take this suitcase."

"Did you bring the dishes?"

"What are you talking about?"

"Jack said I could have his bed and we could have his dishes. He said he was giving his place up when the tour started."

225

"Forget it. You need a bed, I'll buy you one. I'm not taking anything from him."

Rilla was surprised, but he had the good grace to leave it alone. We went right to work. He called the exterminator and we left them to their work and went shopping. The sight of the rows of neat, shiny equipment and tools was almost exciting enough to take my mind off Macky for a few days.

We bought an ocean of steel-blue paint for the garage walls, white paint for the outside trim. We bought signs to hang around the place, and ordered a custom neon "Cooder's Custom Cars" to hang above the entrance. We bought enough tools, for the garage and for the cars it would soon service, to erect a small town. We bought a bed for Rilla and one for me, two dressers and a new desk, office supplies and automotive manuals, dishes and kitchen utensils. Finally, we went to the ASPCA and got two cats.

I let Rilla pick them out, and he based his decision on the certainty of their doom. He chose an adolescent girl cat with yellow eyes, long skinny paws and a black-and-brown speckled face, and a mean-faced yellow tom with a torn left ear. They were due for execution the next day, and Rilla reckoned that the girl was too ugly and the boy too old for anyone but a real bleeding heart to adopt them. We paid for their shots and bought collars for them. The girl licked Rilla's face and the boy tried to bite my hand; Rilla named the girl Angie for the Rolling Stones song and I named the boy Bob for bobcat. They sneezed at the exterminator's spray but then made themselves at home, killing two rats on the first day.

We spent a week on home improvement, doing the

garage by day and the upstairs by night, before the band stopped in to say good-bye. Johnny Streeter monopolized the farewells with a hurried explanation of a job his father had for me until Jack interrupted and said they had to go. Jack and I exchanged a brief handshake without meeting each other's eyes. Delrone gave me a slow fake punch to the chin, Lee a formal nod, Billy an authentically Southern-sounding "See ya, y'all" with a cheery wave, and Eddie a hug. They shook their heads at the condition of the garage and wished me luck. Then they piled into their cars and drove away. Rather than watch them go, I went back into the garage and called John Streeter.

The job was a pretty tall order. A group of film producers were doing a movie about the rivalry between a New York doo-wop group whose popularity was waning and a British Invasion group on the rise in the early sixties, both fighting for the number-one spot and flashing their style. Style, as everyone knew, included cars. Although the chief British car was to be a Morris Mini-Minor that was owned by one of the producers, the American cars had not yet been found.

They needed a '62 Cadillac Coupe de Ville, black, fixed to look and run like new. They needed a '64 Pontiac GTO, a '64½ Ford Mustang, and a Corvette "from whatever year they were really cute." And they needed a paint job on the Mini-Minor, from L.A. silver back to early-sixties London white. They needed other cars to sit in the street and be passed by in the background. They were to begin shooting in March, and that left me only six months.

In the future that I hoped to make mine, I would have been able to wander into my warehouse and pull out the cars they wanted and slap some paint on them and charge the producers a hundred dollars a day to let cars that were hollow on the inside sit on the street and look authentic. But that would be in the future, when the business got off the ground. For now, I took on the special cars and agreed to paint the Mini-Minor. I sent the producers to a fleet rental company for the extra cars. They wanted to lease the special-order cars from me, which was a good thing because I would own them when the shooting was over, but not a good thing because I had no money to put down on them.

I had another meeting with John Streeter, another meeting with the bank, and went deeper into debt. I rented a tow truck and a paint compressor on a long-term lease. I pestered DeMassi about helping me find the Cadillac Coupe de Ville, and he promised to hunt. I visited the Classic Car Club of New Jersey. I ended up with a horrible Cadillac Coupe de Ville with peeling white paint, a smashed-in rear door and a bullet hole in the trunk; with a GTO in very good condition, sold to me reluctantly by a man who had lost all of his property in the past spring's flood; and with a lemon-yellow Pontiac Bonneville.

We worked on the cars from dawn, when we threw open the four rolling overhead doors that made up the east wall of the garage to let the sun in and the dust out, until dusk, when we rolled down the doors, covered the cars and went upstairs to work until midnight on the old offices we were converting into our home. Then we retired for our nightly, lovingly prepared, single-dish dinner and our beer and our brooding. I took care of cleaning up and tucking in the garage and Rilla took care of dinner. Rilla was learning to cook, teaching himself from cookbooks with a meticulous patience that kept me hungry and running for fast food. He was in charge of the kitchen, the accounts, and being nice to people, and he was taking his newfound responsibilities very seriously.

"I was thinking about when we get a regular business going," Rilla told me, sitting in my unfinished bedroom one late night in early November.

I was washing down the last dry gulp of Rilla's version of shepherd's pie with another bottle of long-necked beer. I was staring at a postcard of New Mexico I had pinned to the wall. I had received it a month earlier and had memorized what she'd written on the back.

> Dear Cooder,
> It's very beautiful out here. The shoot went well. They seemed to like me. I don't know when the pictures will appear. Daniel thinks he might be able to get work for me in England after Ireland, so I probably won't be home for Christmas. Hope your business is going well.
> Love, Macky.

"I was thinking," Rilla continued, "about whether it's always going to be like this."

"Like what?"

"Like this," Rilla said, gesturing vaguely. "You know."

We both took a long drink. On the stereo, the Allman Brothers were singing about feeling really bad.

We had moved the stereo up from the garage because it was getting too grease stained from our hands. We put a radio down there instead, even though the jingles for the Hondas and Toyotas and Mercedes Benzes drove us crazy. I would have to write a jingle for Cooder's Custom Cars when I had a minute to think; I would write a sexy bluesy jingle and sing it myself, and it would come out over a car radio and lead a cool guy with a faltering engine to my garage and the answer to his prayers. "If your acceleration, baby/Ain't what it used to be/I'll resurrect your little engine/You just bring your car to me." Macky had left me the acoustic guitar she had learned to play at Wolf's Ridge. She didn't have time for that stuff anymore.

I looked for the hundredth time at the postcard from New Mexico, reflected for the hundredth time that those were no kind of words to send your true love from so far away.

"You know," Rilla was saying, "I wrote that family I lived with. That real nice family? I was living with them when I was busted for stealing that Jag. The mom told me to keep in touch with them, but after a week back there in that place, I couldn't write them no more because it was so depressing. Then I told them I was gonna live here, I was gonna have my own room, I was gonna be assistant manager in this real neat garage. And the mom wrote back and said they were so glad, you know, they were real happy for me to finally have a place of my own."

"So?"

"So this doesn't feel like a place of my own. It feels like a goddamned garage."

"Go to bed."

"You know, I thought this was gonna be exciting. Like when you were down in Paradise Beach. Living

230

with Jack. I talked to Jack, I talked to that chick you were stepping out on Macky with. It sounded like fun. I thought this was gonna be like that."

"Well, you're dumb. This is work."

"I *know* it's work. I'm always *tired*. I look it, too. I look terrible. The mom of that nice family told me to come down for Thanksgiving, but hell, I can't even do that."

"I'll let you off for Thanksgiving."

"Thanks a lot. I can't go looking like this. The mom'll be so worried. She'll cry. She always cried when I was sick."

"You're breaking my heart. What do you want from me? You want the day off, you can have it."

"What about you? What are you gonna do Thanksgiving?"

"Work."

"On Thanksgiving?"

"Who gives a goddamn about Thanksgiving all of a sudden? It's not like I have a big huge family that'll be disappointed."

"Well, like, I'm worried about you. I'm almost as worried about you as I am about me."

"Why are you worried about you?" I asked, not wanting to know why he was worried about me. I changed the records and went into the cubbyhole kitchen and pulled two more long-necks out of the refrigerator.

"I never have any time to myself," Rilla mused.

"I just *said* . . ."

"I'm not talking about a *day*. I'm talking about *time*. Even in jail we had a recreation hour."

"Okay. You can have a recreation hour."

"What good's a recreation hour in this neighborhood?"

"What good was a recreation hour in jail?"

"I want *time*, you know? I wanna, like, go into Manhattan. I wanna meet a Manhattan girl. I want a girlfriend. You know, man, I never even had a date. The closest thing I've *seen* to a girl was a foster sister I had once and if I woulda touched her, boy, forget it. They got rid of me, anyway. They probably read my mind. That's another thing. The way it was going last summer, with all you guys sleeping with each other's girlfriends, I figured this place'd be crawling with girls."

"You're exaggerating."

"Not one girl in this place. Not one. The one at McDonald's is the only one I saw."

"So ask her out."

"No. I don't really want to, and besides, I don't know how to talk to her. She's so flirty, she makes me nervous. You know, though, someone told me about this house down by the train station . . ."

"You've got to be kidding."

"Why not?"

"Don't come crying to me, then."

"What am I supposed to do? What do *you* do?"

"Work."

"Work. *I* work. Does it help you that much?"

"A little. Keeps me from thinking sometimes."

"At least you have something to think about. Boy, do you. And you went and stepped out on her. I never got that. The other chick wasn't even as pretty. I mean, like, Macky was really a fox."

"Don't call her a *fox*, okay?"

Rilla finished his beer and stumbled to his feet to carry the bottle into the other room and put it in the empties box. He brought out two more. He always waited until I was fairly drunk to start talking about girls, always waited for me to give him the one phrase that would put it all together for him.

"You miss her a whole whole lot?" he asked, handing me my beer.

"Yeah."

"That must be really neat."

"Yeah, it's swell."

"Naw, I mean it must be really neat to miss somebody that much. Like, to have a girl that you can think about like that. Ya know, sort of *agonize* over. One particular girl."

"Rilla, shut up. Don't think about it too much. You'll end up like me."

"What?" Rilla asked.

He was making too much of women, I thought, the way I always did. First he had grown up without a mother and looked at every older woman as someone who might have been his mother, every woman, that is, except the foster ones, just as I had considered every woman in town except Aunt Jane Ellen. And then he would move on to looking for too much in women, end up looking for more than a lover, more than a friend, looking for someone who would make it all up to him. He would make too much of his first girl and end up scaring her away. When he lost her, he would reckon that he was born with bad luck, that he was cursed, that the best thing to do would be to lie low and try to keep out of the way of the gods. He would expect salvation from a girl who only wanted

233

a boyfriend. And if he did find something that might pass for true love these days, he would be too afraid to really touch it, certain that it was better to leave it alone, take up something more casual, anything but face it head-on, win it, and then lose it.

"What do you mean, end up like you, huh? What do you mean? Lonely?"

"Yeah," I said. "I guess. Lonely's a good enough word."

6

She walked in off the street one evening, asking if we would be so kind as to store her car for a fair price. Her car was a glossy blue '72 Camaro with Michigan plates. She had driven it over from Manhattan, where she was going to school. She had tried for a year to keep the car in Manhattan, going back and forth between parking garages that charged her more rent than she paid for her dormitory room and spending all her time looking for safe places to park the car in the street. She was always having to leave class to put money in meters or move the car to the other side of the street. Her nerves were on edge, she couldn't pay attention in class, her peace of mind was shattered. A week earlier, all four of her tires had been stolen.

She talked like a debutante, with sterling speech

and manners, but she dressed like a street punk, and a novice member of the street at that. She wore tight jeans, a black T-shirt, a beat-up denim jacket at least four sizes too big for her, and a string of yellowed pearls. She was small featured and very thin, but her thinness was not so much a case of skin and bones as skin and wire, broken-in, supple wire. She pursued me with boneless grace around the garage, shifting from chat to serious badgering to cajoling without missing a beat. I had pointed her to Rilla the moment she walked in, but the moment she walked in Rilla disappeared, and I had to get rid of her myself.

"This is not a parking garage," I said.

"But you have room. You have plenty of room. Look at that corner over there. You're not even using it."

"Look, miss—"

"Oh, you don't have to call me miss."

"Look. There's about four parking garages right over by the subway. They're open twenty-four hours. I'm not. If you decide in the middle of the night that you want your car, and you wake me out of what little sleep I get, I can't account for what I might do to you."

"I'll only come for it during working hours. Maybe around dinnertime. Dinnertime's all right, isn't it?"

"*Nothing's* all right. Look, I'm trying to tell you, I got a lot of work to do here—"

"Doing the cars for that rock-and-roll movie. Yes, I know," she answered, rattling her keys.

"What do you know about it?"

"I know what they've decided to call it. They've decided to call it—" She paused and waited until I lifted my head out of the engine and looked at her,

236

then she finished, with a smile at her own sweet timing—*"Fool's Paradise."*

"Really."

"Seems appropriate," she said, eyeing the garage.

"Are you with the production company, then?"

"Well, no. Not exactly. I read about it and—"

"Excuse me, huh?"

I turned from her and ran smack into Rilla, who had changed from his gray mechanic's shirt that said "Rilla" into one of my good white shirts. He had washed his face, combed his hair back, cleaned the gunk out from his nails. He ignored the narrow look I gave him and answered the girl's smile with a bright one of his own. I left them to each other and shoved my head back into the belly of the Cadillac Coupe de Ville. She gave him the same pitch that she had given me. Rilla agreed that we were not using that corner, and he didn't see why we couldn't just slide her old Camaro over there and throw a drop cloth over it. Her voice was so soft and pleased that she was practically cooing. That was so kind of him, how much would he like to charge her?

"Oh, I don't know. Let's see. Twenty bucks a month? Is that fair?"

The girl coughed and I straightened up so quickly that I smashed my head on the Cadillac's hood. I stomped out of the garage and up the stairs to get aspirin and wash off the blood. I heard them chatter, heard them laugh, heard silence and then thunder on the stairs.

Rilla poked his head into the bathroom.

"I'm walking her to her train. Got it?"

"Go."

237

He didn't come back. I retired the Cadillac for the evening, threw the drop cloth over the Michigan Camaro they had left behind. I sent out for dinner and fed Bob and Angie. I kept looking out the window. When it was dark, I walked to the train station and came home by way of the river, looking for their dead bodies. When I got home, I recaulked the bathroom tile and listened to a rock-and-roll oldies station dedicating a special hour to songs about being on the road. I spent the time usually reserved for beer with Rilla mending a rip in my prized jacket and shaking my head at his absence.

Then, as I realized that I was acting like his mother, it suddenly dawned on me what must have happened. I felt like a fool, and then I felt worse. I took a long cold shower and went to bed. When he strolled into the garage the next morning, whistling a silly Broadway show tune, I grabbed both of his shoulders and peered into his eyes. He held my look for about three seconds and then blushed and turned away.

"Twenty bucks a month, Jesus Christ," I teased, but he gave me one warning, one Cooder-trained drop-dead glare, and I held my hands up for peace and backed away. Only a few seconds later he began whistling again as he picked up his wrenches.

I said nothing else to him, but there was a mysterious effervescence in the air all day. I imagined that I'd get all the grisly details that night at our beer session, but when twilight fell she returned and pulled the drop cloth off her car, and since it was a Saturday night I let him go.

I stayed up all night finishing the grille work on the Cadillac. Then I swept out the garage and tried to fight the misery that was trying to creep in. The air outside smelled like fresh clean snow and the people in Manhattan were probably skipping down the street with their coats open, laughing together. Jack was somewhere in America, Macky was somewhere in Ireland, and Rilla, on a hot drive on a cold night with some city redhead, was somewhere in Jersey. I should have been somewhere myself, trying to have some fun, but the floor was vast and messy, and I just kept sweeping. I began to dance with the broom a little, began to sing a song I used to sing with Dark Mark Clark:

All them girls across the river
Got my whole heart and half my liver
Can't dance chicken foot
Can't dance nothin'

But you needed a fiddle for it to sound any good, and the words "chicken foot" reminded me of Jack's trying to remember the words to "that song by Little Feat, the one that goes 'I've seen the bright lights of Memphis, and the Commodore Hotel' " in the back room of Frank's Place the night that Macky left. The song he meant was called "Dixie Chicken," but Jack couldn't bring the title to mind. And that wasn't all he couldn't bring to mind that night. I should have told him the title. I should have made him tell me the truth.

And now he was gone and out of touch and so was Rilla, and I had a silly middle-of-the-night flash of Rilla walking into my garage to announce his engagement, of me telling him he was a fool and she was a tramp, which is just the kind of idiotic jealous thing I might do. I saw Rilla pulling out of our part-

239

nership and leaving me alone with a pile of debts and two cats to feed and no assistant and no beer buddy. I imagined how I would feel then, imagined it with such fervor that I found myself standing in the middle of the garage with my chin on top of the broom and tears in my eyes.

Her name was Brooke, but at film school she called herself "the Brooker" because "all the guys there think they're so damn groovy." Her mother had named her Brooke Elizabeth with the hope that she would come out in society. Girls still came out, she said, in the ritzy suburb of Detroit where she had grown up. But her mother was dead and the hopes were dashed and Brooke was one tough kid. She had an undernourished, brutal sort of beauty—high arched eyebrows, blades for cheekbones, bright-blue slits for eyes. Her stringy hair was a deep lurid auburn. She was taut and wired and tireless and everything—the tight-lipped twist that served as her smile, the calculated narrowing of her already narrowed eyes, the impatient flick of her wrist—was just a splash of her great rushing rapids of energy and scorn. And, I had to guess, passion, from the way Rilla looked at her. And, I knew, ambition, from the way she kept bugging me.

"God, I hope she's not mad at me," Rilla said fervently one night when we were back together drinking beer.

"Should she be?"

"She doesn't want to see me tonight."

"Well, she's shooting a film, isn't she?"

"I know. I don't know why I can't go with her."

"She's working, for Christ's sake. You don't want

her here in the garage while *we're* working, do you?"

"Sure. I don't care."

"Well, I do."

"You *are* gonna let her do that movie about you, huh? Aren't you?"

"It's not about me."

The original reason she had come to me to store her car, we soon found out, was that she had discovered that I was doing the cars for *Fool's Paradise*. Parts of the movie were being shot near her dorm, and she had approached the director with the idea of doing a homemade documentary about the making of the movie. The director, like me, didn't want her getting in the way and hanging around while he was trying to work. She had gone home to rethink and, being a Detroit baby anyway, had come up with the notion of doing a homemade documentary on one aspect of the making of *Fool's Paradise*: the making of the cars. She had already approached me and given me her pitch. She had given me her pitch many times, in fact; when we met in the kitchen first thing in the morning, while I tried to make eggs and orange juice and gather my thoughts for the day, or when I quit work and wanted to stop thinking about cars. She was there, leaping out at me, waving her skinny fingers in my face. "I can see it now," she had said. "I can see it, you telling me about the cars. We'll go to the actors and get them to tell about the cars. Everybody has a car story. It'll be good for your business and good for my business."

"What's your business?" I had muttered. "Pestering people?"

241

"I can't help it. I see these things in my head and if I can't put them down and get them out, they'll stay there forever."

"Stay there forever," I had repeated, rubbing my arm across my eyes, scratching my ankle with the sole of my foot, concentrating on myself to keep from getting angry. Can't dance chicken foot, can't dance nothin'. Stay in your head forever. "Did Rilla tell you to say that? Did he say I'd relate to that kind of thing or something?"

My voice had that dragging-muffler sound to it, but she didn't scare easily. She only stared at me thoughtfully and answered, "Rilla doesn't tell me what to say."

"You're gonna let her, aren't you?" Rilla was whining. He brought me another beer and held it just out of arm's reach. "It's no skin off your nose, is it?"

"I really don't like being photographed."

"Hell. What if you'd been a rock star, like you thought you were gonna be? You'd be photographed often enough."

"Well, I'm not, so I don't have to worry about it."

"Why don't you just tell her yes? She wouldn't get in the way. She knows about cars. I mean, she grew up in *Detroit*."

"She grew up in Grosse Pointe Farms."

"So?"

"It's like where the Streeters live."

"So? I know she's rich. I don't care. She doesn't act rich. That's okay. I don't care that she has more *money* than me. That's not it. But . . ."

"Well?"

"Forget it, you're in a lousy mood."

"*What!*"

"Look, don't laugh."

"Okay."

"She has more *experience* than me."

"That wouldn't be hard."

"I *said* . . ."

"I'm not laughing. Go on."

"Never mind. I don't know. It's weird sometimes. Sometimes I feel like a jerk. There's times when she just pulls away. I mean pulls away all the way. Won't say nothing. Like 'What's wrong, what's wrong,' and 'Nothing, nothing, you wouldn't understand.' She acts like you sometimes, you know, acts like I haven't been on this earth long enough to understand anything. And then the stuff she *does* tell me about, she gets all mad because I don't get all emotional about it. She's had kind of a messy life and stuff, but I guess I don't go 'Oh, no!' loud enough for her. So she just—slam!— shuts the door. She didn't want to see me tonight, and it wasn't just because she was working on that damn movie."

"I don't think you two are compatible. I think you should give up. What would she see in a guy like you, anyway?"

"You're no expert at this kind of thing, you know."

"Rilla," I said, squinting down the neck of the bottle, "did you ever think that maybe she's just going out with you so she can get to do the movie?"

He said nothing. He went white and licked his lip and stared out the window.

"Did you ever think maybe Macky was just going out with you so she could live in the house with the All-American Band?"

"Maybe she was."

He stood up, shoved his hands into his pockets, and turned away.

"You don't believe that."

"You don't know what I believe," I said.

"God, what's the matter with you lately? You never used to be so mean. Ever since Macky went away, you . . . is it just, is it just—is it just a *girl*? Do you just want a girl or something?"

"Yeah. I just want a girl. Tell Brooke that. Tell Brooke if she sets up a date for me, she can do the movie."

I sat on the steps of the Law Library, facing the hall where the girl was taking her last exam before Christmas. Shoved in between the pages of the *Road & Track* magazine I held in my lap was the detailed map of the campus that Brooke had drawn for me. I finished the article on the Honda Accord for the third time and watched a pair of students argue about who was studying harder. I shivered and checked my watch. I straightened the collar of my jacket and resisted combing my hair. Students began trickling out of the hall across the walk, complaining loudly about the exam and adjusting their scarves against the wind. I looked for a girl with shoulder-length blond hair, a black wool coat and reflective mirrored sunglasses. When I saw her, I raised my arm and waved, once. I waited until she came over to me and then I stood up. She shoved the sunglasses on top of her head and looked at me.

"Hard test?" I asked.

"They're all hard."

244

She hadn't rested much lately, or seen much sun. Her skin was pale; she looked as though she had slept facedown on a pillow of fists, but she was still as pretty pretty pretty as I knew she would be.

"I'm sorry I couldn't come to Jersey," she said. "I just can't stand that state anymore."

I smiled, and her eyes filled with tears and I hugged her. I could feel her crying into my shoulder, could feel the tension down her spine as she fought the tears.

"Come on, Cookie," I said. "I don't look that bad, do I?"

She stepped back and wiped her tears.

"Nobody calls me Cookie anymore."

"Well. It never really suited you."

"You look good," she said solemnly, tousling my hair with one gloved hand. "You don't look desperate to see me. That girl said you were desperate to see me."

"Brooke exaggerates," I said. "I just, I've been feeling pretty down lately."

"I know the feeling."

"And you weren't listed in the phone book and you and Brooke are here at the same school. So I thought she could find you in the student directory or something."

"There isn't a student directory," she said. She turned and began walking and I followed, uncertainly. "She tracked me down through the registrar's office and walked into my Contracts class and said your name and told me . . . Oh, come on!" she cried suddenly, tugging on my sleeve. "Can't you just pretend? Can't you give me some of that old Paradise Beach rock-and-roll kind of talk?"

245

"Desperate," I said quickly. "Wild. I would've walked a million miles."

"You don't look desperate and wild," she said, surrendering a cautious smile. "You still have that worried scowl. I'm glad you came looking, though. What've you been up to?"

I told her about the garage, the renovation, the cars for the movie. She told me about her classes. We occupied an hour with that kind of talk and then we were left looking at the bottoms of our coffee cups.

"I missed you," she said at last.

"Yeah."

Her apartment was cozy and girlish, with lots of quilts and oak furniture and watercolors on the wall and china knickknacks everywhere. There were no pictures of Jack, or any of his ilk. The only clue to her former life was her vast, eclectic collection of albums, stacked wall to wall. With her hair pinned back and her makeup off and her tailored wool clothes, she didn't look like the kind of girl who would normally welcome me into her home. She didn't look like Cookie at all.

"I missed all of you," she said. "But I figured I had to make a clean break. Or I knew I'd go running back. Trudy told me you were back, and I almost broke then. I figured I could talk to you. I figured you'd understand it all. I always thought that maybe if you'd been around when . . . it all came down, it would have turned out differently. I always thought you wouldn't have let me walk away. I knew you wouldn't stand for walking away."

"I walk away all the time."

"No." She shook her head and stood up to pour more coffee. She brought a bottle of whisky along and

246

poured a shot into each of our cups, and then added whipped cream to her cup. She looked at me levelly. Her eyes, which had always sparkled that summer on the beach, now seemed to only soak in the light. "No. You always believed that about yourself. But it isn't true. I knew if you'd been here when it happened, you would've given me some sermon. I could even tell that *Jack* wished you were there. Talk some sense into me. He said something like that! 'God, I wish there was someone who could talk some sense into you,' and I knew he didn't mean the boys. They couldn't talk to me. I think they were always a little afraid of me."

"So was I."

"No, you weren't. You were afraid of hitting on Jack's girl, that's all. Anyway, I guess it's just as well you weren't around."

"Maybe."

"Because you would have made me compromise, and I didn't want to. I mean I couldn't. I couldn't settle for a piece of something. And I don't mean a piece of *him*, his time or his attention. I mean a piece of me. All I would've had left was a girl who loved him. The rest would've had to go. And then there would've been no point to it. There's plenty of girls around who would just be that. It didn't have to be me. It could've just as well been Jean Kenney."

"Jean Kenney?"

"She even looked like me," Cookie said with a hard smile. "Did he tell you that?"

"No. What? Who? Who's Jean Kenney? Cookie, he didn't tell me anything."

"Jean was the girl who was following him. She was devoted to him. I could see that when he threw her

247

out of the room. That night in Boston. Slender little blond thing, quiet as a deer. Jean Kenney. I'll never forget that name. She introduced herself. She knew I was coming. Stevie tried to tell me Jack never saw her again, tried to tell me they probably never slept together. Said she wasn't anything to be jealous of. Jean Kenney. She was the official reason. She *was* the reason, really."

"What are you talking about? A groupie? That was such a surprise? Cookie, it must have been more than that."

"He said something like that," she said, looking away. "He said, 'What did you think that was all about, anyway?' But he didn't just mean groupies and hotels, and all that time on the road, and all that energy going out to little Jeans who were so devoted to him and such big *fans*. No, I knew that. I knew it couldn't be Paradise Beach forever, one big happy family. I knew I'd lose big pieces of him. I knew things would go to his head, things would leave his head. I just never thought I'd lose Jack. God, I sound like such a little girl."

"Go ahead."

"I mean, oh, damn that girl. Of course that part of it hurt. Another girl in his hotel room. He can say he's sorry sorry sorry and it'll never happen again. But who knows what'll happen when you leave? And it wasn't my job to know. It was my job to be kept in the dark. Not ask questions. Keep the home fires burning. Welcome him home from his adventures. Give him a home to come home to."

"And you didn't want that?"

"How could I? That's not what I'm about. All that

would have meant was that I'd be home spinning, building up my own life, and when he came home from the wars I was supposed to unravel everything I'd done and . . . I don't know, cook him a great big dinner. And he said, 'Jesus, Cookie, what did you think this was about?' I don't know. What *did* I think it was all about? I used to have a vision about the two of us married. Married but not settled down. Like we were when I was in college, before he did national tours. Like it was on the beach. But that was already over. It didn't end that night in Boston. It ended Labor Day. It ended the night you and Macky left. The cops started bugging us then because of that stupid boyfriend of hers and we just decided to move on. And he changed. He did. Didn't you see it?"

"Yes."

"His music was always the most important thing. But then Johnny Streeter gave the guys this big football coach speech before they went on tour, about getting out there and winning every city. And Jack kept talking about Macky, how she'd come out to see Paradise Beach. Not Paradise Beach, a town on the Jersey Shore, but the Paradise Beach he wrote about. He got a different picture of himself, like he had some responsibility to every Macky out there. I mean, he'd always been really stubborn, a little selfish about the music coming first, but then he got this real hard core to him. Like he didn't have to explain himself anymore. Like he really *did* have to go out there and win every city, and that was the most important thing. He was pushing me away even then. Like, no girls on the field. Only cheerleaders on the sidelines. And I knew I couldn't change that back."

249

"But he was *crazy* about you. You should have seen him during the spring. He was a wreck."

"Well, so was I! The guys kept saying how much I hurt him and the girls kept asking how could I throw him away. But he was really already gone. I would've just been throwing myself after him."

"He might've come around."

"No," she said firmly. "*You* would've come around. But you're not Jack."

"I *know* I'm not Jack. Lord Almighty, I don't need to hear that again."

"Hear it again? Who else ever said that to you?"

"Macky."

"Oh, she did not. You said it to yourself, that's all."

"Macky," I repeated. "Macky was sleeping with him last summer."

Late that night I came back across the river and pulled into the garage. Cookie had questioned my suspicion with the keen, fact-seeking concern of a future lawyer. I gave her what evidence I had: Macky's wearing of Jack's bathrobe on the night I returned from Trudy's, Jack's evasiveness, Macky's tears, the night of the Streeters' party, Macky's half confession, Jack's muddled pool hall story.

Cookie confirmed my theory as best she could. It was not out of the question for Jack to have taken my girl. It was a natural move on Macky's part; Jack and I were so much alike, once you loved one of us, you loved the other—that was why Cookie had always loved me. I had moved to the couch then and kissed her, stayed on the couch and kept on kissing her, keeping all passion contained in kisses, as if it were my

250

first date and she were my first girl and I were terrified to move out of the safety zone. She kissed me back for as long as we kissed and then she shoved me out the door and looked at me as though she knew the stupidity of all the men in the world but couldn't help loving them in spite of it. And with that look I knew I would have done the same to Jack as he had done to me. Yeah, we were so much alike, and I couldn't fault him and couldn't help but fault him. I'd known all that beforehand, known it since Jack and Macky went away, but I needed to see Cookie to get a clearer picture.

Brooke was studying in my office when I came home. She stood at the door, blinking and yawning, then absently pulled a blanket over her nearly transparent nightgown.

"What are you doing here?"

"I live here."

She checked her watch. "It's early yet. Didn't your date work out?"

"Yeah, it worked out fine," I said, as she frowned at me, and I kissed her forehead and went up to bed.

Now that she had won the fight to make the movie in my garage, Brooke took on the new project of trying to find a girl for me. I allowed her to select wallpaper and curtains for the upstairs rooms, to deck the halls with red and green plastic sprigs of holly from Woolworth's, to string red and green streamers across the ceiling of the garage, to shove a Christmas tree that she never got around to trimming into my bedroom, to spend petty cash money on rock-and-roll Christmas records and elf hats. But I would not let her get past

251

the first sentence of a description of a girl she just knew I would love to meet, I would not take the bait on any invitation to go out drinking with Rilla and her, I would not agree to attend any party held by her silly film school friends. A few times I overheard Rilla arguing with her, telling her to leave me alone, I was nursing a broken heart, and she answered back, Then who was that blonde? Then it would occur to them that they had better things to do than argue about me and the intimate sounds of their whispers, then their silence, from his room down the hall made me grateful for the colder nights when the wind howled strong enough off the river to drown out that telltale quiet.

Only last year it had been Christmas on Ice Caves Mountain, with the blizzard and the fires and the cocoa, and the rings from Con. I twisted my ring every time Brooke mentioned a girl. I touched my ring every night before I went to sleep. I had never taken it off, even when I was with Trudy. Macky had taken hers off when she modeled, and, I supposed, many times since, and I doubted that she had it on now, wherever she was.

Dear Cooder:
The Irish shoot went well, too. There was some trouble with the lamb, who kept running away, and it turns out that I'm allergic to them, but otherwise it went well. The shots should be in a few spring fashion magazines. I know you don't read them, but Peggy Sue ought to be able to find them for you.

As I said, the shoot went well, but the people were not very nice. They didn't do much to make me feel comfortable. The perfume people went out of their way, but here I was less important than the light, and I was barked at a lot. I handled myself well, though. I think you would have been proud of me. There's no one here to lean on.

The London work—that Daniel had—turned out to be Paris work. It's for a designer named Debrisecoeur, who always attracts a lot of attention, and his summer line is going to be all red, white, and blue in honor of the American Bicentennial. Daniel thinks I should go because Debrisecoeur is looking for girls who look—you guessed it—All-American.

I hope you are busy and not missing me too much. I hope you miss me a *little*, because I miss you, but I try not to think about it, not while I'm working. It's all so complicated still, and I still love you so much. It's hard to write this because I keep thinking you might hate me. I'm afraid to call, just as I was afraid to tell you about Jack and me. That's why we decided Jack would tell you. I'm such a coward, and Jack felt so guilty, that we decided he should tell you. I hope he did a good job and explained everything. I'm sure he at least told you it was over.

I keep thinking I see you on the street, even though I know you couldn't possibly be here and even if you were, you wouldn't look so European. Now I know how American you look and I love you for that.

When I have an address I'll send it to you and please write to me. Have a merry Christmas.

Love, Macky.

I was in my bedroom, bundled up with the Christmas mail: Macky's letter, written in brown ink on thin, dry paper; a Christmas photograph of the Stree-

253

ters with a copy of their annual family newsletter; a card from Peggy Sue; a card from one of the producers of *Fool's Paradise*; a card from all my friends down at the bank; a card from the Classic Car Club of New Jersey. Brooke had made eggnog, but I was drinking whisky all the same, with a cherry sunk at the bottom in honor of the holidays. I had Elvis on the stereo, singing a sated, raunchy version of "Merry Christmas, Baby." I had no woman, no snow, no new pair of shoes, no mistletoe, no one to kiss under it, no "Fear not: for, behold, I bring you good tidings of great joy, which shall be to all people."

"Oh, no no no, Cooder, this is not how you spend Christmas Eve."

It was Brooke, wearing a red silk dress under a black fake-fur coat with a red lining. Her hair was up and she wore long fake-diamond earrings. She wore red cowboy boots, which gave the whole outfit a weird effect, and she carried a department store shopping bag illustrated with little reindeer dancing around in circles. In her other hand she carried a bottle of champagne wrapped in festive foil.

"My boy not here?" she asked with cheer.

"He won't be back for a while," I said, sitting up grouchily. "He's gone into the city to buy the necklace he's getting you for Christmas."

"The *necklace* he's getting me for Christmas," she said chidingly. "I guess you're the kind who hates surprises."

"I guess."

"Well, I have one for you-ou!" she sang, ruffling my hair. "And you're not busy, so you have to come now. We have to drive there. Get your coat."

"I don't want to go anywhere."

"You want to sit in your room sulking on Christmas Eve? Come on."

"Yeah. Hell with it. I *don't* want to meet any of your damn girlfriends."

"No girl here. Except me. And I'm plenty. Get your coat."

She took my arm and started tugging, "Come."

I knew she wouldn't let up. I finished my whisky, pulled on a sweater, and grabbed my jacket. She was already skipping down the stairs, whistling carols.

"Well," she said brightly as we sped away in her Camaro. "You're in an *exceptionally* bad mood today! Is it the cars or is it that blonde?"

"Forget about that blonde."

"Well, I tracked her down for you. I have a vested interest."

"Why are you so nosy?"

"Why are you so private?"

"She was Jack's girlfriend," I said. She tossed an earring and raised an eyebrow, and I sighed and fished Macky's letter out of my pocket and read it to Brooke.

"Why does she love you for looking American?" Brooke asked when I was through. "She's American, isn't she?"

"Yeah."

She nodded and turned onto the Jersey Turnpike and gave me a wistful smile.

"Some letter. Poor you."

"I'm still breathing."

"Tough guy. No wonder you're such a grouch. She hopes Jack did a good job telling you, huh? Did he?"

"He didn't tell me at all."

"That's why you wanted to see that blonde?"

"Forget about—"

"I can't forget about her," Brooke interrupted. "You had me run all over school looking for her, and then when I *did* find her and said your name, the look on her face . . . I was jealous. Were *you* two screwing around, too? Or was it more like the coast was clear now that Jack had done it to you?"

"Shut your filthy mouth. I didn't lay a hand on her." I paused and admitted, "Well, a hand, maybe."

"Are you gonna see her again?"

"Brooke, I'm a little unclear on how this is any of your damn business."

"Maybe I'm jealous. Are you gonna see her again?"

"No."

"Not ever? Not even for 'coffee'?"

"No. The moment's gone. I don't know if you can understand that."

"No, I'm too stupid," she said drily, and rolled down her window a crack so that I got a blast of cold air in the face. "Tight little bunch of friends, weren't you-all? Listen. If you and I slept together, who do you think Rilla would be madder at? You or me?"

"Me."

"Really? It's not entirely academic, you see, because Rilla's asked me to move in."

"I thought you already *had* moved in."

"No, I'm serious. Give up my place in Manhattan. I'm being thrown out. You see, the producers of *Fool's Paradise* finally agreed to let me on the set. I knew they'd let me do it eventually, but I never dreamed I'd have to beg so much. I pulled out *all* the stops. I told them I knew *you*, told them I had your *permission*, told them I wouldn't get in the *way*. Finally I had to go for the string section. Tell them I was from Detroit and grew up in a car culture and I think it's just *fascinating* blah blah blah how cars affect our lives as social symbols blah blah blah, and the guy started to melt a little. I could see I almost had him, so I went on with the sociological na da da da, and then I told him I wanted to do the movie in memory of my father. The late great Patrick Leary. Creative director extraordinaire. I told him how Dad used to think up the ad campaigns to sell the cars. In his den he had these folders marked 'Glamour' and 'Luxury' and 'Silence' and 'Speed.' Those were the concepts, like. They'd decide every selling season what concept was in. And then they'd pitch that. So I told him, I told him . . ."

The chatty tone went out of her voice and she glanced at me again. She tried to shove the tone back, but it didn't quite work, and her voice was slightly cracked when she continued.

"So I told him Dad died because he bought his own line and found out it was just a pitch. Dad died because Mom died. He did everything for Mom, and after she died he just couldn't last much longer pretending that luxury really mattered more than speed. I told him . . . I told him Dad's most successful campaign ever was the luxury campaign. It had the line 'Because you deserve what you earn.' That was the tag for print and broadcast. Show this guy with all the finer things—big house, beautiful wife, blond children, lovely roads stretched out, and this three-ton luxury sedan crowning it off. 'Because you deserve what you earn' written in script at the corner. The TV ads showed this car whooshing through the prettiest country you'd ever

257

want to see. The beautiful wife in the passenger seat. Nice music, no chatter. Then at the end, some announcer saying like the voice of God, 'Because you deserve what you earn.' "

"I'd buy that," I said.

"Course you'd buy it. Everybody did. Everybody who could afford it. So anyway, the producer got all teary eyed and agreed. He was almost out the door to go see his kids for Christmas, and I pushed him back and made him sign the contract I'd brought along. I mean, I hadn't risked getting laughed at, telling him all my most personal stuff, just so I could wait a few more weeks to get everything *straight*. So I got the contract. Then I went to the school. I can't do the movie and school, too. So I told them I quit. So I can't live in the dorm anymore. So, like I said, guess who's getting a new roommate?"

Her mouth flickered in a nervous smile, and I scowled at the passing gray landscape. She was now winding the Camaro down a wooded two-lane highway that would have, in the spring, fit into one of her father's commercials. Even in the chill of winter, without benefit of anything green, the woods were so dense and dismal that it felt as if it were the middle of the night.

"So your father sold cars, huh?"

"He sold the lies that sold the cars. Did you hear what I just said?"

"Did he ever write jingles?"

"He wrote everything."

"I'm writing a jingle for Cooder's Custom Cars. I just wrote another verse last night. It's got about ten verses so far, and really long jams in between. It'll

258

have guitars, bass, harmonica, piano, horns, a trio of black girls crooning in the background. The horn section is dressed in identical suits. The black girls are all in red. Sequins. Now use your imagination. I'm at the front mike. I've got shades on. And I sing, 'If your faithful little motor/Is suddenly untrue/You come on down to Cooder/And he'll make it good as new.' I don't have the main riff yet. You know, the riff that says its name. What did you call it? The tag?"

"You can't have a jingle ten verses long. I said, you're getting a new roommate," Brooke repeated, slowly and clearly as though she were teaching me a language. "I will be around all the time now."

"It doesn't matter. It's not like you'd be sleeping in my bed."

"You mean you *would* mind if I *were* sleeping in your bed?" she crooned.

"It doesn't matter what I'd mind. Rilla would mind. And that scene's a mess. I've been there before. It's not worth it. I'm keeping my hands clean from now on."

"So you're saying you've been tempted," Brooke said.

"I'm always tempted."

"By *me*. By *me*. I get all gussied up in this red dress and you can't even say you've been tempted by *me*."

"I thought redheads weren't supposed to wear red."

"You're impossible," she snapped, and slammed on the brakes. "Here we are."

Where we were was facing a thicket of trees on either side of a gravel road that had a chain strung from a post on one side of it to a post on the other side. There were signs hanging from the chain that read No Trespassing, Private Property—Keep Off, and This Area Is Patrolled Frequently at Night.

Brooke said, "Go knock down that chain, will ya?"

I got out of the car, knocked the chain down, and got back in the car. Brooke drove through, and when the thicket of trees cleared the whole field loomed up, and the rest of the day's sunlight seemed to have settled in that lot for one last dance.

It was a drive-in movie theater that looked as if it hadn't been used in years. The back concession booth was covered with taped-up ripped-up plastic garbage bags. The screen, far down on the other end, showed seams and yellow spots. Brooke drove up until we were in the fifth row, and then she parked by a speaker.

"Isn't it great?" she said. She handed me the bottle of champagne she had brought and pulled two long-stemmed glasses out of her shopping bag. I opened the bottle and she filled the glasses and pointed her glass to a corner of the screen. "See up there? Right where those bushes make a little crack? Through that little crack is more of the turnpike, and if you're on the shoulder and lean over the passenger side, you can see down here. They're gonna tear this place down. I thought it would be a great place to shoot one of my films, but now I've quit school and they've closed the place down anyway because they built a mall about a mile on down the road, and there's a quad cinema there, and they don't do enough business here to keep it open. It's a shame, isn't it? Rilla said it was just the kind of place you'd love, and you'd save it if you could, and you had to see it before they tore it down."

"It's beautiful," I said, but that was not quite the

260

word I meant. It had more or less the same faded haunted air as Paradise Beach had had for me before I got used to the place. "But what the hell were you doing way out here on the shoulder of the road?"

"That comes later. I brought you out here so we could consummate our passion before I moved in. But now I guess you don't want to."

"Don't take it personally."

"No, of course not. But isn't this a great place to come out and snuggle up with your lover and make up a movie to go on the screen?"

"Why don't you do that with Rilla?"

"We did come out here once or twice, but he doesn't see the point of sitting out in the cold. And honestly, I might love that boy someday, but he's so goddamned matter-of-fact. No imagination. I figured you could tell a good movie."

"You're the film student."

"Rilla says you're full of stories."

"Sorry, baby. Not tonight."

"Quick. It's gonna get dark. I want to hear it while I can still see the screen. What do you see up there? Some old Western, maybe? You on a horse? C'mon, Cutlas, it's what I want for Christmas."

I did my best for her. I closed my eyes. Then I opened them again. Macky and I had never been to the movies alone. We had always been with the band or the girls. We'd never had a television anywhere we'd lived. We had no common images between us. The only movies I'd seen at drive-ins were surfing movies, with Frannie Kirby and her brothers, but that had been in Florida in the summertime and this was western Jersey in December and the moods were not the same. I couldn't bring that mood back now, on Christmas Eve, shivering in a car with somebody else's girlfriend.

I wanted a love scene, making love in the afternoon, love in the salty heat, when nobody else was home. I wanted bodies larger than life, smoother than life, movie star bodies miming at passion, pretending tenderness, making you believe it was real, showing the lonely hearts in the audience how it was done so that they believed they would know what to do when their time came. But I couldn't see that, either. The only bodies I wanted to see together were mine and Macky's, and we were not, could never be, larger than life.

I thought of James Dean in the desert, rifle slung across his shoulder, wrists over the rifle, dangling down, a self-crucifixion as he mumbled shyly to the beautiful rich girl who would never be his.

"I'll tell you what I see," I said, when Brooke, impatient, poured us both more champagne and nudged me. "I see that scene in *Giant* where James Dean strikes oil and he comes up to the big house where all the rich folks are sitting on the porch. Elizabeth Taylor's sitting on the porch with her blond kids and her big dark jerk of a husband. And James Dean comes up, he's all covered in oil, it's all over him, he's laughing his head off. He comes staggering out of the Ford and he's yelling, *'I'm rich! I'm a rich'un!'* And Elizabeth Taylor says, 'That's fine, Cooder'—or whatever the hell his name was—"

"Jet," Brooke said.

" 'That's fine, Jet. That's just fine. You run along home now.' I see me doing that. I see Macky on the porch with some famous big-shot husband, and me

262

running up all covered in oil, crowing like a damn fool. And Macky saying, 'That's fine. That's just fine.' "

"Cooder. It won't be that way."

"That's what I see. That's all I'm saying."

She kissed my cheek. I slid my arm around her.

"She'll come back," Brooke said. "She'll come back if she's not an idiot."

We drank champagne and watched the screen until the night came down and the screen was shining like a white face in the dark. She gave me a brief kiss on the mouth, nothing to be afraid of, almost sisterly, if you loved your sister very much. Then she handed me an envelope.

"Merry Christmas."

"What is it?"

"It's from Rilla and me."

She turned on the inside lights and I pulled a sheet of paper out of the envelope. On it was written the name of a John D. Deeter of Bristol, Pennsylvania, and directions on how to get to the trailer park where he lived.

"Who's this? My long-lost father?"

"He's a man with a fifty-seven T-bird, already painted blue, in good condition. There's a sad story behind why he wants to sell it, but I won't go into that. Rilla and I will drive you out there, and you will give him three thousand dollars, and you will drive back in the Bird."

"Three thousand dollars? You said good condition?"

"Needs some work, but good enough to drive back in."

"Three thousand? Is he crazy?"

"That's the balance due."

"Oh, no." I started to shove the paper back in the envelope.

"You can't say no. It's a Christmas present. Besides, I'm letting you pay for some of it. Save your pride."

"Rilla doesn't have that kind of money."

"I do."

"No, Brooke."

"Look, I have the insurance money, the trust fund, the money from selling my parents' house. Oh, yeah, I'm a rich'un. Come on, Cutlas. Rilla's been looking for a T-bird for you for months. It'll make him so happy. He feels like you turned his whole life around."

"Okay."

"Big of you. Cheers."

We clinked glasses and I tried to finish my champagne, but it didn't go down well. I gave her a hug until she pushed me away, and then we finished the bottle.

The movie star cars were finished early, three weeks ahead of schedule, which resulted in goodwill, money in the bank, cars on the lot, and the beginnings of a fine reputation. We received an order from the British rock star who had played the British rock star in *Fool's Paradise*. If I was strong enough to kick a business into action, I ought to have been strong enough not to dissolve every time I saw a photograph of a particular model. But it didn't work that way. Peggy Sue had brought me the sheets from the fashion magazines, and I had foolishly framed them and hung them on

264

the walls of my bedroom and my office. I saw her everywhere I went.

She is standing against a red rock in the desert, sunlight blazing all around her, but she is safe in the shadow of the rock. She is wearing those long-pursued famous New World Jeans with a western hippie blouse and white cowboy boots with turquoise and lavender trimming ("Trampy," Brooke had sniffed, but they looked awfully good to me). One hand is hidden behind her back, and the come-close-if-you-got-the-nerve look in her dark eyes leaves what the hand behind her back is holding a mystery. She has style, but it will come off with the jeans. She is beautiful, but she is in the middle of nowhere, no living thing in the picture with her, no one to tell her how beautiful she is. There is no sign in her eyes that she misses me.

Then she is standing in semiprofile on the cliff of a green hill, surrounded by other green hills, a fairy-tale stone village in the valley below. This time she is wearing a white woolly sweater with the jeans. I can't see her face, except that her cheeks are rosy and her hair is artfully braided and she looks fresh and eager and slightly daring. There is a lamb trotting away from her. Its fleece is white as snow. She is looking back one last time. Maybe she is beginning to miss me now, but it's hard to tell, since I cannot see her face. It is a lonely picture. She is learning that style can be a lonely affair.

I stood in my office and in my bedroom and drank my coffee in the morning and my whisky at night and read the caption of New World Jeans—"Wherever you go, you go in style"—and tried to pretend that Macky

265

was just a girl in a picture to me. I was Cooder Cutlas, King of Restoration, and no girl was going to make a wreck of me. I sipped and stared and listened to the Four Tops for inspiration: They laid open their broken hearts, hung down their heads to cry, but they never failed to harmonize and they never lost the beat.

The actor who played Tony of Tony and the Capellas, the doo-wop group on the wane in *Fool's Paradise*, came in to buy the Cadillac Coupe de Ville Tony had driven in the movie. Brooke brought him into her workroom to let him see the editing of her movie about the cars in the movie.

"You know," the actor watched himself say, "I really understood Tony when I saw that Cadillac Coupe de Ville. That chrome. Those fins. That car was more Tony than Tony. You had to listen to Tony's kind of music, that Italian doo-wop, in that car. You couldn't listen to that British stuff. That car is all that Tony stood for. That car is a *monument*."

Brooke spent her days editing the movie. I spent my days repairing the garage and the cars. I heard my own voice on film, talking about cars as though I knew everything in the world, while I stomped downstairs and surveyed those machines and thought, Damn all cars; I hate cars. Business was fine, but we were no longer working at breakneck speed, which left me time to stare at Macky and wonder how I would get her back. We took out ads in the local paper. I continued writing verses for my jingle, but failed to find its identifying riff. The T-bird I had bought from John D. Deeter, my Christmas present from Brooke and

Rilla, sat untouched at the end of the garage. I couldn't bring myself to restore it yet. There was no one around to impress with it.

Dear Cooder:
I'm doing the summer whites for the Debrisecoeur 'Yankee Doodle Dandy' line. He also does menswear, and I'm sending you a shirt that ought to get to you one of these days.

Jack's record finally broke the European charts. It makes me homesick to hear him, but not homesick for St. Louis, or any place I can picture. My home was always where I was with you, so I guess that must mean I miss you.

Are you taking care of yourself? Is someone taking care of you? I want to come home and see you, even if you have another girlfriend and don't want me anymore. You can write me at this address, in care of Albert Debrisecoeur. Please write.
Love, Macky.

The shirt was silk and Blue Marie blue. I put it in the trunk of the T-bird for the day I would need to win her heart by looking cool driving in it. I couldn't look cool now. There was no rhythm in my soul. I was sick of it, sick of the stale coffee and the smell of motor oil, sick of watching the happiness grow between Rilla and Brooke, sick of feeling oh-so-sorry for myself when I saw them together. I was sick of scolding the cats when they meowed to be fed and rubbed against my leg. What I was sick of most of all was having all these things and not caring about them, of nothing ever being enough for me.

267

"Hey, Brookie."

"I'm working, honey."

"Everybody's always *working*. You know, I work, too. I just don't make a religion out of it. I think what we need around here is a vacation. We should just run off to some place. Like *Florida*. I've never been to Florida."

"That sounds nice, sweetheart. When I'm done with the movie."

"The movie, the movie. Oh, there's Cooder again. How much of Cooder is in this movie, anyway?"

"He *is* the mechanic."

"The *designer*. He looks awful. Look at those circles under his eyes. He looks even worse *now*. He's not even working on the T-bird. Have you noticed? It's just sitting there. Maybe it wasn't a good present."

"Honey, did you want something?"

"Yeah. You know that song 'She'll Be Comin' Round the Mountain When She Comes'?"

"What?"

"We used to sing it in the orphanage."

"Honey, do you have to go around saying things like 'We used to sing it in the orphanage'?"

"Well, in the song, in that song, what did you think 'she' looked like?"

"What?"

"We all had different ideas about what 'she' looked like. And who 'she' was. And why everyone was so excited about her coming. And why she was coming around a mountain. And why she was riding six white horses when she comes. I always thought that was

268

horsepower, you know? And since we were all or-phans, we all thought she was coming to adopt us."

March came and went and I paid its bills. I listened to Brooke editing her movie: "That car is a monu-ment. . . . That car is a monument." I listened to Rilla sing from beneath the belly of a car, "She'll be comin' round the mountain, she'll be comin' round the moun-tain, she'll be comin' round the mountain when she comes." I went to Frank's Place to get away from all that noise, and I spent six hours writing half a page to Macky.

> Dear Macky:
> I want you to come home. Home is here. You think it's just a garage and it's just in Hoboken, but it's mine and everything is in tip-top shape because I run it my way.
> Sometimes I feel like chucking it all and taking off, but then you'd have nothing to come back to and I'd have nowhere to go. I guess it's your turn to have the adventures. But I think it's time we had them together. We'll have to work on it when you come home. Please make it soon. I love you.
> Cooder.

That was the three-A.M. version of the letter, the one I had just completed when the owner of Frank's Place threw me out of the back room because the All-Americans weren't there to lock up. When I returned to the garage, I found Brooke waiting at the top of the stairs in one of her flimsy nightgowns.

"Can't you wear a robe?" I grumbled. She stared coolly as I climbed up and raised an eyebrow when I reached her level. "Here. Read this. Tell me if it's okay."

She scanned the letter hastily and grabbed my arm when I turned to my room.

"Cooder, listen. You know that blonde—"

"Her *name* is Mary Catherine O'Donnell."

"Well, Mary Catherine *O'Donnell*," Brooke mimicked nasally, "is in your bed right now!"

She was sitting cross-legged on my bed, wearing one of my blue work shirts and nothing else, peeling the label off a half-full bottle of whisky.

"How can you drink this stuff? Me, I have no head for liquor. I get wild on two beers. So did Jack. Remember? I guess he can drink better now. I guess he can do a lot of things now."

"Cookie?"

She pushed back her hair and smiled up at me.

"I took a little nap while I was waiting," she explained. "I hope you don't mind. Guess who called me?"

Her eyes were red and wandering and smeared with damp makeup. I sat down and touched her face.

"Honey, what's the matter?"

"I'm sorry"—she began, suddenly morose—"that I just burst in here. I'm sorry," she said again, looking over my shoulder, and I turned and saw Brooke watching us from the doorway with a slyly interested expression. "Your girlfriend's mad at me."

"She's not my girlfriend. I'll get us some coffee."

"I don't *want* coffee," Cookie said, shaking her head.

I took her by the shoulders. "Honey, I think you're a little drunk."

"I don't *want* coffee!" she shouted. "I want *Jack!*"

Brooke, who had turned away from us, stopped so sharply that her feet skated and she grabbed my bedroom door for support.

"He called me," Cookie went on. "He wanted me to go up there. I was gonna go. I was gonna *go.* I'm so stupid. I had to fix myself so I *couldn't* go. He's in *Boston.* The scene of the crime! But he didn't call because of that. He called because he went *gold.* 'Night of the Hunter' went gold and he wanted to tell someone. Me. He wanted to tell *me.* He went gold."

"Good for him," I said flatly.

"He wanted to tell you, too, but I knew he thought he wouldn't be welcome. Oh, Cooder, I felt so sorry for him. The boys were all down the hall having a party and he was in his room by himself and—"

"Maybe he'll find a nice little Jean to keep him company."

Cookie pressed her fingers over her mouth and leaned away from me, with reproachful eyes.

"Or a little Macky," I added viciously. I stood up and went over and kicked my dresser. "What do you want me to say? He breaks your heart, uses *my* girl as a consolation prize, turns *me* into a song, and gets a gold record for it. You want me to cry for him?"

"Cooder, it's not *like* that. He really *needs* someone to share it with."

"What's the band for?"

"You know what I mean."

"No, I don't. Unless you mean you. And if you mean you, what are you doing *here*? Why don't you go to him? Why come to me? *I* don't have a gold record."

271

"I just thought of you when . . . I'm sorry, I shouldn't have come. I only wanted to be with you. I thought we'd feel the same way."

"What way is that?"

"*Left out!* Left behind."

"You mean stepped on?"

"No. Just . . . exiled."

"Okay, so we're exiles."

"So is he. He asked me to tell you."

"That he's an exile?"

"About 'Night of the Hunter' going gold. He said he hoped you'd be glad. He said he wished you were there. I want you to go up there. Because I can't. I know you think *you* can't. But you can. You can clear it up, the two of you. The two of us can't."

I studied her face, soft and swollen. I studied her face, because she had her pride, too, wet and shivering though it was, and the price of it was recorded there. I studied her face, and remembered Jack's, remembered my own in the mirror after Macky left, remembered Macky the night she said she didn't want anyone anymore, she was sick of it. Her pride was not a silly thing, not something to dismiss. He had taken too much from her to dismiss it.

"I got dressed to go. I was heading for the train," Cookie said, "and then I just realized I couldn't do it. It's a different life, all that. And I'm an exile. I made my choice. So I came here. Because I knew you'd understand. You went through this before. And you can't go back, you can't let yourself slip . . . but I still miss him. Please, Cooder, please go up there. I'll feel better about not going if . . . please?"

I looked at her and looked at Brooke. Cookie's face

272

was pleading and sweet and Brooke's was calm and expectant. But they could just as well have switched faces. They'd both known all along that there was no way I could refuse her.

The hospitality suite was crowded with people I didn't know: the tour manager, the publicity director, the concert promoter, two men from a local radio station, an accountant, a waiter from room service, and a girl who offered to get me a drink. I accepted her offer. It had taken me an hour to get from the lobby of the hotel to the floor where the All-Americans were staying. The security guard on the lobby level wouldn't allow me up without a room key, so I gave up arguing and began flirting with a maid until she looked away and then I ran for the stairwell and climbed up the twenty flights of stairs. I found a guard posted at the door to the stairwell when I reached the All-Americans' floor, but while I was thinking up a story to tell him, Johnny Streeter walked by and waved at me.

"Oh, hi, Cooder. Run down and get a drink. Jack's being interviewed."

Johnny then disappeared and the guard let me by. The suite was the only room on the hall with the door open, and it had a view of the pool below. None of the boys were in the pool. None of them were anywhere to be seen. I leafed through the concert program with all their photographs in it. Eddie, Billy, Lee, and Delrone each had a spread, and Jack had the rest of the program: photographs of Jack running around the stage, dancing behind the mike, flashing his guitar in all that stagelight. There was a stack of T-shirts next

273

to the programs. The T-shirts read: The All-American Band. American Tour, 1975–76.

The wall decorations were slick-looking posters of drawings of women from the thirties. The carpet was as green and thick as moss. I had never seen such a nice hotel.

The girl brought my drink and sat down on the couch next to me with a glittering smile. I smiled back.

"Are you with the radio station?" the girl asked me.

"No."

"Oh. Journalist?"

"No."

"Oh. You work for the promoter?"

"No."

"Oh." She giggled, "Well, what's left?"

"I'm a friend of Jack's."

"*Oh*. Uh-huh."

The girl spread out her nails to see that they were still shiny pink, and then smiled into my face:

"Jack never sees anyone before the show, you know."

"No. I didn't know."

"Does he know you're here?"

"No. It's a surprise. I drove up from Jersey."

"Well . . ." she went on gently, as though she was sorry to disappoint me and had been through this scene many times before. "You know. Maybe you can see him afterwards at the party or something. I mean, if you're *invited* to the party. But he always comes backstage to sign autographs . . . if you wait to see him after the show."

"Autographs?"

"Yes. He's very nice about it."

274

"Yes. That *is* nice. Autographs for old friends."

"For the fans."

"And fans. Very nice."

She narrowed her eyes, then smiled away her suspicion, cleared her throat, and flashed her nails again.

"You know," she said, with another clearing of the throat, "they really don't like to have people up here, unless they have business."

"There's lots of fans waiting backstage, are there? That's where they belong, right?" I asked, pretending I hadn't heard her last statement, trying to sound pleasant, but my fingertips were growing cold with the beginning of anger.

"Oh, yeah. Lots. There've been lots and lots the whole tour. Especially the girls. But you know," she added hastily, with her hand on my arm to reassure me, "he always waits until he's seen everyone."

"That's nice of him."

"So," she said, after a pause, her voice growing strained and her eyes searching the room to find someone who could throw me out, "where do you know Jack from?"

"Paradise Beach."

"Oh, really? Did you, what, go to high school with him?"

"Is your name Jean, by any chance?"

"What? No, I'm Susan."

"Who the hell are you, Susan?"

"I'm Eddie's girlfriend," she said with dignity.

"Oh. Eddie's girlfriend. Since when?"

"Since *Pittsburgh.*"

"Oh. *Pittsburgh!* Do me a favor, Susan? Go tell Eddie that Cooder's waiting here for him. Cooder Cutlas.

275

Tell him I have a message from his girlfriend—the other one, the one he lives with when he's not on tour."

She turned away quickly and left me a shamed moment to wonder why I was getting so cruel. I followed her into the hall. The Shirelles were singing loudly behind somebody's door. Susan knocked a careful *rap! rarap!* on a door, with a smug, tight-lipped glance that said that she, at least, knew the secret knock, and then she let herself in. The security guard at the end of the hall was arguing with two teenage girls he was trying to push back into the stairwell. "But I've got something for him! I've got something for him!" one of them was wailing.

Behind me, the promoter was telling someone the size of the hall Jack would play in. The publicity director had picked up the phone to talk about "Night of the Hunter" 's going gold. The radio men were impressing one another with famous names. Then Eddie came bounding out of the room across the hall, and to my unending relief, he looked exactly the same.

"*Cooder!* Hey! How ya been? You look great."

He grabbed me hard and then pushed me away to examine me in the dim light of the hall. I saw his face change when he registered that I did not, after all, look great. His hair was cut shorter and his jeans were clean and almost hanging off him, and there were tiny red roads running through his eyes, but other than that, he looked exactly the same. I punched his shoulder and cuffed his head.

"Cooder, you look terrible, you look like us. It's been wild, man, you wouldn't believe it. We came straight here from Cleveland, and then Johnny's secretary called

276

in to say 'Night of the Hunter' went gold. It was *great*, you know, we just went wild. Man, I'm glad you're seeing the show tonight. I wish you could've seen the whole tour. It just keeps getting hotter and hotter. Come on in. Stevie's here."

Bright stripes of sunlight fell across the bed, but the curtains were drawn and the room was fairly dark. The door to the bathroom was open and there was a door on the other side, also open, that led to another bedroom, where I could see Lee on the phone, pacing up and down. Lee waved at me in irritation and turned around to pace the other way. The television was on. Delrone was watching "Leave It to Beaver" with the sound turned down. The girl Susan was leaning over a big rolling tray of sandwiches and snack food and a pot of coffee and an ice bucket filled with Cokes. She twitched slightly when she heard me come in, but she did not look up.

Delrone smiled twistedly when he saw me, pulling himself into a standing position with a long stretch.

"Guess you heard the news. Jack was asking about you last night."

"Yeah?" I said. "What did he want to know?"

"Oh, just, you know . . ." Delrone swallowed and held his throat with his hand. "We're playing New York next, the last three shows. Homecoming. He wanted you to be there."

"He can't talk," Eddie explained, waving at Delrone. "He yelled his head off last night in Cleveland. It was, I think, 'I Fought the Law and the Law Won.' " Man, Cleveland. You shoulda been there."

"Congratulations," I said, looking from one to the other.

"Hey, Sue, you know my friend Cooder?" Eddie yelled.

She threw him a sullen glare and left the room.

"Ask Sara if my shirt's fixed yet!" Eddie called after her.

"Sara still around?" I asked.

"Oh, yeah yeah yeah, she's with us these days. Does odds and ends."

"Things going all right?" Delrone rasped. "How's the car biz?"

"Good. Is Jack really not seeing anybody?"

"He's being interviewed right now."

"You should've seen us before I lost my voice," Delrone said. "It's been pretty hot."

"Pretty hot!" Eddie crowed.

Delrone touched his throat again and shook his head with a faint smile.

"Tell him about it, Eddie."

It was an unfortunate request. I remembered quickly how poorly Eddie told stories as he launched into a shorthand saga of the All-American times on the road, a fragment of an incident, a half-remembered piece of romance, no adventure ever completed, each interrupted as a better episode, in a better town, was brought to mind. The shows were remembered as a constant dialogue between Jack and "the kids"; the kids were no longer the ones in Paradise Beach who had grown up with him, lived like him, dressed like him, the kids were now only a mass that "went wild" at Jack's every command, yearning to be healed by the touch of the evangelist. They ailed only from what they thought their lives lacked after they saw Jack and heard his songs. Soaked in the criminal culture.

278

They thought they ailed, but there was no cure. As long as they waited to see the boys, the boys would come, and as long as they knew the boys would come, they would wait. Jack had to press on, because they were counting on him. They couldn't be "let down."

I was feeling pretty sour by the time Eddie wound down and grabbed himself a beer, and I took a beer when he offered it. Delrone went into the bathroom to gargle with saltwater for his ailing throat, and he inadvertently kicked the adjoining door wider so that we were all let in on Lee's phone conversation.

"Well, what do you want me to do? What do you want? I don't want *this* . . . I know we agreed. I know. I *know*. Look. Why don't you come to Europe when we tour this summer? Come with the tour. You've never been to Europe. . . . Can't you change your mind about summer school? What's *school*? You can make it up later. . . ."

Eddie said, "Sandwich?"

I shook my head and went on eavesdropping.

"No, I don't mean that," Lee's voice continued. "I'm not saying *that*. I'm not saying it's not important. Trudy, *listen*, I'm talking about *us*, I'm not talking about *theory*. . . . Oh, don't bring Cookie up again, that was—"

He broke off suddenly and we heard a door click shut. Delrone spat out the rest of his saltwater and came back into the bedroom, shutting the other bathroom door. He fell into a chair by the window, pulled a curtain aside and squinted into the sunlight. We fell silent. It was so quiet we could hear the soft electronic hiss that the television made when it switched its picture from the Beaver to a commercial to another

279

commercial. We could hear Lee pleading in the other room. I could hear Delrone clearing his throat and Eddie clicking his tongue. Then Eddie spoke so suddenly that Delrone and I jumped.

"Right, like, Trudy's having this affair," Eddie said. "She figures, like, all the guys screw around while they're on the road, why shouldn't *she* screw around while all the guys are on the road? Except it's turning heavy now, and Lee's getting worried and he wants her with him. It's kind of funny, because Lee's about the only one who doesn't screw around."

"Billy doesn't," Delrone said.

"Naw, Billy doesn't screw around, he just flirts. I think Peggy Sue read him the riot act before he left. She was all freaked out, you know, 'cause of all the little affairs," Eddie said to me. "Girls make such a big deal out of everything. I mean, Lee knows about you and Trudy, he doesn't care—"

I jumped and looked at Delrone, who raised his head. His eyes became alarmed, but they were not directed at me, but at Eddie, who continued, watching the ceiling.

"You know, girls just don't get it that it just happens that way. Even when they do it themselves. Like Lee doesn't care about you and Trudy, you don't care about Jack and Macky—"

"What?"

My voice fired across the room like a gunshot, so loud that I could hear the echo in my head, mocking me.

"Did Jack write a song about it?" I asked softly. "Or is it something we just sit around and shoot the breeze about?"

"Good going, Eddie," Delrone snapped.

280

"I'm sorry, man," Eddie said.

"That's okay, Eddie," I said, as I went for the door. "I told Susan about your girl in Weehawken."

In the hall, I leaned against the wall and watched the security guard blocking the door from the stairs with his whole body. He told the girls he didn't want to hurt them. When I heard that, I wanted to slap them all in the face and send them home to their mothers. "If they could have been in love and been happy together, but they thought they had to be something else," Jack had said to me. But he had told a different story to his All-American buddies here; girl for girl, he'd evened my score with Lee. What a guy. I'd never blamed her all that much for Jack, even Cookie said it was a natural thing. Her part of it made sense. His part I couldn't live with. But it had always been a thin comfort to think that he couldn't live with it either, couldn't even talk about it, wanted it buried. Instead, it was just fodder to feed the empty hours on the bus as the band roamed the country.

I felt a hand on my shoulder. I swung around so fast that Delrone pulled his hand away and stepped back.

"You want something?" I asked.

"Settle down. Where you going?"

"I don't know. Out."

"Look," he sighed. "Jack never said a word about it. I guess Macky told Peggy and Peggy told Billy and . . ."

"And now it's just another story."

"Look, we'll go talk to Jack and—"

"No."

He scowled and stuffed his hands into his pockets.

281

"Well, maybe you're right. Maybe after the show is a better time."

"After the show? You think I'm going to the goddamn *show*?"

"Oh, come on. You can't do *that*. Jack's been waiting for you to come. He's been thinking about you. He dedicates songs to you and all. He says, like, 'This is for the guy who owns this guitar.' "

"My guitar," I said.

"Yeah, he plays your guitar all the time. It's his favorite."

"Where is it?"

"In his room, I think. I think he's posing with it."

The battered Strat was on the couch, next to a girl who was putting a new roll of film into her camera. A man by the window was measuring light. Another man was holding a microphone and checking his tape recorder, and another man was writing in a notebook. Johnny Streeter was behind a desk, on the telephone. Sara, the former malt-shop girl, was tugging at Jack's collar. He was wearing a blue shirt and jeans, nothing to be photographed in, particularly. He looked thinner and slicker and strained. The strain flew off his face when he saw me, replaced by an expression of eager mischief, as though I had come to rescue him from a hard math test and spirit him away to play softball in some lot far away from the school grounds. He tried to move toward me, but Sara, without turning, pushed him back into place.

"Hey, man!" Jack cried.

I stood rooted to the ground; for just a moment, we were suspended together in what we'd had. It says

282

somewhere in Proverbs: "To the hungry soul every bitter thing is sweet," and for just a moment that sweet "Twist and Shout" grin of his was the only thing I could think of, and I was as happy for him as I was happy to see how happy he wanted me to be. Then the girl on the couch slammed the camera shut and took a flash picture of that grin. The moment was broken. I turned to her. I saw the guitar next to her. I remembered the look of approval Dark Mark Clark had given that Strat when I had come home with it the day after I joined the band. I remembered Cookie's face when she asked me to go to Boston in her place. I remembered what I'd reflected on during the drive up, that my best fantasy and my worst fear had been realized together: I'd found Cookie in my bed, but all she wanted to do was talk about Jack. I remembered all that, and my hands went around the neck of the guitar. The girl on the couch had moved to the floor, to her knees, and she was murmuring encouraging words to Jack, and the flash was still going, but it wasn't recording any more grins.

"You can tell the whole goddamn world about it, huh?" I said to him. "But you can't tell me."

"Listen, Cooder, don't leave!" Jack cried, but I was already going.

No one came after me. I walked down the hall with the guitar slung over my shoulder. I kept my eyes even with the eyes of the security guard, who had finally rid himself of those desperate girls and when I reached him, I tapped the guitar with what I hoped looked like restorative hands and said, "These babies are so goddamn sensitive, you know?"

"Oh, yeah," he said, dropping the question that had formed across his brow, "Yeah. Hey. Elevator works, you know."

"Rather walk," I said, and ran down the twenty flights to the lobby, half expecting somebody to be waiting for me when I got to the ground floor. No one was there, though, except for a group of girls who let out a cry when they saw the guitar. They turned away when they took a second look, saw me, and realized their mistake.

> *She'll be comin' round the mountain*
> *When she comes, they say*
> *Because she took her car to Cooder's*
> *And now she's goin' all the way.*

When I pressed my fingers into the strings of the Strat, they bit like a backyard dog that has been neglected far too long. But after three days in three different motels, after a concentration that shut down all my other worries, I had the riff for my jingle. It wasn't a masterpiece, a brilliantly original sequence of notes, but I had begun to believe that no riff was all that original anymore, that there wasn't all that much to be done. Everything was a restoration, built from a foundation of what had gone before, improved by the faith that there was an improvement to be made. It was a good and solid riff. I was satisfied with the sound of it.

And when I was through waiting out my exile from Jack's triumphant New York homecoming, when I was through chasing down the ghost of my old talent, "The Ballad of Cooder's Custom Cars" was twenty-one verses long, and I wanted a rest. I wanted to go back to someplace that would afford me the sense of returning. I wanted to go back to someplace simple, someplace where I had once belonged. I wanted to go back to Wolf's Ridge.

The place was overrun with Christians. Mae had surrendered Old Crystal Lodge on a long-term lease to a religious group who intended to employ the grounds as a fellowship retreat for young ministers in need of further instruction and for teenagers on the verge of confirmation, and in the winter for couples who needed to encounter their marriages and renew their vows. They occupied the lodge and all the cabins save one, which Mae had reserved for herself. Their hymn singing, she said, didn't bother her, and they were clean and respectful of the property and had paid in advance. Their timely arrival had saved her from selling the place, allowing her to keep the lodge in the family. She offered me her cabin for as long as I needed it. In return I offered to chop the winter wood.

I brought the axe down hard and watched the chips scatter across the backyard. The blue silk shirt Macky had sent me from Paris, which I had worn to Boston, was dark with sweat. I had torn the sleeves off three hours into the work. I had been up all night trying to coax some heavenly shades of night out of that magic guitar, but all it would offer was that steady riff from my jingle, that simply working walking blues riff, and nothing divine. I had been up at sunrise to chop the wood while the Christians were scrambling eggs and singing "O Lord, We Know It Matters Not (How Sweet the Song May Be)." I couldn't figure out what sect they belonged to any more than Mae could, but they had not yet sung a hymn that I had not also sung, in my boyhood, and it was beginning to wear on my patience.

It was cooler out back, because of the tall skinny pine trees shading out the sun, but I had worked myself into a great heat long ago, and the pine needles' blending with the dry sawdust was making me thirsty and making me sneeze. I sneezed again, dragged my arm across my face, and listened to the Christians, who were inside discussing the Book of Revelations and making chicken salad. The head preacher had sent one of the boys out to invite me to share their noonday meal, but I had no intention of eating with them, and told them that Mae was packing a generous lunch for me. She had closed down the diner in honor of my arrival, and came out at noon with a basket of water and food. She sat on a tree stump and spread a worn quilt across the pine needles.

"Praise God," she said, and winked. "Lunch."

I took one of the bottles of water, drank it down in two gulps, and picked up the axe.

"Ain't you gonna eat?"

"I'll finish this log first."

"I thought you'd take a week or so to do that. I didn't think you'd try to chop it all in one *day*. John Bunyan couldn't do *that*."

"Paul Bunyan."

She tore into a chicken wing and frowned.

"Paul Bunyan?" she repeated.

"And his faithful blue ox, Babe."

"Who was John Bunyan, then? Wasn't there a John Bunyan? Wasn't he a friend of Davy Crockett's?"

"I think he was a preacher."

"Good Lord. I can't get rid of them now. They're

286

on my brain. They're a nice bunch, though. One of 'em told me you were up all night playing that guitar."

"I won't be here long."

"Oh, it didn't bother them none. Were you trying to be like that friend of yours, then? That Jack?"

"I played the guitar long before I ever met Jack," I said.

"And your gal knew you before she knew Jack," Mae said. "Come and eat now."

She had for me a roast beef sandwich, half a roast chicken, a bowl of strawberries, a bowl of potato salad, half a chocolate cake and two bottles of beer and another bottle of water to wash it down with. I was so hungry that it surprised me, and I realized I hadn't had a real appetite in months.

"I haven't eaten like this since I left here," I said.

"No, it don't look like you have. Now, you fatten up before your gal comes back. You don't want her to think you went all to pieces without her."

"I didn't go all to pieces. I got the garage started."

"Work ain't everything."

"I've learned that."

Mae watched me eat, and finally she said, "Your hands are all blistered."

"Yeah."

"I told you to wear gloves."

"I don't mind."

"You don't mind. You wanted to tear something up, didn't you? The wood's not all that important. I can get one of these here boys to do it. It's for *their* people, anyway. But you wanted to take it out on something, didn't you?"

I stretched all the way out on my back, buried my

head in a patch of grass, and chewed on a pine needle.

"We were so happy here," I said.

"It's easy to be happy here," Mae said. "There's no trick to that. Like these Christian folk up here, whenever they frown at me for sayin' a bad word or makin' a joke. I just think, well, it's easy for them to act holier than me when they're up here on the mountain with nothing to do but think about how holy they are. Let 'em go back to work. Let 'em run a business and raise a family and keep church just for Sundays and see how holy they are then. That's the test, I guess. Hang on to it. Take it back with you. That's the hard part. That's what split you two kids up."

"Yeah."

"But you're kids. You'll get another chance."

I looked at her. She seemed awfully sure of herself. She smiled at me until I smiled back, and she packed up the remains of lunch and I picked up the axe again. I chopped until the sun began to set and I heard the Christians making dinner. The preacher sent out two boys to ask me if I needed help, and I sent them off with armloads of wood to set down in the backyards of the far cabins while I swept up the sawdust and tied it up in garbage bags so the raccoons wouldn't eat it and kill themselves. I went swimming in the lake while the Christians ate dinner, to cool out my shoulder muscles, but my arms were already burning by the time I dried off and went back to carry the rest of the wood around.

I was at the last cabin, the one farthest from the lodge, setting down the last bunch of wood. I pulled my shoulders back until my wrists touched, then doubled over, sweeping the ground with my fingertips. I groaned and asked Jesus, who I thought might be tuned in because of all the Christians in the neighborhood, why I could never get a proper vacation. I threw myself back into standing position and swung my arms back and forth. Then I saw a girl standing on the back porch in the doorway, watching me.

She was very pretty, as far as I could tell in the nighttime light. She had on a plain dress and no makeup, but her face was Macky-shaped and sharp, her eyes interested and direct. The sight of her frightened me for a second, because I hadn't heard or seen her coming.

"You all right?" she asked, with some kind of country accent.

"Yeah," I answered in a gasp.

"You keep groaning."

"Just sore. Been chopping wood all day."

"You work here? I haven't seen you before."

"No. Just chopping wood for the day."

"You live in town?"

"No."

"Where do you live?"

"New Jersey."

"I've never been there."

"*Jersey*? Well, yeah . . ." I said. She moved closer and held on to the porch railing.

"My name's Cathy—"

But her announcement overlapped with a cry from inside.

"Cathy! What are you doing out there! Come on back in. We're going up for vespers."

She held my gaze for a few more seconds, waiting for me to say, Come here, darling, come here and rub my back, it hurts so much, and I'll tell you about Jersey, great place, which you've never seen, hell, rub my back the right way and I might even take you there. I said nothing. Over her head I saw a face appear at the screen door. She turned and went in without another word. The face at the screen frowned at me and closed the door. As I walked away it dawned on me gradually why the girl had disturbed me so much.

As a boy I saw bits of my mother in the odd gesture of a movie star, in the smile of a girl in a magazine. When I was older, I found bits of her in girls that I loved, girls, at least, that I told myself I loved as long as it was convenient to think so. The smallest movement could inspire me to think of my mother, the way Maude tilted her head, the way Cookie laughed, the way Macky's fingers stayed curled around my ear, toying with my hair, after she had kissed me. Cathy, standing on the porch, begging for trouble, tugging at the reins, was my mother in the full-fledged fleeting detail of a dream.

I took a rowboat off the dock and paddled out to the center of the lake and settled myself on the bottom of the boat. I rocked from left to right, letting the movement soothe my back.

"So, Mama," I said, talking to her because her spirit was still floating all over the night, "I guess I'll never be anything but a second-rate guitar player, huh?"

I knew my father must have been only a second-rate guitar player. He must have been, to have played in the town where I grew up. He must have been, or my mother would have tracked him down, come back for me, and forced him into making a home for all of

290

us. I knew that was what she would have done. Sometimes, in still purple twilights like the one I was in on the lake, I could feel her right beside me; I could hear her whispering in my ear, "You're a damn fool, Cooder."

I hadn't heard her much in the past few years. When I was little, I used to talk to her when I was alone. When I was older, I used to pray to her instead of Jesus, used to say, "And Mama, take care of yourself," instead of, "And please bless and forgive my mother," the way Aunt Jane Ellen had told me to. When I was little, I had pictured her as a younger, prettier, happier version of my aunt. For a while I stopped speaking to her spirit, figuring it was a crazy thing to do and someday if I wasn't careful somebody would catch me at it.

That night I pictured her as a blend of the best things of every woman I had ever loved. A bird screamed somewhere across the lake, and it turned into my mother's laugh, not a laugh of life, not even a laugh of spirit, but a laugh of memory, a laugh of every girl who had ever left me, every girl but the one who was coming back. They were all laughing at me for imagining a spirit there.

It could have happened just like that. I could have taken her hand and led her away from the porch. I could have told her to meet me at my cabin at midnight. I could have promised that I'd play something on the guitar for her. I could have done the whole thing over again, and it would have been easy, and it would have been nothing, and every woman I had ever known had known that. It was just a seduction, and everyone was willing to go along at one time or another: Macky, Jack, my mother, me. It could have just happened, the way it did before.

They were all at vespers now, singing. Their voices fell clearly down from the lodge. They drowned out the crickets and the birds. I closed my eyes and let the ache in my shoulders fill my whole body. I rubbed my hand up and down my leg. I felt the blisters on my fingers from the guitar, the blisters on my hands from swinging the axe. The Christians had chosen an upbeat but monotonous hymn of praise: "Rise and shine and give God your glory, glory; rise and shine and give God your glory, glory; rise and shine and give God your glory, glory. . . ."

I imagined them swaying back and forth. I imagined their faces. It was easy to be happy here, Mae had said, that was no trick. My hands were stinging so wickedly that I opened my eyes to take my mind off of the pain. The wind rustled in the trees, and the stars were hard and bright. I stared at them for a long, long time.

"I can't believe you took his guitar away."

"It's my guitar."

"But you gave it to him."

"I loaned it to him."

"It was a *gift*."

"It was a loan."

It was a litany by that time, by that afternoon when we lay on the beach soaking up the sun, each wearing different pairs of cheap, funky sunglasses purchased at the boardwalk, protected from the sand by the bright, soft blankets Brooke had purchased at the Hoboken dime store, licking fried chicken grease off our fingers, drinking beer and lemonade—a picnic celebrating the completion of Brooke's movie, starring me. She had finished it and screened it for us just one week after Rilla and I had made a pact to abandon her and the garage if we had to hear that actor saying "That car is a *monument*" one more time. We were on the beach of a Jersey Shore town selected at random after Brooke had lobbied repeatedly for Paradise Beach and had repeatedly been voted down by a two-thirds majority. Brooke had accused me, when I returned from Wolf's Ridge with my hands bandaged and my backseat filled with Mae's pies, of not knowing how to have fun. We had gone ahead with the picnic to show her that I could be as much damn fun as anyone else.

The All-Americans had invaded my garage in my absence, looking for me and possibly for my guitar. Brooke and Rilla had been given backstage passes and had attended all three of Jack's New York shows. Rilla said they were the best he had ever seen, but then he had not seen much. Brooke was a fervent convert to the cause of Jack Armstrong. Rilla had always considered him a pal, anyway, and Brooke had fallen victim to his forlorn charm—that sad, apologetic grin and shrug of his—and the three of them had exchanged wild tales of what had happened in Boston, what had happened with Cookie. Poor Jack, poor Cooder, why can't we be friends? Rilla had advised them both to mind their own business, but Brooke did not understand that kind of language and spent all of her energy fighting for the cause of reunion. She had, she confessed, sent off the letter I had written to Macky, first-class air mail, special delivery.

"It's so *childish*," Brooke said, "taking back the guitar like that. Pick up your marbles and go home. It's so second grade. Can't you just put it behind you?"

I felt a sudden rainstorm on my leg and raised my

head to see Rilla, returned from a dip in the ocean, dripping on me.

"Brookie," he said sternly.

"Oh, *Rilla*."

"I told you to leave him alone."

"I'm just doing this for his own good."

"Leave him alone for his own good."

"And what does he need that guitar for?" Brooke went on. "That *jingle*? That's no jingle, it's an *opera*. It runs on for ten minutes. You know how much ten minutes of air time costs? You could buy another T-bird for that."

"I'll just have to make it a record, then."

"Jack could help you with that."

"There is truth in that," I said.

"*Brooke!*" Rilla yelled. "Change the subject. *Now!*"

Brooke scowled at him and sat up, shaking the sand out of her hair. She pursed her lips thoughtfully and elbowed me in the ribs, pointing toward a group of kids building a sand castle.

"Beach is eroding. See it? You know who I met at the ice-cream stand? This guy, he's a coastal geologist. He was telling me how far the beach has eroded in the past couple years. And you know why? See those jetties? They put them up to stop the waves from coming in so hard and tearing up the shore. These people around here who own summer houses, they wanted to protect their investments. The people who live here year-round, they don't count, they don't have as much money to fight to keep the ocean the way it is. So what happened? They put the jetties up, and now the ocean comes crashing up over them, picks up power, and slams against the shoreline. Gouges out the ocean floor. Drags the sand away. It was all poor planning, you see. They built pretty houses right up against the shoreline when they should have built back. But they could make more money, you know, selling houses right on the ocean. And then they put the jetties in, and now it's getting worse. And they're trying to stop it from happening farther down the coast, down in Maryland, but in some places it's too late. He called it, this geologist, the New Jerseyization of the Maryland coast."

Rilla drank half his beer and ran the bottle over his forehead, the way Jack used to do with his bottles of Coke.

"I know there's a point to this," he said. "And I know it better not be about Cooder."

"See, it's New Jerseyization. Short-term solutions to long-term problems that only end up making the problem worse."

"Like what?" I said. "Like stealing back a guitar that belonged to you in the first place?"

"Like running away."

"So endeth today's lesson."

Then nagging me was forgotten for the rest of the day. Brooke and Rilla buried each other in the sand. We stopped on the way home for fried clams and more beer. We returned home at the beginning of a lazy, balmy night and went up to my room to play Monopoly, listen to records and pet the cats. We were sunburned and sleepy and focused our energy on the fight for money and property. Brooke was a very competitive player.

"If you buy the Boardwalk, you sleep alone tonight," she told Rilla.

"I really don't see," he said, blinking in surprise at the board and raising his head slowly, "what one has to do with the other."

"Oh, go ahead," Brooke cried, suddenly merry. She threw her hands around his neck and kissed him. "Buy the Boardwalk. You're so calm all the time. I never think about how lucky I am. You could be like Cooder."

"I don't want the Boardwalk."

"Hard and unforgiving."

"I am *not*," I objected, "hard and unforgiving."

"Buy the Boardwalk! Put a hotel on it."

"You're so confusing."

"You're so cute. Isn't he cute?"

He accepted another kiss, his eyes still puzzled. He glanced at me. The cats stampeded down the length of the room, in pursuit of a plastic Monopoly house Brooke had thrown at them. Brooke settled back in her chair and threw the Boardwalk property card at Rilla.

"You can have it for free. Don't build the hotels right on the shoreline, remember."

"You can't play that way."

The phone rang and Brooke shouted, "We're closed!"

She seized the dice and began rattling them violently in one hand, warning me as I walked to the phone, "Cooder, if you go out to fix somebody's damn tire or give them a jump start . . . You're not the only garage in town, you know."

I answered the phone.

"Hi," she said. "It's Macky."

I sat down on the desk and took a deep breath. My heart began clanging around my body like an angry pinball. I was afraid it was going to try to escape through my throat and choke me. I began to breathe very carefully. I felt every breath I was taking.

"Hello? Cooder?"

"Hi," I whispered. "Where are you?"

"Paradise Beach."

"Paradise Beach?"

"Paradise Beach," Brooke sneered, "No, I don't want to go back to Paradise Beach. No, it's too *heartbreaking*."

I held my hand up sharply, signaling for quiet.

"Are you busy?" Macky asked.

"I wouldn't call it busy, no."

"Do you want to come down? I'm in a hotel."

"Which one?"

"The one across from the Sandpiper. The tall one. Ocean Towers."

"What are you doing there?"

"Waiting for you. Are you coming?"

"Yes."

I hung up. I kissed Brooke on the top of her head. I ran to the closet and changed my shirt, ran to the bathroom and washed my face, sat on my bed and checked my wallet.

"You can't go down there for fun," Brooke complained, "but you can leave in the middle of our game and go haul up somebody's car."

Brooke picked up my property and gave it back to the bank.

"We finally get you to go to the beach and have fun, and then you turn around and tow cars all night. When

298

are you gonna learn?" She glanced up at me, finally, and did a double take. "Oh, my God."

Rilla raised his head, turned to me.

"What?"

"Was that *her*?" Brooke asked.

I nodded. I walked to the door. Their eyes followed me. They both looked very earnest.

"Be careful driving down," Brooke said.

I gave her a salute, but she didn't have to worry. I drove like an old lady on my way down. A bunch of teenage dragsters, thinking that the T-bird had to be owned by a hot-rodder, tried to goad me into racing with them, but I ignored them.

When I arrived in one piece at Paradise Beach, I parked the car by Carl the Corvette Specialist's. It hadn't been that long since I had been there, but the whole place had changed, and I might never have been there in my life, the way I felt walking down the boardwalk. I strolled past the carousel but didn't give it more than a glance. I walked slowly, taking in the summer courtships in their various stages. I walked past the malt shop and looked inside, but there were all new girls there. Passing a souvenir stand, I saw Jack's face on a T-shirt. I walked all the way down to the Outer Limits and found that the new house band was called the Band of Thieves. There might have been a few of the old faces hanging around outside the door, but they weren't the kind of old faces you'd remember. One face saw me and started to nod, then looked away coolly, as if it was understood that no warm greeting was necessary after an absence of two summers.

I turned around and started back to where I had

begun, but I didn't recognize anyone else and no one recognized me. I studied the ocean for what must have been only a few minutes, but seemed like half a life-time. Then I walked into the Ocean Towers Hotel.

It was a quiet, clean hotel, mostly for young mar-rieds or couples who could do fair imitations of young marrieds. It had a carpet of aqua blue that was sup-posed to represent the ocean floor, and the wallpaper in the lobby was patterned in waves. The desk clerk neither questioned me nor offered to call when I asked for Miss Simmons' room number. He just told me the number and I went on up.

The door was cracked open two inches, and I pushed it farther without knocking. There were crumpled tis-sues on the dresser, and a bucket of ice with a bottle of Jack Daniels sitting next to it. There were a few fat magazines next to the bottle. There was one king-sized bed and she was perched on the end of it. She was staring at the television with empty eyes, her hands folded faceup in her lap, a few crumpled tissues scat-tered around her.

Her body was longer and leaner and less like a girl's. She sat with a haphazard confidence. Her hair was cut very short, and it gave her face a strange elegance. She was wearing an expensive-looking, simple white dress that must have turned quite a few heads when she walked down the boardwalk. Probably, I told my-self, one of the Debrisecoeur Yankee Doodle Dandies. Her shoulders were bare and her neck stretched long when she bent her head to her lap and sniffed, knead-ing the tissues with her fingers. I was tracing the line of her legs when she glanced up.

"Beautiful, beautiful brown eyes," the old hillbilly

song went, "I'll never love blue eyes again." Her eyes were shy and welcoming, her face open. I clutched the doorknob harder. She was tan all over, an even coffee-with-a-lot-of-milk tan so I couldn't see her blush after we stared so long, but I knew she was doing it because I could see it in her eyes.

"Hi," she said.

"Hi," I said. "You look beautiful."

She stood up and gave me a turn in one fluid, practiced motion. A quick, raised-eyebrow smile melted into a bashful one. She turned down the volume on the television set. She came to me and kissed me, awkwardly, kissed my lower lip. I still held on to the doorknob as urgently as if it were a gun and I was surrounded.

"Come in," she said. She pushed the door so that I had to let go of the knob. I stuffed my hand into my jeans pocket. "You look good, too."

"Yeah?"

"Yes, you look just the same. I was hoping you would. I thought about you so much, and I always pictured you just like this, and then after we hung up I was afraid maybe you'd . . . changed."

"Naw."

"How's the business going?"

"Good."

"Really good?"

"Yes. Really good."

"Um . . . you want a drink? I had them bring Jack Daniels for you."

"All right."

I walked over to the dresser and began fishing cubes out of the ice bucket. "You?" I asked.

"Yes. Please."

I poured out drinks while I examined her dresser. There was only one small makeup bag, a hairbrush, the fashion magazines and dozens of crumpled tissues. Her tissues on the dresser in Jack's flat had always been smeared with black or pink, but these looked clean. There was nothing else to look at. There was a small suitcase by the bed, a briefcase leaning against the night table. A bathrobe hung on the hook of the partially opened bathroom door. The curtains were drawn. A black-and-white movie danced on the television set, elegant Katharine Hepburn teasing Cary Grant. I left the drinks on the dresser and turned to her. We stared again for a while.

"So you have a new look," I said.

"Yes."

"Is it for a job?"

"No. It's just . . . me."

"I like it. You don't wear as much makeup."

"No." she said. Her hand fluttered to her face and fell.

"There's a lot of tissues around."

"Oh, I was . . . crying. Earlier."

I sat down on the bed. She met my eyes for as long as we could take it, then we looked away.

"Crying?"

"Jittery, I guess."

She smiled, a sweet pulse of a smile that would have torn away my defenses, had I put any up.

"How long have you been back?"

"I've been in the States two weeks. I flew straight to St. Louis to see my daddy."

"It's been a long time for him."

302

"Yes. He was glad to see me."

"Yeah. So am I."

"Are you? You're not . . . mad?"

"Why should I be mad? You're back, aren't you? Are you? Unless this is just a visit."

"No, it's not just a visit."

"You got my letter?"

"Yes."

"And you came back. Right?"

"I missed you. I missed you so much."

"That's what I wanted to hear. So why would I be mad?"

"I was afraid. . . . I'm still afraid."

She ran her hand through her short hair in a way that made me want to do that, too. So I did. I ran my hand over her hair. It was like petting the cats, but softer. Much, much softer. I cradled her head and kissed her, a kiss for each lip, each eye, each cheek, a line of kisses all the way down to her nose, then back to her mouth, which was ready for me. I slid my arms around her waist and her hands went around my neck. I lifted her to a higher place on the bed and leaned her down very slowly. She stroked my face with the tips of her fingers. I saw her shudder, her eyes still questioning, her eyes so dark I could see myself reflected in them, could see myself but not what was frightening her. I got up and turned off the lights.

I picked up every part of her and met it again, met her skin and her mouth and the sounds that she made. We traded off and I let her run all over me. She told me that she missed me, and the things only I could do. She told me that there had been men between us, men who didn't matter and one who did, one who did

303

and was not good to her. She told me that while she was away she had met the loneliest part of herself, but she had worked her way back from it before coming back to me. She didn't want to come home lonely. She had to conquer it herself and bring her victory back as a gift. I told her that there had been no one, no one, no one in her place the whole time she was gone. I had waited for patience and it had finally come. The heat shimmered off her body and dissolved into water. We spoke with our hands and never said a word.

There was nothing that she didn't see. There was no part of her that I couldn't reach. All the anger and loneliness of the past months burned slowly away, replaced, if it had to be replaced, by a drifting sorrow at what it had cost to get here, a sorrow that was no match for our greed for comfort. It was more than comfort, more than consolation, more than reward. It was where we belonged.

There was white noise on the television set, and we lay limp in each other's arms, our legs tangled, her head nestled under my chin, damp, still, our breathing now so quiet that I couldn't even hear it over the static. The white of the television stabbed my eyes. I took breaths to speak, lost my thought, kissed her shoulder and her neck until she turned and slid across me and kissed me and we fell asleep that way, until the news of the morning on the television woke us up.

We stayed in bed all the next day. I told her small stories through our morning coffee, and then we stopped talking again and waited until our room service dinner arrived. We picked at it while Macky told me stories about Europe.

"The cars are so small," she said as I buttered a roll for her. "They thought I was so *stupid* for saying that. They thought I was stupid anyway. It was like being back with the malt-shop girls, except I didn't have the status of being your girlfriend. It was so lonely, sometimes. I mean, modeling is, anyway, I think, but there I had no one to talk to. And the cars were small and the countries were small. I tried to tell them about the cars you worked on, the Cadillacs, the Pontiacs. They laughed. They said, 'Oh, those big old American dinosaurs.' I just wanted to get in a big car on a big American highway and drive and drive and have you with me and find ourselves in the middle of nowhere. Like we did. There, you could cover a country in one day. You were always *somewhere* over there. Somewhere famous, some little village renowned for cheese or wine.

"When I was in Rome, I wanted to cry. I spent the whole time with this photographer, this Texan, because he had this collection of country-and-western records. I spent the whole time in his hotel room listening to Patsy Cline singing 'Seven Lonely Days' or Loretta Lynn singing anything at all. Just hearing them reminded me of you. I spent all day on the couch with ice packs on my face so I wouldn't cry and swell my eyes up, listening to country and western. That was what I saw of Rome. That was around the time I got a letter from Peggy Sue saying she'd delivered my pictures to your garage. She said there was this spiffy-looking redhead there, making fun of you. She said you two seemed real chummy, like this girl knew everything about you. So I figured I'd lost you. And I figured I deserved it. And I didn't see any point then in coming back to America. But then when I wrote and asked you if you had a girlfriend, and you wrote back and didn't mention one, I thought maybe I had a chance. I figured you would have told me if you were hooked up with someone else."

"No one else," I said.

She pushed the tray away, stood up, went to the window, pulled back the curtain, and studied the sunset. She opened the window and the curtains billowed in wide pale rays of fading sunlight. I raised myself on one elbow and pulled the dinner tray to me.

"That redhead," Macky said. "She lives there, doesn't she?"

"Brooke? Yeah. She's Rilla's girlfriend."

"Brooke. You like her, don't you?"

"We're friends." I paused long enough to finish the green beans. "She's nosy. She'll probably pounce on you as soon as you walk in. But she has a good heart. She mailed that last letter I wrote to you."

Macky turned, curious.

"You weren't gonna mail it?"

"I couldn't decide."

"Why wouldn't you mail it?"

"I don't know. Pride."

"Pride? You have nothing to be proud about."

"Thank you."

"I mean . . . pride. You mean you thought I'd read your letter and say, 'He loves me. Well, that's his tough luck'? Your letter was the first thing that cut through everything and really touched me since . . . since I left you, I guess. Well," she went on, after I fumbled for an answer, "I guess I have no room to talk. I was too proud to go to your garage. I wanted to meet you on neutral ground first."

"It didn't feel real neutral last night."

She smiled, a pretty sexy smile, and walked back to sit on the bed.

"That's not the part I was worried about," she said. "But we've always lived in other people's places. The garage is *your* place and I didn't want to walk in un-announced. I had to see you first. I had to be invited. Because it's your place and I didn't help you build it and you and Rilla and his girlfriend have your habits down. And if I just walked in, I'd be treated like a guest. And I don't want that. I want to pull my weight and I want to belong."

"Okay," I said. "What about only wanting to be with me? Has that fallen by the wayside?"

"That goes without saying."

"Say it anyway."

Now, sometimes you miss your calling
In the home of the brave
But Cooder's never seen a woman
Or a car that can't be saved.

I was driving past his house on my way back from getting charcoal for the barbecue. I knew where he lived because Brooke had taken me there, parked the car on the curb, pointed at it, an unpainted cottage

307

with falling shutters in an unkempt jungle of a front yard, off a secluded road. "That's where Jack lives," she had said, and I had answered, "Looks like it," before regaining possession of the steering wheel and heading back for the garage.

But I soon found myself, when I was out in the car alone, driving past his place in spite of myself, like a high school boy in love who drives past his girlfriend's house to see if the light in her window is on.

He didn't live that far away. His house was halfway between Hoboken and Paradise Beach. I never told Macky that I was driving past his house, never took her there when we went on our drives. We spent evenings walking along the river together, planning her future career moves, looking at the city, talking about where we'd like to go for dinner. We took drives together and talked about nothing at all. We spent weekends at the beach. I gave her the side room with a view of the vacant lot as her base of operations so she could have a room for herself while we got used to each other.

"I can see what all the sulking was about," Brooke said grudgingly. Macky had only spent a few days sniffing around "that spiffy-looking redhead" Peggy Sue had warned her about before they formed an alliance.

Rilla's birthday was the week after the Fourth of July, and since this Fourth of July was the big Bicentennial, and since this birthday would see Rilla out of his teens, we were planning a big surprise barbecue for him. I had driven way out into the heart of Jersey to a special hardware store that was having a sale on charcoal. I drove back in a way that forced me to pass the house where Jack lived.

I sat in the car, engine idling, and watched Jack in the front yard, bent over the belly of a tan Rambler. I stared for a while, a good long while, and watched while he got into the driver's seat of the Rambler and tried to start it. I winced at the sound the engine made, and then, in spite of myself, I was out of my T-bird and walking down his driveway.

"Oh, *Cooder*," he said, when he looked up and saw me. "I can't get the damn thing started."

I held out my hand and he gave me the wrench he was trying to work with. He held on to the hood and watched me look at the engine. I stepped back and shook my head.

"You ever think of changing the *oil*, Jack?"

"Well, the guy who sold it to me said he'd just changed it."

"Great. What made you want to buy this thing? And who sold it to you? Why don't you buy your cars from me?"

"I can't afford you, man," he said, and I stared at him until I finally smiled.

"I might make a deal for you," I said.

"Well, I couldn't count on that."

"How far were you planning to go in this thing?"

"Just for a drive, you know, man. I'm getting a little restless, you know?"

So we went for a drive in my car. I didn't know where we were going. He said he knew the way and told me when to turn. It was his favorite scenic route: north, west, a tiny two-lane highway. I adjusted my shades and Jack adjusted his. I fiddled with the radio while we drove from shade into sunlight and back again.

"Man," Jack said, petting the dashboard, "you finally got a T-bird of your own."

"Yup."

"You know, I've driven past your garage. Just out driving, you know, and I'm going past your garage. I've looked in and seen the lights were on. I've seen how the place looks. All bright and clean. You did a real good job, you know, man. It's a cool-looking place. You know, maybe I could stop in, get my oil changed."

"You need a whole new car. That's no car for a solid-gold rock star."

"Yeah, well. I don't feel like a solid-gold rock star."

"That'll come soon enough, I guess."

"I guess. Hey, listen, Cooder?"

"Yeah."

"I'm sorry, man."

"Yeah."

"And you know, actually, something else. I've seen this car before, too, you know, when I'm just sitting home. I've seen it, like, come past my house. I thought maybe I was dreaming or something. But hell, I guess I knew I wasn't. Like I said, I've been by the garage. I've been by, you know. I know she's back. I know she came back. And I've parked there, sometimes, you know, and just listened. 'Cause when I was passing by, I could hear this guitar. *The* guitar. Playing this riff."

"You like it?"

"Yeah, it's a good riff, man. I like it a lot."

"I'm gonna play the whole song at this party we're

310

having. A barbecue. For Rilla's birthday. Rilla, Jack, he's gonna be twenty."

"Twenty," Jack said. "Twenty, man, that's *old.*"

He flashed me his grin and his eyes were sparkling and I couldn't help but laugh. I kept on driving, driving until it grew dark enough for both of us to take off our sunglasses. Then it grew dark enough for me to turn on the headlights. I turned the T-bird around and headed back to where we'd come from. Jack told me a story about his sister's married life. I played with the radio and found Dusty Springfield singing that the only boy who could ever reach her was the son of a preacher man. We turned up the volume and rolled down the windows to let her voice soak us and the wind rip away the rest of our talk. I drove him back to his house and went in with him to turn on all the lights. He asked me to stay but I had to tell him some other time. It was getting late, and I had been gone far too long. I knew Macky would be getting worried, and I had to get home.